MY BETTER LIFE

SARAH READY

CROWN

ALSO BY SARAH READY

Stand Alone Romances:

The Fall in Love Checklist

Hero Ever After

Josh and Gemma Make a Baby

Once Upon an Island

Soul Mates in Romeo Romance Series:

Chasing Romeo

Love Not at First Sight

Romance by the Book

Love, Artifacts, and You

Married by Sunday

My Better Life

Stand Alone Novella:

Love Letters

Find these books and more by Sarah Ready at:

www.sarahready.com/romance-books

Sign up to receive bonus content, exclusive epilogues and more at: www.sarahready.com/newsletter

MY BETTER LIFE

When East Coast elite and wealthy bachelor Gavin Williams wakes up in a rural West Virginia hospital, he doesn't remember who he is or where he's from.

He doesn't remember his heiress fiancée, his luxury homes, his exotic travels, or his private plane.

And he especially doesn't remember insulting local country-girl and fiery redhead Jamie Sutton, smashing her dreams, and leaving her in a pinch.

So when a redhead in overalls stands over his hospital bed and convincingly tells him he loves banjos, hound dogs, and rustling chickens, what's he supposed to do?

Suddenly Gavin is scrambling to fit into a country life that doesn't feel familiar and that can't possibly be his. A wife? Kids? A chicken coop?

His life is full of holes and secrets, desires and dreams, and as Gavin learns more he begins to wonder—will he ever remember? And what happens when he does?

my better life

SARAH READY

CROWN

W.W. CROWN BOOKS
An imprint of Swift & Lewis Publishing LLC
www.wwcrown.com

Published by W.W. Crown Books an Imprint of Swift & Lewis Publishing, LLC, Lowell, MI USA
Cover Illustration & Design: Elizabeth Turner Stokes

Library of Congress Control Number: 2022910417
ISBN: 978-1-954007-38-3 (eBook)
ISBN: 978-1-954007-39-0 (pbk)
ISBN: 978-1-954007-40-6 (large print)
ISBN: 978-1-954007-41-3 (hbk)

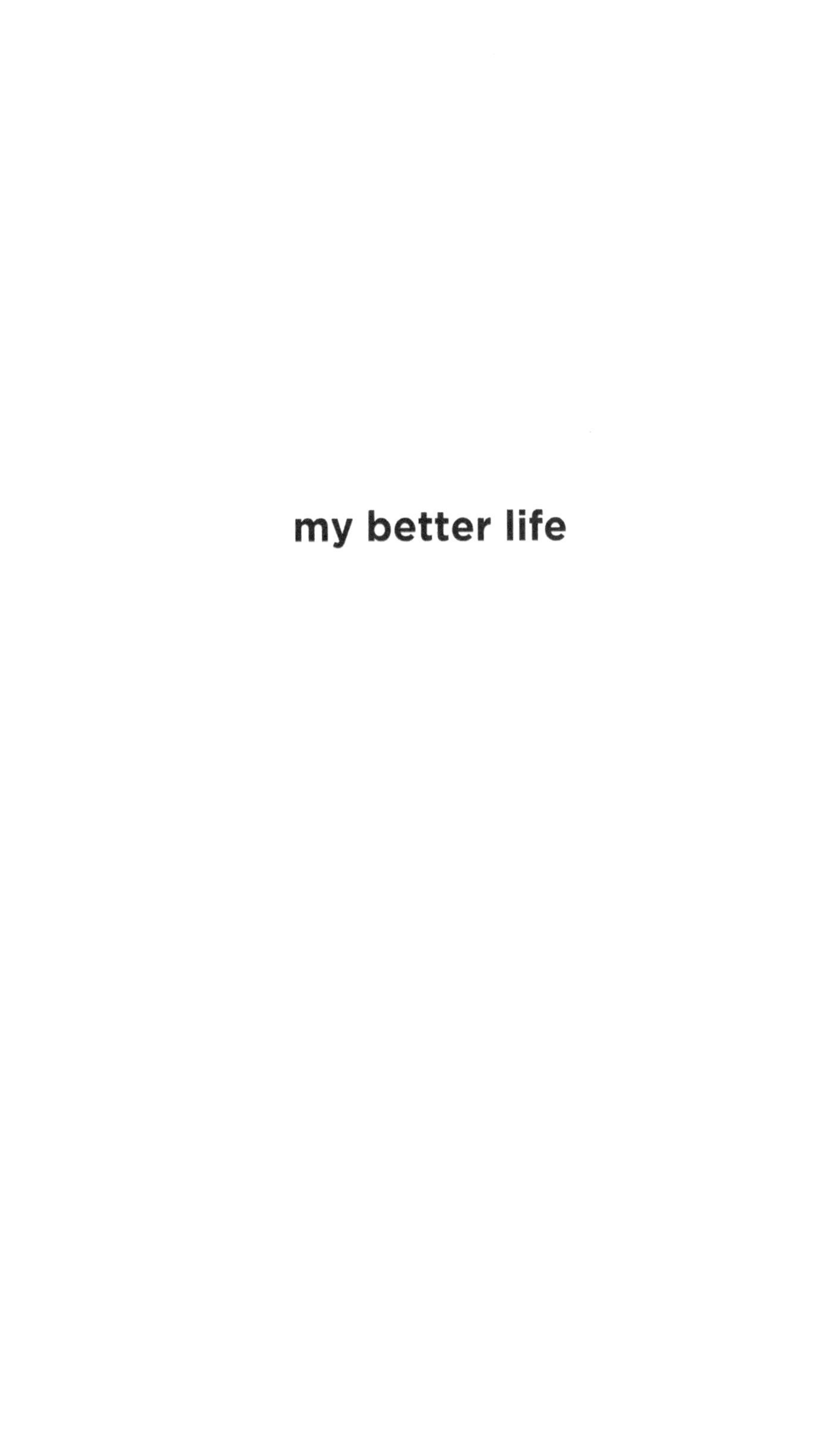

my better life

1

———

A PIECE OF GLASS CAN BE AS COLD AND DESOLATE AS THE depths of a lonely man's heart, brittle and eager to be broken. Or a piece of glass can burn, a bright, wild inferno that blazes as hot and desperate as first love, undulating with passion as I fill it with my breath.

The blue-green waves of glass curl with white froth, the promise of a rising wave, right before it breaks. I run my hand over the cold, smooth surface, and even though I know a glass sculpture can't love you back, I put enough sweat, tears, and heart into this piece over the last three months to pretend that it might. My studio, an old stone barn that squats like a tired donkey at the corner of the property, is tinged with the sweet scent of seared cherry wood, and the acrid smell of smoke lingers on my overalls.

The early morning is dark, full of country racket—the percussion of the bullfrogs and the melody of the cicadas, interspersed with the occasional crow from our resident rooster. Out the barn door I can see the crescent moon and the morning star hanging low in the indigo sky. It's nearly six, the kids will be up soon, but not yet.

I still have a few minutes before the mad school rush where eating breakfast, bathrooming, packing lunches, and managing to get three kids dressed with two matching socks *and* matching shoes, becomes as impossible as using ice to melt glass.

I stick my thumbs in the pockets of my overalls and breathe out a long sigh.

The sculpture, a three foot by five foot iridescent wave, is one of the best things that has ever happened to me. It's our ticket to a better life, the chance I've been praying for, and it's all thanks to a man I've never met.

Gavin Williams.

I don't know much about him. We only corresponded by email. Short, terse, uninformative emails. But I know enough. Mainly, he's rich. At least, rich enough to commission a ten-thousand-dollar piece of art and pay a ten percent advance. Which is the best, the absolute best thing that's happened in this little corner of West Virginia in a long, long time.

I stroke my hand over the cold azure glass. I can still feel the waves of my breath flowing through it. Gavin wanted the sculpture to represent rapids on the Cambodian river where he met his fiancée. It's a wedding present, which is nice for the fiancée but even better for me.

Ten thousand dollars better.

I stroke the line of white froth at the edge. The glass is as soft as a kitten's paw. I smile. That's some nonsense Bobby would've said. He was a pure romantic, always coming up with ridiculous metaphors and turns of phrase. Me, I never had time for romance. And with Bobby gone, there isn't any call for romance anyway.

Besides, I'll take cold, hard cash over love and romance any day of the week. I'm no fool.

That old curmudgeon rooster crows again, and I expect the kids will wake up soon. But before I start grilling pancakes and sliding bacon into the oven, there's one thing I have to do. A cool breeze from the open barn door stirs up dust from the dirt floor and lifts the scent of beeswax and smoke from my overalls. Bobby said that smell was the best, most exotic perfume in the world.

See? A romantic.

I tug the silver chain necklace from around my neck, lifting the dented heart locket from under my overalls. I don't take off the necklace unless I'm working glass, but I do now, lifting the warm, delicate chain from my neck. The necklace coils in my palm, the links settling into my hand with a soft metallic hiss. The heart locket is dull, the metal is discolored and scuffed. It clicks as I pry open the latch. Most people put a picture inside, but Bobby wasn't most people. I drop the sliver of glass into my palm. The orange-tinted shard glints against my skin.

I can hear the memory of the shattering stained-glass

window, a thousand shards raining to the stone floor, the noise of all that senseless destruction an echo of my life.

Six years ago I took this shard, dug the needle-sharp end into my pointer finger, pushed out bright red blood, and promised that I'd keep going, that we'd be okay.

Today, after six years of sweat, struggle, and clinging to okay by the skin of my teeth, I've finally done it.

I press the shard into the same spot, right over the white star-burst scar on my pointer finger. I ignore the sting and grit my teeth until the glass slices into my skin and the warm tang of blood slides over my finger. I stare at the crimson drop welling up, as round and new as a dew drop on a curled leaf. I can almost taste its coppery tang.

Then I curl my hand into a tight fist. Holding onto the locket, the glass shard, my promise.

"I did it. I promised I would, didn't I? The kids are going to be okay. We're all going to be okay. You can rest easy now. Alright? I told you we'd be okay."

The breeze drags its fingers over the back of my neck, rustling my hair, and although it's only the wind, I'll take it as a sign. From this day forward, everything is looking up.

Elijah will finally get a pair of new shoes, heck two pairs. And I'll have enough money for gas to drive him to play on the little league team, and enough money to pay the club fee. I'll be able to afford a math tutor for Tanner and finally take him on that weeklong camping and rafting trip he's been begging for.

And Shay, she really, really wants that cedar shake treehouse, the one that looks like a miniature replica of a seaside mansion. It's been stationed in the parking lot of

Beaner's hardware store for a year now, and every time we go shopping, she parks herself in that treehouse and sits cross legged on its wood plank floor for the whole thirty minutes I'm in the store. I'd be able to get her that little house. My heart nearly doubles in size at the thought of how happy the kids will be.

And me...I'm dreaming of a meal, one with crispy-skinned chicken where the salty grease drips down your chin, hot yeasty rolls that flake off and melt in your mouth, sweet corn slathered in creamy butter, and greens braised with salty bacon. I'd have gallons of iced tea with fresh lemons and fancy sugar, and there'd be pies, peach pie with double the peaches, and lemon meringue with the meringue so high it's excessive, and strawberry shortcake, with gallons and gallons of strawberries, and while I'm gorging on the best food I've eaten in years, I won't be worrying, I won't be worrying about anything at all.

And it's all thanks to Gavin Williams.

Like I said, I don't know much about him, but I do know that he's an angel.

2

GAVIN

"YOU ARE SUCH A PRICK. I TOLD YOU LAST WEEK, WE'RE done. D-O-N-E. The wedding is off." Lacey has a death grip on the metal scalpel she's holding, her knuckles white, and I think about backing up, because by the look in her eyes, she just might be considering plunging the sharp point into my heart. Or jugular. Whichever would kill me faster. And she'd know, considering she's a doctor.

Even in ugly lima bean-green scrubs and a long white coat, she still manages to look poised and, of course, pissed.

Not that I'm afraid, but I step around the stainless steel patient table and put some space between us. The cold smell of antiseptic pinches my nose, and the patient room, barely big enough for two adults, much less the swabs, gauze, cupboards, syringes and scalpels, presses on me.

Ever since I was a kid I hated being inside, hated being stuck, and this six by eight room, with anatomy posters on the wall and a flickering, buzzing light, is making my skin itch. I want to grab Lacey's hand and pull her out to the fresh air. Take us back to the lush jungle where we first met, to the perfume of orchids and vine-covered trees instead of the tang of antiseptic, to the hum of insects instead of the buzz of artificial lighting.

"Do you remember when you saved my life? How I fell in love with you while you saved me from that snake bite?"

She narrows her eyes. "A good deed never goes unpunished."

It's then that Lacey realizes she has a death grip on the scalpel. She carefully sets it on the cracked laminate counter and lets out a long-suffering breath.

"Gavin."

The way she says my name makes me step around the stainless steel table and reach for her. The room, the way sounds are muted inside, with all the cupboards and boxes and clutter, makes me feel trapped. It also makes me feel like I'm nine again and I'm standing in my dad's office, my head bowed, waiting for him to say whatever it is he called me in to say. I'd breathe in the harsh cleaning solvent used on the tile floors and eventually that smell became synonymous with his disappointment.

"Gavin—" he'd say. My name, I came to realize, meant a thousand things, all of them bad. Gavin meant—Why can't I sit still? Why can't I remember the multiplication tables? Why can't I read better? Why can't I be more serious? Why can't I be more respectful? Why can't I be more like Will? Why can't I stop being a disappointment? Why can't I be anyone, anyone at all, except me?

The way Lacey says "Gavin" is exactly the way I hoped to never hear again.

It hits a sore spot that I've buried deep and run away from. I've spent years avoiding any situation where I got close enough to someone for their disappointment to matter. To trap me. Until I met Lacey.

"Please. I love you. I messed up." I reach out, and although Lacey's face is colder than the winter I spent in an igloo in the Arctic Circle, she still lets me take her hand. I pull her close and fight against the overwhelming urge I have to run, to fly to New Zealand for cliff-diving, or to Iceland to chase the Northern Lights. That's not me anymore. I love Lacey and I'm going to prove it. So instead of focusing on the pressing claustrophobia of this closet-sized patient room at this depressing free clinic where Lacey's volunteering, I'm going to focus on her.

Her hand is cold, her fingers dry from scrubbing with sanitizer and constantly changing out rubber gloves. I rub the back of her hand, and her eyes narrow.

"Honestly, Gavin, you don't know what love is. I value myself too much to waste my life on a man-child who thinks so little of me that he believes a bunch of old ladies when they tell him another woman is his soul mate. It's asinine. I knew you were having a hard time adjusting to the idea of settling down. The idea of picking out kitchen towels terrified you, for goodness sake. Fine. I understood you didn't feel prepared to run a charity with me. I was prepared to make accommodations and compromises with your desire to roam. What I'm not prepared to do is marry a man who can't discuss his hesitations like an adult and who kisses other women days before our wedding."

Lacey's eyes cut me, not with the anger she's wielding like a scalpel, but with the disappointment so clearly written there.

I grip her hand and struggle to draw in a bracing breath of the antiseptic-coated air. "I know. I know I was wrong. You're right, I was an idiot. I was scared. I let my fear cloud how much you mean to me—"

"How much?" She tugs her hand away.

"What?"

"How much do you care? Would you be willing to give up your lifestyle for me? Give up all your international trips for me? The skydiving, the parasailing, the climbing, the scuba diving, the rafting, visiting all the exotic locales, would you give all that up for me?"

My skin goes cold at the thought, but... "Of course—"

"Really?"

"Yes. I love you. I want a home. A family."

Lacey crosses her arms over her chest. She taps her heel against the old cafeteria style floors, the click, click, click, loud in the suffocating room. "I'm not sure which of us you're trying to convince when you say that."

I shake my head in denial. "When I saw you for the first time, all woozy from the snake bite, your face shining above mine, I knew we were meant to be."

Lacey studies me, her blue eyes as cold as the stainless

steel table. "Would you still think that if I told you I wanted us to live here the rest of our lives?"

She gestures around the dingy room.

I raise my eyebrows at the peeling, cracked walls, the cupboard full of blue cotton exam gowns, the smell of antiseptic, and below that a hint of mold, and grimace at the "Remember to wash your hands" poster circa 1978.

"Live in this clinic?"

She rolls her eyes. "No, Gavin. Not in this clinic. In that log cabin you bought six months ago the last time I volunteered here. We'd live in Hollow Creek, West Virginia. I'd run this free clinic. You'd volunteer on the business side. We'd live in this town for the next forty years, until I retired. We'd be too busy for vacations or travel. Instead, we'd stay here. Every single day of the year. On this mountain. We'd settle down, have kids. Live, work, and die. Here. Here for forever."

She points at the brown and gray tile floor, stained with decades of grime. The walls of the room crush me, the weight of forever stuck in one place making it hard to breathe. Decades of never, never leaving one place? I wouldn't be living on a mountain, I'd be buried under a mountain. I can already feel it crushing my chest, heavy and constricting.

Lacey scoffs and shakes her head. "That's what I thought."

"You really want to live here?"

I can't imagine it. Lacey Duporte comes from a family as wealthy as mine. She grew up in New York City, has traveled the globe, volunteers in countries around the world. She eats at the best restaurants in every city she visits, shops on Madison Avenue, has a penthouse in Manhattan—I can't imagine her in this crummy little ramshackle town in the middle of nowhere, where a basket of fried shrimp is considered fine dining, a drive-in theater is cultural entertainment, and the only place to shop for clothing is the five and dime. There are more churches than stoplights, and the accents are thicker than the beards on the old men, which is saying something.

I like people, that's not the problem. I get along with everyone. The problem is, according to the hand-painted welcome sign at the edge of town, there are only two hundred and twelve people in Hollow Creek. I doubt a single one of them has ever left this mountain top.

If I lived here for the rest of my life, if Lacey asked me to stay here, I'd... I shake my head.

Lacey walks to the small sink and turns on the faucet. It spits out rust-colored water then turns clear. She rinses her hands, scrubs with a hot-pink soap, and then yanks down the paper towels. When she's through, I know she's finished with our conversation.

"I'll live here, if that's what you want. I'm willing to do whatever it takes. I'm willing to work hard for it. Make any sacrifice." A drop of sweat trails down my forehead in protest.

Lacey brushes past me, the abrasive scent of sanitizer clinging to her. Her heels click coldly on the tile. She pauses at the door. Without turning she says, "That's the thing, Gavin. Love isn't supposed to be hard work. It isn't supposed to be a sacrifice. Love should be easy."

That's possibly the stupidest thing I've ever heard. "Since when?"

What she's describing isn't anything like the love I've known.

I follow Lacey down the dank hall of the free clinic. Old yellow smoke stains coat the popcorn ceiling and walls, from decades past when smoking was not only acceptable but encouraged by physicians. The hallway is narrow, and the flooring sinks to the left. The clinic is in a 1970s double wide after all. It's only open two weekends a month and Lacey volunteers here a few times a year, which is why I bought the cabin. I thought it'd be a nice vacation spot for a couple days a year. There's hiking, rafting, climbing. It's okay.

For a few days.

Not for decades.

Not...

I shake my head and ignore the musty scent and the creaking floors. The reception area is empty. It's early yet, and patients haven't started to arrive.

I'll do whatever it takes to prove to Lacey that I really do love her.

I'll do whatever it takes to keep her from saying my name with so much disappointment.

She unlocks the front door and holds it open for me. I take in the morning light glinting like the Saharan sands on her golden hair. "I flew around the country looking for you. It took a whole week to figure out where you were."

"Congratulations. Now that you've found me, you can go." She nods to the parking lot and my rental car. A cherry red Jag, her favorite, which is why I got it. I picked it up at the airport in Charleston when I got in early this morning. I left my plane there and drove hours into the sticks.

"I'll stay here with you, if that's what you need to prove I love you."

She shakes her head, and the look that I once thought was intelligence and poise now I think might just be disinterest. "I don't want to live here. I was making a point. You are completely incapable of loving anyone more than you love indulging yourself."

"I love you—"

"No."

"I love my brother Will."

"You kissed the woman he loves because you felt like it. How is that not indulging yourself?"

The sore spot in my chest expands and I step outside of the walls of the clinic onto the dirt-packed parking lot. I breathe in the mountain woods air and let the wide, blue bowl of the expansive sky settle me.

"I don't have an excuse for that—"

"Then don't give one."

"But I apologized."

"An apology isn't enough."

"Give me another chance. I'm willing to live in this dank little town, on this backwards little mountain, all because I love you."

"Maybe. Maybe not. I'm not willing to wait around to find out. Because from what I can see, I rushed into our engagement and then I found out that you're selfish, you're incapable of taking life seriously, you'll never settle down, you don't have any direction or career, you'll be a rotten father because you're still a child yourself, your work ethic is non-existent, you lean on your brother to fix your messes, and you don't take responsibility for your own actions. I'm glad that I found all of this out before I made the mistake of marrying you."

She shrugs and then nods at the parking lot, telling me to go. It's funny. I've been on the end of enough break-ups to know how this goes, but it never hurt quite this much.

I once fell twenty feet down a cliff in South Africa when I was free-climbing. I hit a few of the ledges on the way down, banged my head against the jagged rocks and broke my wrist when I hit the ground. That moment feels a lot like right now.

Probably because I realize Lacey's right.

And maybe, contrary to what my brother Will believes, our dad was right too.

Some essential thing that makes people capable of loving in the right way was left out when I was born. Will got it, but somehow it missed me.

Because if the people I care about most can't see it in me, then I don't imagine it's there.

"I'll come by the cabin at noon to give you back the engagement ring. I don't have it on me right now."

I shake my head. "I don't...you should keep it."

The edges of Lacey's mouth turn down. "What for?"

I can't think of an answer that she'll like or one that she'll believe.

A rusted pick-up truck pulls into the parking lot,

throwing up a cloud of dust. Its tailpipe lets out a series of clangs and bangs. The engine cuts off with a cough, and a tall man with a large gut swathed in flannel and suspenders jumps out.

"Well, if it ain't Doc Lacey. I'm come about old Arthur. He's been troubling me of late, horny as the devil poking his wife on the night of the full moon."

The man scuffs across the dirt lot. He's red faced, the type that burns after five minutes in the sun and then peels to ghost white again. His beard is shaggy and his eyes are bright, stuck on Lacey's warm smile.

"Oh no, your arthritis is acting up? Well let's take a look."

Lacey's already forgotten me, and it hurts, even though this is what I love about her. She cares about her patients, she has passion for her work, she cares about everything and everyone.

As she leads the man toward the clinic door, she turns distractedly back to me and says, "I'll see you at noon."

"I'll be there," I answer, but she's already led her first patient inside, and the door shuts with a loud, indifferent clang of finality.

3

―――――

Jamie

"Here kitty, kitty, here puss, puss." I crouch down and crawl on my hands and knees across the worn, wide wood planks of the old kitchen. I slide the bowl full of oatmeal under the table, letting the smell of melting brown sugar and butter waft toward my six-year-old, who decided last week that she's a cat. If I do this right, I'll coax her up to the table, to eat in a chair with a spoon like a good little kitten should.

Shay huddles under the table, sniffs at the air, and then licks her hand like it's a paw. I have to give it her, she has cat mannerisms down. Not for nothing, I'm really glad she decided to move on from donkey. The kicking was getting out of hand.

Tanner and Elijah sprint around the table, shoving

chairs out of the way. The pounding of their feet, their excited shouts, and the vibrating floor make it feel like I'm in the way of a stampede.

"Mom! Billy's in the house again!"

Oh for crying out loud.

It's then I see him, the old rooster, flapping his wings, pecking the air with his sharp beak, threatening to poke the living daylights out of anyone that comes near him.

"Well, get him then."

Billy's beady eyes latch on me with a malevolent gleam. It's like he knows I'm the reason he can't stay in the nice, warm kitchen where there's plenty of food dropped on the floor. In fact, I'm crouched in the sticky remains of last night's pea soup, a spoonful dropped next to Tanner's chair.

Elijah lunges for Billy, the old, cantankerous cock. Billy squawks and flaps his wings, beating me with them on his way past. I flinch and then scramble under the table next to Shay. I've been pecked enough to know when to duck for cover.

Shay giggles at me running scared from a rooster, but then she remembers she's supposed to be a cat so she ends her laugh with a staid meow.

I wink at her.

"Mom, are you 'fraid of ol' Billy?" Tanner asks as he sprints around the table, his shoes thumping on the floor. There's the clatter of silverware above, and I imagine Billy's found the bowls of oatmeal. Mine has walnuts, one of Billy's favorite things. I spent a whole day with Gran harvesting those walnuts, and there's no way I'm letting some bad-tempered dinner bone steal them from me.

"I'm certainly not." I crawl out from under the table and jump up with a fierce expression.

Billy, sure enough, is perched on my table, his bright orange claws scratching the soft pine. His curved golden beak is strategically positioned over my steaming bowl of oats. He cocks his head and holds still, considering whether it's the time to eat or the time to fight.

Flight never enters Billy's mind. He's a chicken not a coward.

"Eat it and die," I tell him in a menacing voice.

"Golly," whispers Tanner.

"He's gonna get it. He's gone and made Mom mad." Elijah elbows Tanner and they both stare at Billy like he's on a morning walk to the gallows.

Billy clucks and warbles low in his throat, and his rust red feathers puff out around his chest. I take a warning step toward him and he puffs his feathers more, doubling his size. He really is a beautiful rooster. His comb is apple red, his eyes beady bright, his breast feathers shiny russet with an iridescent blue and black tail to make a peacock proud. The only thing that ruins it is the fact that he's old, wiry, and only has one eye. He lost his left eye in a fight he picked, and won, with an eagle that swooped down and tried to eat him.

I suppose that eagle didn't know. Nobody's gonna eat Billy without Billy's permission. Trust me, we've tried.

I tiptoe toward the table, the plank floor creaking

under my feet. Billy narrows his eye and makes a warning squawk.

"Who let him out?" I say, edging closer while pretending I'm not getting closer.

"Tanner."

"Elijah."

The boys point at each other.

"Meow." Shay crawls out from under the table and licks her paw.

The smell of buttery oats, walnuts and brown sugar stirs up again when Billy flaps his wings, warning me not to come any closer. My stomach growls.

"Why'd you let him out?" I look at Tanner. He always tells, especially when he did it, he's like one of those villains in kid's cartoons who can't help but gleefully describe every step of their evil plan, because all they really ever wanted was someone to appreciate their genius.

Tanner sniffs and wipes the back of his hand across his nose. He looks to his brother. Elijah, being ten to Tanner's nine, is the leader. With his okay, Tanner nods.

"Cause...See...I was testing out my robotic arm egg collectin' system, the eggs came down the chute, and the arm, it's like that claw in the toy machine, 'cept it actually grabs the eggs, it doesn't rip you off, and then the pulley was supposed to open the gate just enough to drop the egg in the basket, but Billy snuck through the opening cause he doesn't have bones, he's liquid, and he knocked the basket over, and all the eggs got cracked, so Elijah and I were getting the eggs, and Billy ran past, and Shay was pushing the front door open with her head to see what the noise was about, because she's curious since she's a cat, and Billy ran past her, and then..." He stops talking when Elijah elbows him.

I'm beginning to see exactly what happened. Tanner looks exceptionally proud, even though there's a rooster on our breakfast table and all our fresh eggs are cracked, so I expect his pulley robot thingy worked. Granny Allwright keeps giving him metal scraps from the junk yard, and he keeps building more and more contraptions.

"Good job on the robotic arm."

Tanner and Elijah grin.

Billy clucks. I lunge forward, swipe him off the table in one quick grasp. He pecks me, a quick, hard hit against the bare skin of my arm and I bite my tongue at the painful sting. That's gonna bruise. He flaps and squawks and wriggles, like he's in a fight to the death. I hold his wings down at his sides and press him against my body, trying to limit his movements.

"Settle down. I'm not gonna eat you. Today. Ornery old coot."

"She got him!"

Tanner and Elijah let out a loud cheer and Shay meows her approval, hopping up on a chair to have a look. The boys lead the way, Shay follows on all fours, and in the backyard, we close Billy back in the coop with the hens.

Down the mountain, I hear the rumble of the school bus. Sound travels here—you can hear Granny Allwright singing in her garden in the mornings even though she lives two miles up the mountain—but by the sound, I know the bus is only a few minutes down the road.

"The bus! Shovel that breakfast in, get your backpacks, and your shoes, and—"

The kids take off, even Shay forgets to be a cat and runs after her brothers. When I make it to the kitchen, breakfast is already gone. Oatmeal is smeared on Shay's face. I wipe her red cheeks and kiss her on the nose.

Tanner and Elijah race through the kitchen, hopping into their shoes. There's a hole in Elijah's left shoe, right at the tip, and I see his white sock poking through. The bus honks. It's at the end of the drive.

"Bye Mom!"

"Bye!"

"Love you!"

They run out the door, Elijah the fastest, Tanner right after him, and Shay's little legs spinning wildly to keep up, her hand-me-down blue camo backpack thumping against her back. I glance around the kitchen, at the dirty dishes, the spilled oatmeal and milk, and the feathers and dust motes still floating in the breeze from the opening and slamming front door. The kitchen may smell comforting, and you might be tempted to relax, but it's an illusion. This place is the eye of the hurricane, the deceptive quiet between the chaos of the past and the chaos of the future.

I sigh at the mess and think, someday, someday I'll have a moment to give it a good clean. I'll have a minute to fix the faucet that shoots jets of water every which way when you turn it too far to the left. I'll tighten the loose knobs on the cupboards. I'll get a stove that doesn't need me to light the pilot light every time I cook. I'll mend the torn screen in the windows. Then I'll move on to the rest of the house. Fix all the things. Someday.

But not today.

The whooshing of the airbrakes on the bus hisses and the door closes. I wave from the kitchen window, as the yellow bus pulls down the road. I can barely make out Shay's pigtails, or as she calls them, cat ears, as she climbs into the front seat. Tanner and Elijah run toward the back.

I rub a hand down my face and consider a shower.

But the kitchen clock reminds me that I don't have time. I have to get the sculpture over to Gavin Williams' cabin before his fiancée or wife or whatever she is arrives. His directions were clear in his email. Deliver the sculpture this morning before ten a.m.

Leave without disturbing the house or the occupants.

Payment upon delivery.

For that kind of money, I'll follow his directions to the letter. Even if it means I'm dressed in dirty overalls, covered in chicken feathers, and I smell like chicken poop, scratch seeds, smoke, and oats.

I shrug. Bobby would've told me chicken poop is nature's finest beauty treatment. I'll go with that.

Besides, today is the first day of the rest of my life. And from here on out, it's going to be a good one.

4

Jamie

THE CUSTOM-MADE WOODEN CRATE IS IN PLACE, FOAM AND bubble wrap swaddle the sculpture like a baby. Nothing's going to happen to this piece on my watch. It's good that we arrived an hour early. I need at least this much time to unpack and clean up before Gavin and his fiancée arrive.

The cabin is sparkling. You might never be able to know wealth by sight, but you sure can smell it. It smells clean, nothing definable, just noticeable by the absence of dust, dirty dishes, and clothes waiting to be washed.

The ceilings are so high, the wooden beams so golden, the windows so tall and open, that it almost feels like I'm standing in a cathedral in some faraway, exotic land. The furniture is white and minimal, the stone fireplace is two stories tall, and the kitchen is just off the living room. It looks like a kitchen from a magazine. It makes me smile to wonder if there's ever been a chicken running around it.

Diedre, my best friend, spins in a circle and lets out a low whistle. "This place sure is something else."

"Yeah, it's okay."

Diedre clicks her tongue and gives me a laughing look. "Okay, huh? I'd put up with a lot to be set up in a place like this. Wonder what this guy's like."

I shrug. It doesn't matter to me. I'm not after the guy, or the cabin. "Who cares what he's like? The only thing I care about is that he likes my art and I'm getting paid."

I flip my braid over my shoulder and she snorts. "When'd your heart get all moldy and shriveled? I swear, Granny Allwright gets more action than you."

I pry the box open and carefully lower the wooden side to the gleaming hardwood floor. "Don't want action."

Diedre won't believe this. She's been my best friend since she moved here ten years ago and thinks she knows exactly what I need. Mainly, a whole lot of wild, no-strings attached sex. She claims good sex cures just about any ill. In that case, it sounds a lot like Granny's blackberry moonshine. Delicious in the moment, but you sure pay for it in the morning.

"Jamie, your heart is shriveled, not your lady parts. Be honest here."

I pry loose the next side of the crate and ignore Diedre. I need her and Big Tom's help lifting the sculpture, but that doesn't mean I have to converse.

Big Tom's out in the truck, scheduling his next drop-off. He runs a port-a-john business, mostly supplying construction sites, parks, and events. You'd never believe it, but supplying toilets is a real busy job.

Diedre picks at her bubblegum pink nails and narrows her eyes on me. Diedre smells like vanilla cookies and hairspray, mostly because she already did a photo shoot this morning for her social media, and she likes to smell good as well as look good. She's made a living off affiliate marketing and ad revenue, based on, from what she tells me, "looking real big and real sexy in butt cheek-baring shorts and a crop top, barefoot in the woods, while holding an ax, a dead badger, or any other country kink those repressed city boys like. They can't get enough of me."

I've seen most of Diedre's photos, and there are quite a few I wish I could unsee, especially the pseudo nudie ones where she used Granny Allwright's taxidermy squirrels as props. Those squirrels, wearing red gingham shirts and hats, have always given me nightmares.

I feel Deidre's calculating gaze on my neck as I carefully peel away the bubble wrap and packing tape. The bubble wrap crinkles and snaps as I tear it free.

Careful. Careful.

Diedre walks around the box, her high kitten heels click-clacking. Finally, she stops in front of me and clicks her tongue at the nearly unwrapped sculpture. "It's a beauty. That's for sure."

A jolt of pride fills me. If I had a different life, I'd try to get my art into galleries. I'd...

Diedre frowns. "Do you ever think about everything that's out there? Do you ever wonder what it'd be like if you could leave Hollow Creek, travel around the world, sell your art in New York or Paris? Do you ever think about all you're missing by staying here?"

I pause, my fingers scratching against the last of the bubble wrap. A clock ticks on the opposite wall and I consider the big, wide open, million-dollar cabin that I'm kneeling on the floor of. The clean smell, overlaid by my chicken poo and smoke scent. I think about how this cabin is the most exotic place I've ever been. Even in sixth grade, when all the other kids went on a field trip to Charleston to see the capital building, I had to stay home because I had chicken pox.

I let out a wistful sigh. "Sometimes," I admit. "Sometimes I think about it." There are galleries in New York, art shows and competitions in cities around the country, exhibits in Tokyo or Rome. Years ago, I used to dream about, not showing my art in galleries, but even just stepping inside one. Even just that little thing seemed like enough.

"And?" Diedre asks.

I shrug. "And then when I'm done thinking about it, I wrap all those thoughts up in a box," I tap the wood of the crate. "I tape it, nail it shut, and then bury it, so deep down that I don't ever have to think about it again. Not unless I want to. Which I don't."

Nobody's got time for that.

Diedre stares at me like I'm short a few screws. "Okaaay. That sounds really unhealthy. You know that, right?"

I grin at her. "Sure do."

"As long as you realize your coping mechanisms suck.

Anyway, I'm sure some good old-fashioned lovin' would cure what ails you."

"Aww, come on, Dee. I had my once-in-a-lifetime with Bobby. I don't get another."

She lets out a long sigh. "I'm not talking about a love like that. I'm just talking about some fun. You need a man."

I frown and shake my head. "I already have three men in my life."

"What? Who?"

I count on my fingers, "Elijah. Tanner. And...ol' Billy."

Diedre throws back her head and lets out a full belly laugh. At that moment Big Tom comes inside, and I see what I've known for a while now. Big Tom is madly, deeply, and unrequitedly in love with Diedre.

Unfortunately, he has the scruffy, bearded face of a hungry groundhog and is as shy as a sinner in church on Sunday. Neither scruffy faces nor quiet blushes catch Diedre's attention. She prefers bombast and flash pasted on pretty men. So as far as I can see, Big Tom doesn't have a chance.

"Oh there you are," Diedre says, throwing Tom an off-handed glance. She puts her hands on her hips and taps her foot. In heels, she's at least three inches taller than Big Tom. "Why do they call you Big Tom anyway? Never could figure it out."

Tom's face blazes carnelian red, and he ducks his head. But Diedre's already turned from him to inspect my sculpture. "It really is a beauty. I wish you'd let me set you up online."

I gesture for Tom to come over. "Thanks for helping out."

He nods, which in Big Tom speak means, "you're welcome, glad to do it."

"Don't say much, do you?" Diedre asks.

Tom looks at Diedre, a deer-in-the-headlights expression on his face. This is the usual expression he wears whenever she speaks directly to him, but I think he's also stunned because she's still wearing her photoshoot outfit. The butt-hugging jean shorts and flannel crop top show off her lush curves for those horndog, repressed city boys. The scent of vanilla floats around her like sugar cookies left out to lure in naughty boys. Her words, not mine. But, by the look on Tom's face, Diedre's magic is working.

She waits a full five seconds for him to respond, but when he doesn't she shrugs and looks at her nails. Then she glances at me. "Did you show this to Granny Allwright before boxing it up?"

Diedre loves my Gran, mostly because Granny's a character with a capital C. Granny was born during the Great Depression, she grew up in Hollow Creek, and she loves to play the crazy mountain lady for any hikers or unsuspecting outsiders that come through.

"I showed her last night."

Diedre's eyes light with interest. "What'd she say?"

A lot. Too much. Mostly about how I'm plum wasting my life and if she had talent like me she'd have gone and left instead of squatting on a mountain top.

I told her I had kids to raise, bills to pay, jobs to do.

She said, "Can't never could do nothing!"

Which since I was five years old has always made me grind my teeth, because it's her way of saying my negative attitude and excuses are the only thing stopping me from succeeding.

I narrow my eyes. But what did she say about my sculpture? Oh, right. "She said"—I put on her accent, which Diedre loves—"this here's making me grin like a mule with a mouth full of briars. You done it, Jamie girl. I asked the Lord, me and him are real good friends, I asked him to make you an artist, and he done it. For a minute there, I thought he wouldn't, but I don't chew my cabbage twice, so I waited, and there it was."

I smile at Diedre. Gran was real proud of me.

"Um, cabbage?" Diedre stares at the glass sculpture. "What's this have to do with cabbage?"

"It means she doesn't repeat herself, that's all."

Big Tom grunts, which means, "that's right."

Diedre lifts an eyebrow at him.

"Ready?" I ask.

They are.

We move the four-hundred-and-twenty-three-pound sculpture very, very, carefully to the art table Gavin ordered specifically for this piece. It's positioned in the center of the room so that his fiancée can see it as soon as she walks in.

I stand back and appreciate how the light shines through the curves and lines of the glass, making it look as if the sculpture is really moving, like it's real, flowing water in some far off river, all the way across the world.

"You need us to help clean up?" Diedre gestures at the crate and the bubble wrap.

"That'd be—"

Tom picks up the large crate with one arm and walks out the door.

"Or that could happen," Diedre says, staring after him. "He sure is an odd one."

I shrug. "Aren't we all."

"You ready?"

Big Tom's engine revs. Sounds like he's ready to go.

"I'm going to stay here, clean up, make sure everything's set."

Now that my piece is here, I'm nervous. I want Gavin to love it, I want his fiancée to love it, I want everything to be perfect. I'm itching to dust it off again, wipe away any fingerprints, maybe see if I can position any lighting to hit it just right.

"Alright, alright, I see you're itching to fix it up. You'll be okay walking home?"

"It's just a few miles."

"Sure. Call me if you want a ride."

I give Diedre a quick hug. After she saunters out, I pull my handkerchief from my overalls and start wiping the glass down. Everything, and I mean everything, has to be perfect when Gavin arrives.

5

———

JAMIE

I'M JUST FINISHING MY FINAL WIPE DOWN WHEN I HEAR THE rumbly engine of a car coming down the long drive. Oh gosh. My hands shake and I shove the handkerchief into my pocket.

Gavin didn't want me here when they arrived. It's like those old British dramas Granny watches. The aristocrats don't like to see the staff. They like to pretend the beds make themselves and the dust magically disappears. Not that I mind. I don't need to be seen, I'm covered in chicken gunk and wearing my dirty overalls. Nope. I'm happy not being seen.

My glass art can and should be what everyone looks at.

I look around the cavernous cabin for a back door I can slip out of. But for a great room that's five times the size of my whole house, there doesn't seem to be any door but the front door. Out the towering windows, a bright red sports car slows to a stop. The car's gorgeous, it looks almost like a piece I made last year for Diedre's Christmas present. I made it after a lick of bright red flame, dancing and bending in the fire, motion crystalized in glass. In the second I take to stare at the car, another pulls in, an old pickup—that's Rusty Drukenmiller's truck—and a woman climbs out and Rusty pulls away.

I should leave. I really should hurry and find that back door.

But...I've never seen anyone like this woman. Diedre, she's gorgeous in an earthy, lush, sensual way. I'm used to her type of beauty. But this lady...I always thought those women in magazines and on TV were touched up and fake. That illusion shatters like glass striking the floor.

She's beautiful like ice is beautiful. It's cold, and flawless, and if you stick your hand against it too long, it hurts. She's so pretty that looking at her feels like getting frostbite. She's in a tight blue silk dress, one I never imagined existing but realize must be the height of fashion, and the way she moves is like a snowflake floating down to earth.

As Tanner would say, *golly*.

Diedre asked what she'd have to do to get a man that could afford this place. Well, here's her answer. You'd have to look like that. I suppose, it should've been obvious.

Granny Allwright always says *beauty never made the kettle sing*, but I think she only ever said that to make me feel better. I've never been beautiful. Nobody would even consider me especially pretty.

I've known it my whole life. I've got a mirror, don't I? My hair is too red, my eyes too big, my lips too wide. I'm too skinny, too fair, too everything. Maybe alone, each piece is pretty, but all together? I'm like a bird decked out for mating season—too, too much in every way. As an artist, I can appreciate my uniqueness, but beyond that, I know I'll never turn heads. And it didn't ever matter to me.

But when Bobby and I had our shotgun wedding, the good people of Hollow Creek wondered if I wasn't maybe too plain to keep a man like Bobby at my side. Because Bobby, he was special. Everyone expected great things of him. Big things. City things, money things, beautiful wife things. They didn't expect him to end up shackled to someone like me.

But Granny, shotgun in hand, toasted us at the reception. Drunk on her blackberry moonshine, she said, "You got yourself the best bride you could ask for. Don't forget it. All you grumblers that say Jamie ain't pretty enough for Bobby. I'll tell you. Beauty never made the kettle sing." And that was the last word on that.

I'm not pretty. But I work hard and everybody knows it.

Beauty has never mattered to me. But at this moment, I finally see what everyone meant all those years ago. This is the kind of woman they expected Bobby to marry.

I didn't get it before. Now I do.

The front door of the sports car slams and I jump. I yank my eyes away from the woman, and there, stepping towards her is…

Goodness.

If the woman is ice, he's the fire.

Suddenly I'm hot.

Real hot.

I pat my cheeks and know they're burning chili pepper red.

Diedre was right, my lady parts aren't out of commission. The evidence is there right now, because I'm heating up like the molten glass in my furnace. In glassblowing the tip of the blowpipe is heated and then dipped in the molten glass. I've never thought about how suggestively erotic that is until this very moment.

Because apparently, my lady parts wouldn't mind Gavin Williams dipping his blowpipe into my furnace.

In the last six years I've never, ever, not ever experienced want, or lust, or even a spark of desire. Diedre would point out a man and say, if that doesn't light your fire, then your wood must be wet. And I'd say, it's wet, it's permanently wet.

But I was wrong. Because my wood just combusted.

I shake my head. Get ahold of yourself, I scold. He's engaged to be married. You're...you. Pull yourself together, you're here to drop off your work and get paid. And...you're not to be seen!

Dang it!

I let out a squeak and frantically look around the great room for a means of escape.

Gavin (he must be Gavin) and his fiancée (she must be his fiancée) walk toward the front door, their voices muted through the cabin walls. He tilts his head toward her, they're in a deep, intense conversation. The urgent look in his eyes sends goosebumps all over me. He's so rugged, so good-looking. It's like he's the original artwork and all those movie stars and male models trying to look manly and rugged are the poorly done reproductions. It makes me dizzy just looking at him. But his fiancée doesn't seem to notice. Like I said, she's ice, and she must be used to him, I suppose.

Oh well.

I take one last, wistful look at my glass work, flowing like a crashing wave and then I run toward the kitchen, my shoes pounding on the wood floor.

Door, door, where are you door?

Not in the kitchen, that's for sure.

There's a hallway off the great room, leading to bedrooms maybe? Perhaps there's a door that way. I fly over the floor, worried now. They're almost at the front door. I sprint down the dark hall. It seems like there's a dozen doors and I open them at random. An office, decked out with a computer and multiple flat screens. A massive bedroom with a bear rug and the biggest bed I've ever seen. Another bedroom, this one with a fireplace and a jacuzzi, it smells like roses and massage oil. A home gym. Another office. Another bedroom. Ugh. Is all this really necessary? And why don't any of these rooms have a patio door to *go outside*?

Why didn't I leave earlier with Tom and Diedre? Why did I stick around? Why?

I reach the end of the hall. There's a tall mirror, and my reflection stares back at me. My hair is a wild flame, my braid frizzing, my overalls are more stained than I realized, and my eyes tell me exactly what I already know—I'm in trouble.

I'm about to be caught up in a romantic interlude, looking, smelling, like this.

Then I remember, there was a laundry room off the kitchen, which might lead to that big garage. And a door!

I take off, running toward the kitchen. As I race through the great room I hear the ping of the electronic door lock and the grinding of the bolt.

I'm too late. Gavin's opening the door.

"—you should stay. I promise I can convince you—"

Gavin holds the door open wide for his fiancée, the sound of wind rustling the leaves, and the smell of damp tree bark blowing in. I'm directly in front of them, twenty feet away, right near my glass art.

"No, Gavin. I don't love you. I'm not going to marry you."

Oh.

Okay.

That's awkward.

Gavin grabs his fiancée's hands, and levels her with a smoldering look that would have most women kicking off their underwear. "Please. Give me another chance."

He leans forward, maybe to give her a kiss, and I think this probably isn't a good moment for me to interrupt. So I do what any normal, polite person would. I drop to the ground and hide behind the ugly white modern couch.

I feel like Shay, crouched like a cat on the smooth wood floor.

I cock my head. It's quiet up there. So maybe they're having a nice, long, passionate embrace. One with lots of tongue. Gavin looks like he'd use tongue.

Huh.

Maybe if they're really going at it, like humping against the wall, I can crawl across the floor, slide into the kitchen and scramble out the (possibly there) back door.

Slowly, I crawl to the edge of the couch and poke my head around the corner.

There's no kissing.

There's no humping.

There's not even any smoldering looks.

It's just the fairy princess dropping the biggest diamond ring I've ever seen into Gavin Williams' hand.

"I...I'll wait...if you change your mind."

"I won't."

I dig my hand into the corner of the couch, the soft fabric giving under my fingers. There must be something seriously wrong with this guy if she's cutting him loose like this. Maybe he's a nudist. Diedre dated a nudist for a while. She liked it at first, but then she said it got old real fast. She said it was like birthday presents without the wrapping paper. No fun.

"Can I have the keys to the jag?" The woman holds out her hand.

Well, she's got balls, I'll give her that.

"Why?"

"I just booked a flight in Charleston for this afternoon. I hired a car service for the trip down, but there isn't enough time to call them back. I'll drop the keys for you."

"I can drive you."

Embarrassment crawls up my neck. This guy doesn't know when to quit.

"I booked the flight to get away from you."

Gavin tugs the car keys from his pocket and drops them in her hand. His shoulders slump.

"Thanks. By the way, you should get cleaners in here. It smells like a garbage heap."

I cringe and then bury my nose in my overalls and take a breath. That's...yeah, that's me she's smelling.

The woman spins on her heels, and then seconds later, she's revving the car's engine and kicking up stones as she speeds down the drive, the backend of the car fishtailing on the gravel.

Gavin lifts his face to the ceiling, closes his eyes and lets out a long, defeated breath. I'll give him this, he still manages to look like the sexiest man alive even when he's miserable. He's in an expensive-looking leather jacket, real nice jeans, leather boots, his sandy-brown hair is styled like he's getting ready for his own photo shoot. Diedre would eat this up.

Gavin grasps the engagement ring in his hand and sighs. He looks sad, lonely, and...preoccupied. Now's my chance to crawl past and out the door.

I'll email about payment later.

After he gets over his broken heart.

Like, in a day or two.

I press my hands into the wood, rubbing my fingers over a knot, and slip out from behind the couch. The floor lets out a high whining squeak. I pause, one hand in the air, stretched out like a cat. I twist toward Gavin.

He's not forlorn and preoccupied any longer.

Nope.

He's staring at me.

His blue eyes are as wide and thunderous as the mountain sky before a storm.

"Who the devil are you?"

When Gavin was sad and pleading, like Elijah when he begs to go out and play baseball instead of doing his homework, I sorta felt sorry for him. But now, he's looking at me like I'm a diseased rat that somehow, incomprehensibly ended up in his pristine world, and all my feeling sorry evaporates.

I stiffen, because honestly, I do have some pride.

"You have two seconds to answer me, or I'm calling the police."

Not for nothing, but "the police" is Daryl Jones, my second cousin. That's not going to help Gavin. All it'll do is embarrass me. Daryl will get a good laugh out of this.

Gavin pulls a phone out of his pocket and holds it up threateningly.

"Tell me your name and what you're doing lurking in my home."

Slowly, I stand. I don't want to startle him after all. When I do, he gets a good look at my dirty overalls, my roughed up boots, and my frizzy hair. His eyes widen and his nostrils flare. I get the impression he just got his first whiff of ol' Billy.

I really should've taken a shower.

I would've if I'd known this was going to happen.

"My word, she's a squatter. I've got a squatter in my home." His jaw hardens and he thrusts his hand toward the open door. "Out. Get out." He motions at me like I'm some mangy stray.

"Hey!" I put my hand on my hips. "I'm not a squatter. I'm Jamie Sutton."

He stares at me, his expression uncomprehending. "What did you say?"

I blow out a long breath, the hot air stirring the hair sticking out from my braid.

"I said," I annunciate and talk real slow for him, "I'm not a squatter. I'm Jamie Sutton."

He shakes his head like he still doesn't understand and then he takes slow, careful steps toward me, like he expects some loony behavior on my part. When he's only a few feet away, he wrinkles his nose and looks at me with utter distaste.

"I don't know what jammy sudden is, but I want you to remove your person from my home."

Oh lordy. He can't understand plain English.

"Jamie Sutton," I say slowly pointing at myself.

He stares at me, uncomprehending. No wonder the fairy princess left him. He's gorgeous, but his head is full of rocks. And he has a temper. I know it, because he steps forward and grabs my arm, his fingers hot and calloused.

"That's it. If you won't get out, I'll take you out."

He drags me toward the front door. It's funny, a second ago, I would've loved to go out a door, now I don't want anywhere near one. I dig in my heels and tug in the opposite direction. But he's strong. Real strong.

"Hang on!" I shout, starting to put up a fight like ol' Billy. "What's wrong with you? You gave me the code to your place. I'm dropping off my work. Hello. I'm Jamie Sutton. The glassblower. Jeez Louise, you're yanking me like Granny pulling up a radish on a Sunday. Let go!"

He's having none of it.

"Unbelievable. I can't understand a word she utters," Gavin says in a completely dumbfounded voice.

I step on his foot. Hard.

"Let go! Understand that!"

He stops tugging me. We're a few feet from the door. I'm panting hard, and I bet anything, that my face is redder than molten glass. Worse, even though I'm infuriated, him holding onto me is sending an SOS through my insides. The message travels up my arm, down my chest, and all over my body, telling me that all that heat I'm feeling means it's time to strip down naked and cool off the old-fashioned way.

For crying out loud.

Gavin leans forward, towering over me, and brings his face close to mine. I can feel the warmth of him and I can smell the cologne he wears. It's like fresh air, strength and vitality. Or maybe that's just him.

My breath comes in short, painful pants, and my heart drums in my ears. In all this mess, I've nearly forgotten what I'm here for.

My work.

To get paid.

To start a new life where I can stop working three jobs and start giving the kids all the things I've always wanted to.

"Why'd you do that?" Gavin asks between clenched teeth. He jerks his head toward his foot. Apparently, it hurt when I slammed my boot down on his toes.

I try to jerk my arm free, but he keeps ahold of me. I glare at him. Now I know exactly how Billy feels when I trap his wings.

"Because. You won't let go." I say it real slow so the words can get through his thick skull.

He frowns and then releases my arm. My brain likes that, but my body doesn't. It wants that SOS, and my skin still tingles where he was touching me.

Gavin clears his throat and rubs at his nose. Yeah, yeah, I smell bad. Deal with it.

It's time to take charge. I stand as tall as I can, which isn't much compared to Gavin, who's more than six foot. I stick out my jaw and try to look as professional as I can, then I hold out my hand.

"Jamie Sutton. You're Gavin Williams?"

Apparently, this is too much for him to handle. "How do you know my name?"

I roll my eyes. "You hired me."

"I hard you?"

Oh my word.

This is probably the worst pseudo-conversation I've ever had in my life.

"You hired me to create glass art. The wave you commissioned. I dropped it off, like you instructed in your email." I point to the wave, sitting in its place of honor on the art table.

Gavin looks from me to the wave then back to me again.

I lick my dry lips and wait for him to connect the dots.

Before, I thought this cabin was expansive, but now it feels claustrophobic. Gavin's standing entirely too close. Studying me too carefully.

A slow, trickling flame licks over me, and I try to turn it off.

"No." He shakes his head. "I don't want it."

Well, that does it. The flame is off. It's completely off.

"What do you mean you don't want it? You commissioned it. You can't just—"

"She keeps talking and I keep not understanding a word. Is it fair to say I hate this place? I've been to the depths of the Cambodian jungle, the heights of Machu Pichu, the isolation of Antarctica, I've galloped on horseback across Mongolia, I've been to remote islands in Oceania, but never, never have I been confronted with so much..." He waves his hands at me. Speechless.

"So much what?" I ask, crossing my arms.

"You realize you're covered in chicken poop? And feathers?"

"Yes?"

He shakes his head, then a trapped-in-a-corner sort of look enters his eyes, and he says, "I have to ask, have you ever left West Virginia?"

I purse my lips.

"I'll be generous. Have you ever left this part of the state?"

I refuse to answer.

"This mountain?"

I look away from him. What does he want me to say? No. No I haven't. I've dreamed of it. My heart has left. My dreams have left. But my body hasn't. What of it? What does that have to do with anything and why does he think he has the right to ask?

He scrubs a hand down his face, and if possible his expression is even more horrified once he realizes I've never left this mountain. I cross my arms over my chest.

"We have a contract. I've delivered. I've upheld my end of things." He looks slightly ill, so I gesture at the door and say, "Sorry about your fiancée getting cold feet, bad luck there, but that doesn't mean—"

He turns away from me mid-sentence and paces across the room to stand in front of my work.

"Yes. We had a contract. I told you I wanted a wave the color of the Tonlé San River, shaded with jungle leaves and flashing under a lapis lazuli sky. An artist who has traveled and lived, they would know what I meant. But you..." He gestures at me and I flush. "You. This blue, this so-called wave, is as drab, ugly, and uninspired as—" He stops suddenly, and I get the feeling he's saying but not saying, *you.*

He shakes his head and continues, "Plain, lackluster, uninteresting. I commissioned a piece of art, not a glass blob. A customer has the right to refuse if the piece doesn't meet their requirements. This isn't cerulean, this isn't a wave, it's not what I asked for."

Needle-hot anger and embarrassment sting me, like I've fallen in a patch of nettles. "You signed a contract."

"I'm not paying for this. Take it and leave."

The locket around my neck burns hot, I can almost feel the sliver of glass inside, the one I made my promise on.

"I spent months working on this, I did exactly as you asked. Maybe you don't have enough artistic merit to see it, or maybe you don't have enough heart to appreciate good art, or enough brains to realize the difference between cerulean or azure, maybe you think it's red—"

Gavin throws up his hands. "What is ray-ud?"

That's it. "Red!"

"Listen, Miss Sudden. Or can't you understand English? Are you too busy rustling your chickens and rolling in their feces to understand—"

He. Did. Not. Just. Say. That.

"—what I'm trying to tell you? I don't want it. Your craftsmanship is poor. Your execution is terrible. I don't pay for subpar work. Take it and get out."

"No." I hold out my hand. "You owe me nine thousand dollars. I take bank check, wire transfer, or cash. Cold hard cash."

He laughs. "Get out."

I narrow my eyes. He's not going to pay. I could take him to court, but I don't have the money. He's won and he knows it.

I keep my hand extended. "I'll take that ring then."

His eyes turn hard. "I said get out. Go back to your

mountain home and run around barefoot feeding your chickens or whatever it is you do for fun."

"I paid for all the materials. I paid with my time. This isn't right."

He steps forward to grab my arm again, probably to drag me out of his stupidly beautiful million-dollar cabin. I bare my teeth at him. I hate him. I hate him so much. All that lusty furnace heat has turned to unadulterated loathing.

He's not an angel. He's not an angel at all.

I wonder, if I knocked Gavin over the head and kneed him where it counts, would Daryl side with me? Probably. He doesn't much care for snotty, stuck-up peckerwoods from the city. At least, not since his wife ran off with a bottle plant manager from Pittsburgh.

Gavin's hand brushes my arm. There's that awful zing again, racing over my skin. I flinch away from him, darting to the side. But I forgot where I was standing. I step away from Gavin, and away from the door, right into the table holding my glass.

I trip when I hit the table, my feet tangling, and I grab at the hard sides, trying to right myself and stop the table from wobbling. I don't manage either.

My heart stops and time stops too. The table tilts to the side, and my glass, my beautiful glass wave, slides, slides, slides through the air. It's tumbling now. The light from the windows strikes it and even if Gavin says otherwise, to me, it looks like a river flowing, deep in the heart of the jungle, full of secrets and mysteries. Then, the wave hits the floor, right at a corner, just the right angle, with just the right amount of force, to make the whole thing shatter in a crashing, cracking explosion.

The shards blow outwards, and I roll, hitting the ground too. The table breaks my fall, and I skid over it, and land, sprawled at the edge of the glass field. All the air sucks out of the room, and I'm left in a vacuum of silence. There was the bang of shattering glass, and then, nothing. Slowly, I start to hear again. My heartbeat. My breathing. The tinkling of the last bits of glass skidding across the floor.

I lift my palm from the ground. There's a shard stuck in the meaty bit. I wince and tug it out. A bit of blood wells to the surface.

I drop the glass to the wood floor and then lift my head to look at Gavin.

He's fuzzy, all blurred out, and I realize it's because there are tears in my eyes.

I drop my chin and blink them back.

"Jeez," he breathes. "What the..."

That's it. That's really it. My stomach drops and I feel like I'm going to be sick. There isn't any coming back from this.

It's not like I can piece it back together and sell it to someone else. It's not like Diedre can post it online for me and try to find a buyer. It's not like any of the hopes and dreams that I finally thought were coming true will.

No.

My chest cracks, shattered like the blue glass pieces around me. All that blue glass looks like my heart's blood.

Because blood is blue, isn't it? At least, it is until you're bleeding.

I almost hate myself right now. For six years I didn't really dream or think about the better things we might have. I just worked hard and accepted things as they were. But finally, finally I let myself imagine, and this morning I thought we'd made it. But I was wrong. And now that it's been taken away, it hurts. It hurts real bad. I wish that I'd never dreamed of it or thought about all we could have, because if I hadn't believed in it, then it wouldn't hurt when it was taken away.

I wipe my hand against my cheeks, wiping the hot, wet tears away. Then I look up at Gavin. He stares at the mess around me.

"I'm still charging you," I say, a painful lump in my throat. "I delivered. Payment upon delivery."

He scoffs and shakes his head. "I felt bad...then you had to go and ruin it."

I push to my feet and wipe my bloody hand on my overalls. Gavin watches and then winces.

"Pay up."

He shakes his head. "This will have to be cleaned. I'll pay the cleaning fee and then we'll be square."

"Like hell."

He frowns at me. "I seem to remember paying you ten percent up front. Be happy I'm not asking for that back."

I cross my arms and shake my head mulishly. "I'm not leaving 'til you pay."

He might not ever pay. But what do I have to lose by trying? Nothing.

Gavin walks around me, and I try not to wince when his shoes crush the glass under his feet. It feels like he's crushing my heart. He sighs and then lifts his phone. I tap my foot as he types something in and taps the screen. "I'm calling the cleaning service. You'll have to move when they arrive."

I lift an eyebrow. Yeah. Good luck with that.

He holds his phone up to his ear. In exactly three seconds my phone starts to play "Foggy Mountain Breakdown." Granny keeps changing my ringer. She thinks it's a big laugh. Gavin stares at me, but he hasn't caught on yet. I lift my phone out of my pocket and hit answer.

I glare at him as I say into the phone, "Mountain Top Cleaning Services, how may I help you?"

Gavin swears and hangs up.

"Rude," I say into the phone.

He paces back over the glass. I'm the only cleaning service in town, and now he knows it.

He swings around and glares at me. "Fine. I don't need it cleaned up. I'm leaving. You can sit in here until you rot for all I care. I'm not coming back." He stalks towards the door, and then probably at the same time I do, he remembers that he gave his rental car to his ex-fiancée.

I smirk.

Without looking at me, he scrolls through his phone again. Looking, I'm sure, for a taxi.

He holds the phone up to his ear, his shoulders tight, the line of his back tense. In exactly three seconds, "Foggy Mountain Breakdown" starts up again.

"Hello, Hollow Creek Taxi Service, how may I help you?"

Gavin spins around, an astonished expression on his face. "You?"

I smile at him, a cat in the cream. "Me."

"Are you the only person that works in this town?" He seems absolutely outraged.

Apparently, Gavin Williams has never heard of the concept of *working* for a living.

"Where do you need to go?" I ask into the phone. The reception is bad and the line crackles.

Gavin growls in disgust and hangs up. "The airport," he says. "How much?"

I put my phone back in my pocket. Then I make a show of counting on my fingers. "Let's see. Gas multiplied by mileage plus time, aww heck, a country girl like me doesn't know how to do math. Let's just say...nine thousand dollars."

Gavin's eyes flare and I stand my ground.

"And how much to clean up this mess?"

"Nine thousand."

He steps forward and looks me up and down, clearly not liking what he sees. "I really, really don't like you."

I clench my hand, the blood reminding me of everything I just lost. But then, I never had it, did I? "That so? Well, I reckon I really, really don't like you either."

He shakes his head in disgust, then he turns, stalks out of the cabin, and slams the door behind him. The door shakes and the angry sound echoes through the big space.

"What do I do now?" I ask the empty room.

Wait, I guess.

He can't walk all the way down the mountain. He'll be back.

But five hours later, I have to head home to meet the kids at the bus, and Gavin Williams is nowhere to be seen.

6

———————

GAVIN

THE WIND SMACKS MY FACE AND NEEDLES OF COLD AIR HIT me. I drag in a breath and brace myself against the sheer edge of the cliff. What the heck is wrong with me?

The wind whips past, tugging at my limbs, and I wonder for a minute if I should turn around. This route, a deer trail really, is more technically difficult than I realized. It's not a marked trail, just a path down the mountain, near my cabin. The ledge along the cliff-face is only six inches wide and littered with loose gravel from past rockslides. It's a warning I'd usually take by turning back. But I don't want to turn around yet. If I do, I'll have to confront that nasty-tempered red-haired woman, and then I'll have to apologize.

I was an ass. But I felt raw, exposed, undone by what

Lacey said, and then when I thought I was alone, safe to lick my wounds, I opened my eyes and there *she* was.

That half-feral, boney, frizzy-haired, smelly, awful woman. She was on her knees looking at me like I was someone to be pitied. Me.

Lacey saw that I couldn't measure up, and then this woman, who smells like chicken poop, has feathers in her hair, and has never left this mountain top, looks at me as if she feels sorry for me.

I'm okay being envied, desired, or hated, but never, ever pitied.

When she told me I owed her for the artwork she delivered, my wedding present for Lacey, I lost control. I don't have an excuse. To be honest, I barely glanced at the glass wave. It hurt to look at it. I didn't want it anywhere near me. The light hitting the glass and sparking off it was a potent reminder of everything Lacey said, and everything I'd just lost.

Lacey claimed I don't know how to love. I don't know how to stay still. I don't have direction or purpose. That I'll make a terrible father and a terrible husband. That piece of glass, the blue shining wave, was a monument to my delusions. I thought I'd changed. But I haven't.

Because even now, my chest is twisting, my hands are itching, and I'm preparing to run.

I'll hike the Andes. I'll dive the Maldives. I'll go and I'll do what I always do, and I'll prove Lacey right.

My brother Will is going to be disappointed. He's finally shucked off all our dad did to screw him up. Because he's a better person than I am, he thinks I can do it too. He thinks Lacey is the best thing that ever happened to me and that I'd be an idiot to screw this up. Well, I'm an idiot.

That's what our dad always said. Will was the smart one, I was the dumb one. Will was the serious one, I was the fun one. Will was the success, I was the failure. Will was...he was my twin and my best friend.

When he was nine, our dad realized he was a mathematical genius. He decided that he'd mold Will into the perfect financial, business machine. There were hours of tutors, books, lectures. Will wasn't allowed outside to play, wasn't allowed friends, our dad even put down his dog. I knew what was happening, I hated it. So I did my best to disturb the lessons, sneak Will out of the house, play pranks on the tutors. I did everything a nine-year-old could to make sure my best friend and brother could come outside and play.

A month into my strategic assault on tutors and lectures, my dad decided he'd had enough. Nothing would prevent Will's talent from blooming, especially not his less useful, less intelligent, less obedient brother. So in the mornings, and in the evenings, really, every minute we weren't in school, Will was sent to the office to study with his tutors, and I was sent...

At first, my dad locked me in my bedroom, but I just climbed out the window, down the tree, and then went to find Will to see if I could make a distraction big enough to let him run off. But then, my dad caught on, and instead of locking me in my room, he locked me in a closet in the basement. There were no windows, no lights, there was just darkness, and me, hitting my shoulder against the door and yelling and yelling.

The first day, when my dad let me out, I ran upstairs to find Will, to tell him everything that'd happened. But Will was crying because Dad had put down Riley, his Jack Russell. Will thought it was dad sending him a message, that his studies were more important than anything else. But I knew it wasn't a message to Will. It was a message to me.

"Where were you?" Will asked.

I shook my head, shrugged, and said in a cocky voice, "Outside playing. I'm sick of hanging around, waiting for you to come and play."

After a week of sitting in the dark basement closet for hours and hours while Will studied with his tutors, Will stopped asking where I was, why I wasn't there trying to distract his tutors anymore. After a month, Will stopped trying to get away to play and just started studying all the time.

When he asked what I did while he was learning, I told him that I hiked in the woods, climbed trees, swam in the pond nearby. I told him dozens of stories about all the wonders of outside. The scratchy bark on the trees that I climbed looking for bird nests, the tadpoles I chased in the pond, the deer tracks I followed deep into the woods. I told him about all my adventures. It wasn't a lie, because while the tight, concrete walls of the two by three closet pressed on me like a stone coffin, I closed my eyes and imagined I was in the bright woods, under the open sky, breathing in the leafy air, listening to the robins, feeling the wind on my skin and the cool, damp earth on my bare feet.

Three years later, I was twelve, taller, and stronger, and my dad stopped locking me in the basement closet. When Will's economic tutor pulled in the driveway and my dad didn't come, I sat in my room, shocked, confused, and then, with slow realization, I knew I was free. He wasn't coming. I was free. That first day I sprinted into the office, barging in on Will and his tutor. I still remember the flushed heat of my skin, the wild beating of my heart, I was free, and Will and I were going to go outside. A trace of sweat lined my brow, my dad was there too. All of them looked up at me.

"Will," I said, my voice breaking, my heart pounding.

He lifted his head from the large book he was tracing his finger down.

I swallowed down the fear at seeing my dad. What would he do? Would he take me back downstairs? I didn't care. I felt wild and free.

"Will. Let's go outside. Let's..."

My dad's lips curled into a cruel, amused smile. He knew something I didn't, and I realized, too late, that I'd walked into whatever he'd planned.

"Let's go outside?" I stuttered, gesturing at the window and the beautiful, blue sky.

Will stared at me blankly.

My heart thundered, and the sweat on my skin turned cold.

"I'm busy, Gavin," he said in a patient voice, like he was

speaking to a child. "I don't have time to play. I have work to do."

Will turned back to the book and murmured a string of numbers to his tutor. My dad though was still watching me, his smile curving wider. I took a step back. Another.

I hadn't realized. I didn't know. All those years I was locked in the basement, in the dark, dreaming of outside, Will was locking himself away in another kind of closet. I was let out, but Will, he was still trapped inside.

My dad had what he wanted. He didn't need to keep me locked away anymore. Will, my twin, my best friend, had become exactly what my dad wanted him to be.

I shouldn't have pretended. I shouldn't have told all those lies. I shouldn't have pretended to be happy, to be free, just to keep Will safe. Because it didn't work. It'd trapped him.

I took another step back. Then another. Until I was out of the office. Out of the house. Until I was running.

I sprinted into the woods. Ran until I didn't have any more breath. Tree branches reached out and scratched at my skin, tore at my clothes, briars caught in my hair and birds cawed angrily and fled in front of me, the cuts and the stings burned, almost as much as the burning tears, but I kept running, until I came to the pond, the one I always dreamed about, and I tore off my shoes, sobs choking out, and then I dove in, my clothes weighing me down, I swam to the middle of the pond, and sank to the bottom, where there was no sound, no sight, no tears, and I looked up through the rippling, air bubbling, murky water at the azure sky, and I promised myself I wouldn't ever,

ever, ever, ever be trapped, or held down, or forced to stay in one place. I wouldn't ever be trapped again, and someday, Will would be free too, someday, he'd be free.

What I didn't count on was that I'd never really made it out of that closet, and Will got free before me.

I grip the rocky ledge. A stubborn patch of grass growing in a crack tickles my hand, and I breathe in the scent of river stone. It smells like the damp concrete of the basement closet. And even in nature, out in the open, with the clear sky and the wind whipping past me, and a wide, churning river, sixty feet below, I feel trapped.

I have to go.

I have to leave.

I'll call Will, apologize for nearly ruining his chances with Jessie. I'll call Jessie, make sure she and Will are okay.

And then I'll go.

I turn, inch back on the cliff edge. It was a stupid idea to come on the hike. I need to get out of West Virginia, out of this town. This place is as much a trap as the basement closet. The people who live here never leave. They live and die here.

That red-haired woman is a prime example. She's what happens to people who stay in one place too long. I can't even imagine what life is like for her. What if that were my life? What if I were married to her? Life would be an unending hell, that's what.

She was mean-tempered, loud, demanding.

But that doesn't excuse the way I spoke to her. For a minute, I felt like my father, and that's something I never want to feel.

I'll apologize. I'll pay her the money. Then I'll go.

I shuffle my feet, and a cluster of rocks fall, knocking loudly against the cliff wall until they splash into the swollen brown water below. The river bends like an undulating snake, the white rapids its scaly skin, as it slithers through the gorge. I swallow and wipe at the sweat on my forehead and try not to think about the fact that I'm on a narrow ledge on an unmarked trail.

No worries. I've hiked worse.

My mouth is dry, filled with the acrid taste of river stone. I turn my face, breathing in the sharp air. Then, I hear it. The distinct groan, the creaking, cracking grumble that precedes a rockslide.

I jerk my head up. Above, a mountain's worth of dirt, and gravel, and boulders, slides towards me, picking up speed. The grumble becomes a roar, and the second I realize I better run, it's too late.

A boulder slams against my shoulder. I fling myself to the side. Shield my head with my arms. The thick cloud of dust and dirt hits, and I choke on the dirt-filled air. Sharp gravel pelts me, a hailstorm of rocks.

The landslide is a booming roar, and I'm consumed by the sound, blinded by the cloud of dirt and choking on the thick air. I stand, try to dodge the boulders, make it off the cliff. Fear scratches at me, drawing blood. I realize that I could die. In all the extreme sports, the cliff-diving, the skydiving, the whitewater rafting, I never once considered that I could die.

Fear chokes the breath from me. Stupidly, horribly, my life flashes before my eyes, but it only takes a second.

Because all I've ever done is run and run and run.

The only person I'll leave behind that loves me is Will, and with Jessie's help, he'll get over my death soon enough.

Another crack sounds. I throw my arms over my head. A boulder the size of a man crashes down the wall. It's coming right for me. I dive to the side, barely balancing on the thin ledge. I tip back, my arms pinwheel. I manage to grip the rock with the tips of my fingers. Then, the boulder hits the ledge next to me. It smacks the rock with a bang, the wall vibrates like a bucking horse. I'm thrown up in the air. My teeth slam together and I taste the copper tang of blood. Then, when I slam back down, the ledge is gone. It's crumbled beneath the weight of the boulder and joined the rockslide.

There's nothing for me to hold on to. My hands claw at the cliff. I grab the grass sticking from the crack in the wall. The roots give way. And then I'm free falling. My stomach plunges faster than me. The river is below. If I can only hit it right. The air is yanked from my lungs. Rocks smack into me, spin me around.

The cliff wall flies past, the blue and green trees streak by, the brown river looms closer.

I try to right myself, but I'm struck by another rock. The air yanks at my clothes and my hair. I've jumped from planes, cliffs, bridges, but never has falling felt like this. The air whooshes through my ears, making me deaf to everything but its roar. My chest hurts, my teeth grit, my muscles tense. I'm about to hit.

I understand physics. I know that when falling from a great height, water doesn't give. In fact, it hurts when you hit. You can break a leg. Or a neck. I know exactly what to expect.

It's likely that in seconds I'll be gone.

All I can think is—

I'm sorry Will.

I'm sorry.

I'm sorry Lacey. I wish I could've been better.

I'm sorry Jessie.

I'm sorry.

I'm sorry Will.

I slam into the water. The river doesn't give. No. I hit the surface and it's like hitting a concrete floor. Then the water cracks and swallows me. The cold is an electric shock. It only takes a second to realize I made it, I'm still alive.

I kick at the churning water, struggling for the surface, my lungs burning.

I'm alive.

I'm...

A boulder stabs the water, and shoots toward me. I kick my feet and jerk to the side. But I'm too slow. The boulder glances off my head. Starbursts of pain explode through my skull. The world is a riot of churning panic and pain. Another rock slams into me and I spin in the water, sucked down the raging river, kept under, away from the air I desperately need.

I claw at the water. Kick. Fight.

I spin in the current. Slam into a rock. Spin around again.

The world grows fuzzier.

The fear vanishes as quickly as it arrived.

The water rushes past me, a clear brown maelstrom, full of frothing rapids. I blink, the water stinging my eyes, and I look up through the murky water at the azure blue sky.

My limbs stop working, my lungs stop begging, my clothes weigh me down, and I start to sink in the deep, cold river. I'm back. I'm back in the pond. Somehow, I made it back to the pond.

I smile as the current pulls me deeper.

Then, I hit another rock. My head cracks against it. I hear the sound of my skull hitting stone, even under water. And strangely, I don't see the water anymore, I can only see a million pieces of shattered blue glass.

Then even that fades and the world descends into nothingness.

7

Jamie

The kids didn't take the bus. No. On my way home I was called into the school to speak with Ms. Crum, the principal. Luckily, Granny Allwright was bombing down the road in her old banana yellow Mustang, on her way to pick up some nightcrawlers from the tackle shop, and she offered me a lift.

She's waiting in the school parking lot now, since the last time she came inside the school was three Christmas pageants ago, and the less said about that, the better.

Elijah, Tanner, and Shay sit in a row in the little blue plastic chairs, right outside Ms. Crum's office. When I walked past, Shay looked at me with big eyes, but the boys stared at their feet. None of them made a peep, which is how I knew right away that this was real serious.

Hollow Creek School is a series of brown and white double wide trailers, connected by concrete sidewalks. Kindergarten through fifth grade is in one trailer, sixth through twelfth grade in another, music, art, and the cafeteria in the third, and the offices in the final trailer. Ms. Crum's office smells just like it always does, like soggy carpet, pencil shavings, and stale coffee. The noise of her tapping her pencil against her metal desk is the only sound in the room.

She's resided as Hollow Creek's principal for forty years, molding the destinies of generations, and she's silently reminding me of that fact.

Granny Allwright always claimed Elvira Crum has the squished, lumpy face of a toad and the personality of a rat, and I can't say I disagree. As a kid, I had nightmares about being sent to her office.

I lean forward in the vinyl chair, a spring in the padding digging into my thigh, and I clear my throat. "Ms. Crum, what did you want to talk—"

"Jamie Sutton," she snaps. Her eyes are swamp green, and when she frowns her wide mouth nearly sags over the entirety of her chin.

I sit up straight and the chair's spring pokes me again. "Yes?"

"I've seen some bad eggs in my time. Bad eggs that amount to nothing."

I hear one of the kids' chairs scrape, and I imagine they're leaning in closer to hear.

Ms. Crum slaps her pencil against her desk. "But I've never seen any eggs as rotten and spoiled as yours."

"Now see here—"

"Your daughter refuses to recite her letters. She refuses to speak. She will not read. No matter what we try, the only thing she can do is meow, or bray, or neigh. Is learning a joke to your family? Do you deride education in your home?"

I flinch. "No, of course not. But she's only five, she should be allowed to play—"

"She is not here to play. She is here to learn."

There's another scuff of a chair in the hallway. I'm itching to turn around and look at the kids, but I keep my eyes on Ms. Crum and the pencil sharpener, the pile of pencil shavings, and the stack of papers that have surrounded her for decades.

I grit my teeth. "I was a late reader. It isn't unheard of—"

"Yes." Ms. Crum stabs her pencil at me. "You were one of my greatest failures."

I wipe my sweaty palms on my overalls. "Is that all?"

Ms. Crum's eyes flicker to the kid's seated in the hall, her gaze reminds me of a toad tracking the flight of a fly. "At afternoon recess, your daughter pretended to be a cat, and rightly so, Cody Thorn told her to stop. Your sons then used the pulley and rope on the flagpole to hang Cody by his underwear. He was ten feet up the pole and it took us a half-hour to get him down. Do you understand me?"

Ms. Crum's voice has reached a high fever-pitched squeak. Her face is a florid red. I take that in, but I'm having a terrible time keeping a straight face. From what I know, Cody is just like his dad Doug, mean as an adder and big as a bull. I think Cody must've said something a little worse than "stop" to Shay, and I bet the boys decided he needed a lesson in how to treat their sister right. It's not hard to imagine. What is hard to imagine is how Elijah and Tanner managed to hook Cody up to the pulley system.

Slowly, I turn in my creaky chair and look past the peeling wallpaper on the office wall to my kids lined up in the hall. All three of them look at me with the sweet, wide-eyed expressions of innocent little angels. I hold back a snort and turn to Ms. Crum.

"No. I don't quite understand what you're getting at."

She thrusts a finger at me. "Your daughter is unmotivated and undisciplined. Your sons are deviants and troublemakers. In the last week alone your sons have jerry-rigged the classroom windows to open at their command, used a string to yank all the tests off their teacher's desk, wired into the sound system and played 'Foggy Mountain Breakdown'—"

That has to be Granny's influence. I cover a snort.

"It is not funny!" Ms. Crum slaps her desk. "What would Bobby say if he saw his children? What would he think? They are spitting on his memory."

I clench my fist and take a deep, steadying breath of the stale coffee-tinted air. In his early days, Bobby was in this office a fair share of the time, getting his own reaming. I imagine he would've asked the boys why they didn't hoist Cody higher than ten feet, and then he would've cuddled Shay in a big, warm hug. Then again, if Bobby were still around, we might not live in Hollow Creek anymore, and our whole lives would be different.

"That's another thing," Ms. Crum continues. "Tanner has been telling stories, claiming he has a pa. A new pa at home."

I swing around and look at Tanner. His freckles stand out as his face goes white. He looks down at his shoes.

When I look back at Ms. Crum, she's adjusting the pencil sharpener, inching it around her desk, lining it up with her stapler. "I expect, I'd prefer if he were telling the truth. Because from my perspective, if you don't clean up your kids' act, if you don't get them to take learning seriously, we're going to have problems. What they need is discipline. What they need is a father."

I frown at Ms. Crum. She's as old as Granny, she's old-fashioned and she's fairly awful, and right now, her swamp green eyes have taken on a pitying look.

I want to snap *I don't need a man.* But that'd be a lie, because if the good Lord told me that I could have Bobby back, I'd take him up on that offer in a second.

And then, I wonder. Why has Tanner been telling tales? Does he want a dad that bad?

I grip the dirty jeans of my overalls and glance around the office, at the windowless walls, covered in water-stained wallpaper, at the filing cabinets overflowing with years of school records, at the collected records of generations of Hollow Creek's finest.

"If you don't fix this situation, I'll be forced to hold your daughter back. And I'll be forced to expel your sons. Do we understand each other, Mrs. Sutton?"

I dig my boots into the dank blue carpet, and the dirty drab blue suddenly reminds me of horrible, awful Gavin

Williams. I can see him sneering at me, telling me this is exactly what he'd expect of someone like me. How my kids will become just as ugly, drab, and uninspired as I am. If he'd paid me what he owed, I could've gotten Shay reading tutors, I could've hired math tutors, we could've... should've...would've...

"We understand each other." I stand and take a final look at the little room, overflowing with paper and files, Ms. Crum squatting like a grand dame in the center of her kingdom.

"Good. I expect changes."

I hustle out the office door and jerk my head at the kids. "Let's go."

They scramble out of their chairs, like they've been shot out of a potato gun, and hurry down the hall to the front door. At Granny's Mustang, they all pile into the back. The brown vinyl seats creak and the springs groan. The car is forty-five years old, and it shows every single one of those years. The brown vinyl is more cracked than whole, and foam squirts out of the seats like toothpaste. The floor in the back is missing in a few places, and you can see the undercarriage, and the road flying past. The car, of course, has an ash tray, and in the tray and the fabric, you can still smell the pipe tobacco that Grandpa Allwright smoked in here for the twenty years preceding his untimely death.

It's a comforting kind of smell, and it settles me as I climb into the car and shut the groaning front door. Granny Allwright looks over at me and lifts an eyebrow. Apparently, she can tell it's been a long, long day.

"That bad, huh?"

I nod, then buckle in. Shay reaches over the seat back and rubs her nose against my hair.

"Meow?"

I sigh and run my hand over her cheek. "You're alright. But maybe, in school, you could pretend to be a little girl?"

In response, she licks her hand like it's a paw.

We'll work on it.

Elijah helps Shay buckle in.

Granny looks in her rearview mirror at the kids while she puts on a bright shade of orange-pink lipstick. "What happened? What'd you boys do this time?"

Elijah puts his arm around Shay's shoulder. "Aww, Gran. That Cody troll shoved Shay down and told her if she was a cat then she'd have to eat bugs like a cat—"

"Cats eat bugs?" Granny frowns at them.

Tanner nods. "Some do."

"He had a roach, and he shoved it in Shay's face."

"Rawrra-meow." Shay's kitten meow is extremely affronted.

"Well, I never. Me and the Thorns are going to have a nice little sit-down chat."

"We took care of it, Gran. We hooked Cody to the flagpole and used the pulley to send him up. It gave him a wedgie that'll take years to get out." Tanner bounces in his seat, eager as usual to tell all about his mechanical brilliance.

As his mother, it's my duty to tell Tanner, "That wasn't the right way to handle the situation."

"But it sure was the best way," Granny mutters so only I can hear.

Tanner and Elijah look down at their hands folded in their laps, the picture of contrition. They heard Ms. Crum as well as I did. They know what expulsion means.

"You boys can't keep getting in trouble at school."

Tanner looks up quickly, his eyes flashing with youthful outrage. "We're bored! We hate sitting in there doing nothing but nothing. How would you like it if somebody made you sit in a chair all day and do stupid worksheets that have no point?"

Elijah nods. "We want to build things. We want to have fun."

"Rawr." Shay wrinkles her nose to add to the point.

I shake my head. We've already had the "school is important for life" conversation about nine thousand times.

Granny revs the engine and glares at the kids. "Listen to your mother. You'll do good at school, you'll behave, and that's that."

"Yes, ma'am," the boys chorus.

I give Gran a grateful smile. She winks at me, then pulls out of the school parking lot, the car vibrating so much it's almost like a massage. The engine noise is so loud, it's about all you can hear.

But still, I turn around and ask Tanner. "Why are you telling stories?"

He knows what I'm asking about. Why is he telling the other kids he has a new dad?

His jaw goes hard and he frowns. "You wouldn't understand."

As soon as Tanner turned nine, he had a whole slew of things he thought I wouldn't understand. He's more sensitive than Elijah, more volatile in his emotions. While Elijah remembers Bobby, Tanner doesn't, and I think it eats at him. "Try me."

He shakes his head and looks out the window.

Granny flicks on her blinker and turns to start heading up the mountain. The tailpipe backfires, and then pops again. We all learned years ago to ignore the various hissing, rumblings and pops the mustang makes. This car is twenty-five years past its prime, but Gran won't give it up.

I glance at her. She's what most people would call a bag of bones. Her skin sags over her frame and hangs loose like clothes flapping on a line. It's what comes after nine decades of scraping out a life in the backwoods. For half her life she didn't have electricity or indoor plumbing. That didn't come to the mountain until the late seventies. She's stubborn, proud of her independence, and she swears she'll die with a shotgun or a fishing pole in her hand, on her own land. She's a glimpse into the future, and what I can expect to look like sixty years from now. Her face is as craggy as the mountain side, her hair has lightened to a foggy orange, and it's like the wind has whittled her down to leave only the essentials— stubbornness and wicked humor.

She turns her sharp gaze on me and purses her

orangey pink lips. "You dropped your glass off today. At that Wilbur fellow's place."

"Williams."

A needle of anger works through me, and I squirm. Gran narrows her eyes.

"What happened?" Gran doesn't miss much.

May as well get it out. "He didn't want it."

The car backfires, and I think it's because Granny punched the gas in either anger or shock. "What's that?"

I grip the fabric of my overalls. "He didn't want it. He said it was..."—ugly, uninspired, drab—"not what he asked for."

"I'll talk to him. I'll tell him what's what." By the look in her eyes, I can imagine exactly what that "talk" would entail—mainly, the end of a rifle.

I shake my head, the horrible feelings of earlier starting to seep back in. "He left town. He isn't coming back."

Granny lets out a disgusted grunt. "You worked months on that piece. You put all that time and money into supplies, he can't just—"

"He did." I cut her off. I don't want to talk about it. If I do, I might cry. And I don't want the kids to see how much this hurts. How much I was counting on this making a difference in our lives.

But Gran knows. She reaches over and squeezes my hand, her papery skin soft on mine.

Tanner wiggles in his seat. "If we find him, I've got this new idea about using a trip wire to dump a basket of rotten eggs—"

I shake my finger at him. "Don't you waste my eggs."

"Aww Mom."

"Don't 'aww Mom' me."

Gran turns down our drive and the Mustang bumps over the pitted gravel. Up ahead, I see my home in a different light than I did this morning.

When I left this morning, it was home. It needed a lot of fixing, but it was home. Now I see it the way Gavin Williams would see it. The way Ms. Crum likely sees it.

It's an A-frame with moss and grass growing from the roof. The cedar log walls are a bit green, a lot dingy, one of the windows is broken and patched (temporarily) with duct tape. The house is tiny, the squat stone barn is nearly as big. The yard has never been mowed, tall grass and weeds grow wild, until they butt against the encroaching mountain woods.

Tanner's contraptions litter the yard. To us it looks like imagination, but to a stranger it'd look like piles of junk. The chicken coop takes up most of the side yard, and the grass is gone where they've scratched down to the dirt digging for grubs and bugs. Our dog Scooter, a twelve-year-old bloodhound-Lab mix, rests like a muddy puddle next to the coop, not bothering to lift his head more than an inch at our arrival.

The laundry I put out this morning hangs on the line between two trees. There's socks, shirts, underwear, towels, all clothes pinned close together, with not enough space for an ant to slip through. Under the clothesline, Tanner and Elijah's bikes lay in the grass.

Finally, parked under the rusted metal carport is the

old station wagon we bought when Elijah was born. "Hollow Creek Taxi Service" is painted in neon blue letters on the wood paneled door.

Looking at my home, all I can see are the weeds, and the junk, and the rust, and the broken down. The ugliness and the drabness.

Gran pulls to a stop and parks at the front door.

"Go on then." She waves the kids off. They spring out of the back. Tanner and Elijah run for their bikes and Shay heads over to pet Scooter.

When they're gone, Gran taps her fingers on the steering wheel. "What really happened? Don't you tell me a story."

"I'm not gonna lie." I sigh and shift in my seat. When I do, Grandpa's tobacco scent drifts to me.

"Tell me then."

I take a deep breath and tell Gran everything Gavin Williams did and said, ending with, "It hurt. There's a part of me that thinks he was right. I know I'm not beautiful, or traveled, or as la-di-da as him. But Gran, just because I'm not those things doesn't mean I don't feel and don't dream. I can imagine the things he talks about. I have dreams too. When my glass broke, it felt like my heart broke. I worked so hard."

I taste the salty sadness of tears, even though they're not falling.

Gran clucks her tongue. "Oh Jamie Lynn. If I could skin him, I would."

I nod and watch Tanner and Elijah speed past on their bikes. They've almost outgrown them.

"I was counting on that commission. I was going to fix the house. Get the kids new clothes. Find a tutor for math and reading."

"Well, you know what they say."

"Don't count your chickens before they hatch?" Or in Tanner's case, don't count your chickens because all the eggs are going to be smashed with a robotic arm.

"No. No."

"If wishes were horses, beggars would ride?"

"No. Not that one."

"What can't be cured must be endured?"

Gran purses her lips, her wrinkles pulling tight. "Jamie Lynn, haven't I taught you anything?"

I bite my fingernail to keep from answering. This seems like a trick question.

Gran rolls her eyes. "They say, the Lord works in mysterious ways. Trust me. It'll all come out in the wash."

"Ohhh. That one. Okay." I nod. I'm not so sure, but I'll give Gran the benefit of the doubt.

I lean across the stick shift and give her a hug. She's as pokey as a bundle of sticks, and if she weren't so stubborn, I'd think she was fragile. "Go on now. Go get those kids some supper."

I wave Gran off, then head inside to make mac n cheese. Comfort food.

THE DAYLIGHT HAS SLIPPED AWAY LIKE WATER DOWN A DRAIN. The loft is swathed in darkness and the kids are bundled up under the blankets on their beds. Shay is already asleep, curled in a ball, her breath even and quiet. Elijah stares at the cedar ceiling beams, his hands behind his head. I lay next to Tanner, the soap smell from his bedtime bath strong in my nose. I showered off too, so we're all squeaky clean. He rests his head on my chest.

They've already had their bedtime story and said their prayers, but by the way Tanner holds onto my hand, I know he has something to say.

I lay quietly and wait for him to share. Tanner is like a clam with his emotions, the more you pry, the tighter he closes up. You just have to wait patiently and eventually he'll open up on his own. Finally, he lifts his head from his pillow.

"I told Cody and Dale I had a new dad because they're always teasing me that I don't have one."

I nod and don't let my face betray how much his words hit me right in the chest.

Elijah sits up. "We do too have a dad."

"But I don't remember him. And he's not around, is he?" Tanner glares at me, daring me to contradict.

I squeeze his hand. "That's all true. But why would you lie? They all know you don't have a new dad."

He looks away. I wait for long, quiet minutes. Elijah falls asleep and snores softly, his mouth open. Tanner's eyelids flutter and then he falls asleep too.

I brush his hair back from his head, then carefully pull my hand from his.

He won't say why he'd lie, but I can imagine. After all, I'm not the only one with dreams.

Two nights later I'm making liver and onions with Gran, the smell pungent and hanging in the air, when Diedre bangs on the door.

"What? What?" I use a hand towel to wave some of the smoke out of the kitchen.

The boys are out back working on another egg delivery contraption, and Shay is practicing jumping off the picnic table and landing on all fours.

Diedre raps on the door and frantically waves her arms.

"She's drunker than a boiled owl." Gran frowns at Diedre, all dressed up in tiny shorts and a sequin crop top.

"She is not." I roll my eyes. I wave my towel at her to come in. "It's unlocked!"

Diedre swings the door wide and storms in, stomping across the wood floor in her platform heels.

"Granny Allwright!" she calls, bringing in her vanilla and hairspray scent to mix with the liver.

"Diedre, you here for liver and onions?" Granny frowns at Diedre's bare stomach. "You could use some more on the middle."

Diedre snorts. "No. I can't stand the stuff."

Granny shakes her finger. "Just put some sop on it."

Diedre cringes. "I already ate." She won't be distracted. "Jamie." Her voice goes low and serious. "Have you heard the news?"

I frown at her and shake the skillet. "What news?"

Diedre's eyes widen. "The six o'clock. The gossip hour."

"We don't listen to gossip." Granny narrows her eyes. "And neither should you."

The six o'clock news, aka the gossip hour, is aired on Hollow Creek's local radio station. The station has a range of about five miles and plays only classic bluegrass, but every weekday at six o'clock, Cudder Ross gets on the airwaves and relays *all* the gossip. Who got in a fight at the bar, who got fired, who hit the stop sign on Saturday night, where the fish are biting, who fell asleep in church, who is courting, who is not, and...well, it's like a bunch of busybody clucking hens on steroids.

"You should this time." Diedre tugs a portable radio out of her purse and turns it on. The station crackles, buzzes, and then Cudder's voice rings out, loud over the sizzling liver.

"That's all the news folks. Again, if any of y'all have information on the unidentified man at Memorial Hospital in Brunswick, contact Dr. Lewis. For your listening pleasure, here's that interview again."

I frown at Diedre. "What is this?"

"Shhh. Listen." She hushes me and holds up the radio. Granny crowds in closer.

"Cudder Ross here, for Radio Hollow Creek. I'm here at Memorial Hospital in Brunswick at the bedside of a man found yesterday morning at the edge of the river. Mister? Have you remembered your name? Do you know who you are?"

There's a scuffling, grating noise on the mic, then, "Get that microphone away from me. What's wrong with you?"

A chill runs down my spine. I know that voice. I *know* that voice.

"Has anything come back to you? Do you know where you're from? Anything to identify yourself by?"

"I said get out." It's *his* voice again.

A scuffle ensues, the mic cuts off for a moment, then Cudder comes back on.

"And there you have it, folks. The man, approximately thirty years of age, six foot two, light brown hair, blue eyes, no tattoos or distinguishing marks, except that he's meaner than a striped snake and tougher than a pine knot, was found two days ago at the river's edge, with no identification or cellular phone. He's lost his memory folks, but not his personality. If you have any information regarding his identity, the Memorial Hospital asks that you contact them immediately."

Diedre clicks off the radio.

I stare at her as the liver and onions crackle.

"Onions are burning," Gran says, reaching for the skillet.

"He…" I nod at the radio. "That's…"

"Spit it out." Gran pulls down six plates, even though Diedre definitely won't be eating.

Diedre smirks. "I thought it might be him. He sounded just like that peckerwood you described."

"Hold on. That man's Wilbur?"

"Gavin *Williams*."

Gran waves that away. Obviously his name isn't the point.

I shrug. "Fine. Whatever. I'll go over after dinner and let them know." Then I perk up. "Maybe he won't remember that he didn't like my work. Maybe I'll convince him he loved it and he was going to pay me. Wouldn't that be nice?"

Gran sets the plates on the counter with a hard click. She looks at Diedre and Diedre nods.

"What?" I feel like I'm missing something.

"Me and the Lord had a long talk after that Gilbert hurt you."

I shake my head, deciding that Gilbert is at least closer than Wilbur. "Thanks, Gran. I appreciate you praying for me."

Her mouth stretches into a wide smile. She's in a gray house dress and work boots. At my thanks she widens her stance and puts her hands on her hips.

"I already told you, Jamie Lynn. Me and the Lord are good friends, what d'ya think just happened?"

Diedre heads over to the fridge and pulls out a pitcher of iced tea. "I think Gavin Williams just got a biblical smack on the head." Diedre grins at Gran.

"Not yet he didn't." Gran hands a glass to Diedre. "Pour me one too."

Gran takes a long swig of the iced tea and then lets out a happy sigh.

"See, girls. This Wilbur boy, he acted the way he did because he don't know no better. From what Jamie Lynn says, he's a high-flying, big-headed, richie rich—"

"Peckerwood," Diedre adds.

"Who thinks he's better than everyone else and who thinks he can treat people poorly just because he has money."

"Okay?" I'm not catching on, but by the sparkle in Gran's eyes, she's thinking of something big.

"Oh. Ohhh." Diedre laughs and then claps her hands.

Gran nods. "You want the money he owes you. But what if you can get something better?"

"What's better than that?" I frown at them both.

Gran grins, and there's a bright, mischievous twinkle in her eyes. "I'll tell you what's better. A good ol' fashion helping of just desserts."

8

Jamie

Memorial Hospital in Brunswick is a small community hospital serving the area's rural population. It was built in the early nineteen seventies and is just as ugly as all the other institutional buildings constructed in that decade. The building sticks up like a beige band-aid, jutting off the scabby terrain of the brown hillside.

Brunswick was once a coal mining town, now it's mostly a half-dead ghost town with a supermarket and a three-bed hospital. It's on the northern side of the mountain and only fifteen miles away, but it takes an hour to get there, traveling narrow, winding, hilly roads, that cling to ravine edges and have construction yellow rockslide warnings posted every hundred feet.

The kids, Scooter, and Gran are in the station wagon in the gravel parking lot waiting for me to bring out Gavin.

Or Billy as we're going to call him.

That was Gran's suggestion. She said we couldn't call him his real name, and she wouldn't remember it anyway, so we might as well name him after the other ornery cock in our lives. Billy.

Gran also suggested I lay on my accent nice and thick, thicker than I've ever done. Just to give Gavin a nice treat. She wants to make sure he gets as much mountain living as he can take. He thought accents, banjos, and chickens were hillbilly? Well, he's gonna get a nice heaping pile of it, and Gran thinks it's exactly what he deserves. I can't say I disagree.

I walk across the parking lot to the front door of the hospital. There's a cigarette ashtray station at the door, and an old bench with green peeling paint. The glass door has the names Dr. G. Lewis, Internal Medicine, and Dr. M. Tinker, Family Medicine, the hours, and the phone number.

The rumbly sound of a lawn mower cuts through the air, and I smell fresh cut grass and cigarette butts. My feet scuff on the gravel and I turn around. Okay. Never mind. I can't do this. I'm not going to do this. What were we thinking?

In the car, Gran sees my expression. She waves her hands, and then pointing at the hospital, she gives me two big thumbs up.

No.

Nope.

No.

Then I see Tanner. His nose is pressed against the window, and he's watching me, an intent expression on his face. And it's as if my heart slides sideways, like an automatic door, and all I can do is walk on. I raise my hand and wave.

I'm doing this.

From here on out it's thick accents, banjos, and barefoot chicken rustling. That's just desserts. Lord help us all.

I push the door open, an arctic blast of bleach-tinted air conditioning hits, and my shoes squeak on the polished linoleum floor as I walk to the front desk. The 1970s institutional facade matches the interior perfectly—puke-green walls, tan floor, drop ceiling. I almost feel sorry for Gavin Williams having to stay here so long, considering how much he hates drab and ugly. I imagine, even without his memory, he's upset about his uninspired surroundings.

There's a nurse in fuchsia scrubs with bedazzled glasses behind the desk. She smiles as I walk in. "Morning, hon. Can I help you?"

This is the test. Hollow Creek is a very isolated town. Nobody in Brunswick knows me. And they don't know Gavin either.

If I can pull this off, I can pull off anything. I bite my tongue and send up a prayer for forgiveness. "You sure can. I'm here for my husband."

She leans forward in her chair. Keen interest lights her expression. "Your husband?"

"Mhmm. Billy Sutton. I'm told he has...amnesia?"

She pushes away from the desk, her cheeks flush with excitement. "My word. You've come for him! Praise be."

I get the distinct feeling she's sending up praise, not because she's happy for me, but because she's happy to get rid of Gavin.

"I'll be right back. Right back. Don't you leave." She waves her arms, pushes back her chair, stumbles over it, then hurries into the back.

"Where would I go?" I try to peek through the door she left ajar but can't see anything.

My heart's pounding from the lie I told. It tastes wrong on my tongue, like bitter tea left to seep too long.

In less than thirty seconds, the nurse shoves through the door, and a white-haired, harried doctor rushes out behind her. Dr. Lewis, his white coat says. They stop and stare at me like I'm the answer to all their prayers. Another doctor, a round, gray-haired man, Dr. Tinker, stumbles out after them.

The nurse waves her hands at me, like she's pulled a rabbit from a hat, and says proudly. "She's here for her husband."

I think Dr. Tinker mumbles, *Thank God.* But I can't quite catch it.

"Wonderful! Wonderful." Dr. Lewis rushes around the desk, his white coat flapping behind him. He grabs my hand and pumps it up and down.

"She has to see him first, doesn't she? Maybe her husband is a different missing person?" Dr. Lewis frowns at me, but I get the feeling he's willing to give me Gavin, even if he isn't my husband.

The nurse nods. "He's sleeping now. You can just look in on him."

At the room, one of three patient rooms in the hospital, I hover in the doorway. It's him. I mean, I knew it was. I recognized his voice. But still, seeing him in the hospital bed, it makes my insides twist all around themselves.

I don't like Gavin. That's as clear as a white stripe on a skunk. But it still twists me up to see the purple bruise covering the left side of his face, the swelling on his eye, the cut over his lip. He was so rugged and handsome, so full of vitality. Now, he seems so vulnerable.

Dr. Lewis watches my expression. "Is that your husband?"

My breath comes in short, tight gasps and I blink away tears from (I'm sure) the sting of bleach. I nod. "It is."

"Awww, she's all emotional. There, there. He's alright." The nurse pats my arm reassuringly.

I give her a wobbly smile.

Dr. Tinker lets out a long, grateful sigh. "I'm certain it's the head injury, but your husband has been quite... uncooperative." He winces.

The nurse nods. "Sore as a bear with a rotten tooth."

I frown at Gavin. A lock of his hair has fallen over his eye and I have the urge to push it back from his forehead. "What do you mean 'uncooperative'?"

The nurse taps her foot on the floor. "Never wanting to stay still. Never wanting the door shut or the lights off. Complaining about the food. Moaning about the hospital.

Claiming he could buy the whole place, saying he's certain he has money, loads of money, and we better let him out so he can find his family, cause he..." Her brow wrinkles as she looks over my outfit. "Did he remember right? Do you have loads of—"

"Ohhh. No. Nope. Although, it's always been a fantasy of his, being rich." I give a bright smile.

Dr. Lewis looks from Gavin to me, a hopeful smile on his face. "Not that I don't believe you. But do you have identification? We'll need proof of identity, paperwork filled out."

"Of course I do." I open my purse and pull out a night's worth of work.

Diedre brought her computer over and found photos online of Gavin Williams, then she used all her photoshopping might to create twelve years' worth of false memories. We've got wedding photos, honeymoon photos, family photos. Gavin at the house, on the porch, holding a chicken. I knew she was a master, but when I saw the photo album she made, I almost believed it was real myself. Diedre even made a marriage certificate and called Big Tom up to request he hire Gavin. She even has a fake driver's license promised through one of her less reputable internet contacts. That'll be here in a few days. It's scary really that you can manufacture an entire life in one night.

I fan the documents and photos out for them to see.

"He had his wallet on him, so I don't have his driver's license or social security card, but I figured this was proof enough. The kids are in the car waiting for their daddy."

Dr. Lewis's smile stretches across his wrinkled face as

he takes everything in. "Who are we to keep a man from his family?"

"I'm ever so grateful." I smile back. But all I can think is, you're going to hell, Jamie Lynn, you're going to hell for this.

9

GAVIN

MY HEAD HURTS.

There's a crowbar in my skull tearing my brain apart. I can't think it hurts so much. I want to peel the pain away, scratch it out of my head. It's been like this for two days now, ever since I woke up in this horrible place.

Amnesia. Who gets amnesia? Isn't that something that only happens in made-for-television movies? The doctors don't know who I am. No one knows. Not even me.

And the doctors claim I may *never* remember.

I try not to think about that, because if I do, I feel as if I'm entering a dark, tiny room, and for some reason, that terrifies me.

The doctors also said that my memories may come

back all at once, or in a slow trickle over time. But there's nothing I can do but rest and wait and see what happens.

I don't know anything about myself. But I do know that I don't like to wait and I don't like not moving. Even now, I itch to get up and leave. There's someplace I'm meant to be, someone I want to see, I can feel it. I just don't know where or who.

I pray that I'll remember, or that they'll find me.

I glare at the woman standing in front of me. She's not pretty. I don't know why this strikes me as something I care about, but there it is. She's not cute.

I don't recognize her. Not at all.

"Who are you?" I flinch at the noise of my own voice. It feels like nails punching into my head.

She blinks at me. And I decide to amend my earlier opinion. She's not pretty, but her eyes, her lavender blue eyes, are stunning. She nervously licks her lips, her pink tongue darts quickly over her wide mouth and she looks down at the hospital sheet pooled around my hips.

"Billy," she says, her voice soft like flowing honey. "It's me, Jamie."

I start to shake my head, but then stop. Because that hurts too. I want to say, who is Billy, but then I realize *Billy* must be my name.

I can't remember...I can't...I can't remember my name.

Billy.

Okay.

Billy is short for William, and when I think William, there's a whisper there at the edge of my lost memory.

"Who are you?" I ask again.

She clasps her hands in front of her chest, innocent blue eyes wide, frizzy red hair a halo in the hospital light. "Baby, it's me. Jamie. Your wife. I'm here to take you home."

My wife? Her face blossoms into a beatific smile, like the Madonna under the shining light of heaven. I can't say anything, except...

"No."

Because I don't know who I am, I don't know who she is, and I don't know what's going on. But I do know one thing. I never would've married a short woman with red frizzy hair, a flat chest, unflattering clothes bought off the rack at a discount superstore, and a southern drawl that sounds like it's echoing off a hillbilly's mountaintop.

I would *never* do that.

I don't know who I am. But I do know that I have a certain taste in women, and this Jamie person doesn't hit the mark.

At all.

"Sorry. No."

She grins at me. "Aww. Come on, Billy baby. Gran and the kids are waiting in the station wagon."

That's when my world screeches to a halt.

"Kids?"

"Course. Elijah, Tanner, and Shay. Lord almighty, Billy. How hard did you hit your head?"

She leans forward and brushes her fingers, cool as a spring morning, over my forehead.

I stare at her with rapidly expanding horror.

We're *married*?

We have *kids*?

I'm...Billy?

I grasp my pounding head in my hands.

"I'm Billy?"

The woman, Jamie, drops a sharp peck on my cheek. Her innocent smile has a jagged edge.

"Always the jokester. Come on, honey, you've got work in the morning. Pumping the poo outta the outhouses."

And that's when I know. The reason I can't remember who I am is because I don't want to. An unattractive wife? A station wagon? A horde of snotty-nosed kids? Pumping poop?

Apparently, my life is hell.

And by the stubborn look on the woman's face, this nightmare life of mine, it's not going away.

10

Gavin

The back of the station wagon smells like oily fish and wet dog. I grip the edge of the backwards facing seat and try to ignore the large, slobbering dog, with his maw less than two inches from my face.

You always sit in the rear with the dog, on account that Granny gets carsick, my wife said. I shake my head, ignoring the pain, because...my wife.

Granny is an ancient, stick-thin woman, with garish orange lips and narrow beady eyes. She didn't say anything when Jamie tugged me out of the hospital, gripping my arm, like she was afraid I was going to make a run for it.

I nearly did when I saw our car.

But Granny, she stepped out of the front seat, looked me up and down like she was taking my measure, and then spit on the dirt parking lot. I get the feeling my grandma-in-law and I don't see eye to eye.

Then the kids tumbled out of the back and swarmed us, hugging my legs and jumping all over me with cries of *Daddy!* and *We missed you!*

Jamie pointed to them and said their names—Elijah, Tanner, Shay.

I figured I should've felt some sort of paternal love or some memory of holding them as babies. But all I felt was a massive headache and the urge to dunk them in a bathtub, give them haircuts, and find some flea powder. They're filthy. They're unkempt. They're scabbed and dirty and missing teeth, and...the smallest boy, the one with orange hair and freckles like his mom, leans over the back seat and stares at me.

"Hi Trevor." I try on a smile.

"His name's Tanner." The older boy, the more serious one with brown hair, rolls his eyes.

The little girl—she'd be cute, if she weren't covered in oatmeal—meows and then licks her hand. I flinch. That hand is filthy. Then I sniff the air and gag.

Tanner waves his hand in front of his nose. "That's Scooter. He got into the coop and ate chicken poo this morning. It gives him gas."

I cough and then edge as far as possible from the overgrown, smelly mutt, but the darn dog just climbs closer. A long string of drool falls from his mouth and lands on my shoulder.

The station wagon hits a bump and my head jackhammers. My wife drives like she's in a police chase, taking hairpin corners at speeds that leave my stomach behind. I feel like I might be sick, and I can't decide if it's the smell coming from the dog, the kids staring at me, or my wife's driving.

The car rumbles and coughs and we bump onto a gravel drive, moving into the shade of big pine trees. The whole drive, Granny's been fiddling with the radio, trying to find the best reception for her banjo station. Now that we're here, it comes in loud and clear.

We passed the town limits a few miles back. The sign said Hollow Creek, but Jamie pronounced it Holler Crick.

I take a deep breath and wipe my hands over my face. It can't be that bad. My life can't possibly be that bad. I've lived it, according to Jamie, for thirty years. I've survived, healthily and maybe happily, for decades. It can't be that bad.

We pull around the bend in the drive and I lay eyes on our home.

It's that bad.

The station wagon jerks to a stop. The kids cheer and practically somersault out of the back. The dog leaps over the seat and bounds after them. I shove open the back door. It swings wide with a rusty screech.

I step out into the tall grass and take it all in. The moldering A-frame, the metal wire chicken coop, the piles of junk, the sound of a crowing rooster, the banjo still playing on the radio, and the musty scent of rotting cedar and wood smoke. My skin runs cold. This can't possibly be my home.

I thought I was wealthy. I'm poor.

I thought I was single. I'm married.

I thought I was happy. I'm...

Jamie stomps through the grass and then stops next to me, looking out at the kids playing an impromptu game of chase around the chicken coop.

She beams at me.

I shake my head. This doesn't feel right, it isn't right, this isn't where I'm meant to be.

"This..." I stop, my stomach knotting. "This is where I live?"

She squeezes me to her side. "Mhmm. Home sweet home."

I'D LIKE TO CLAIM THAT THERE IS NOTHING OF ME INSIDE THE house, but I can't. There are pictures on the mantle of Jamie and me at our wedding, of me holding a chicken in the front yard. I pick up one photo, pasted in a rustic wooden frame.

"What's this?" I hold it out to her. She and I are standing in front of a tent.

Out of all the things I've seen today, only that tent feels right to me.

"Our honeymoon. Down by the river." A bright red blush covers her cheeks and spreads down her neck. I lift an eyebrow and set the picture back on the wood mantle.

I wonder what happened on our honeymoon to make her blush so much. I can only imagine. Literally. I can only imagine, since I don't remember being intimate with this woman. Come to think of it, it's incredibly strange to be standing next to a woman I've slept with at least enough times to make three kids and not remember a second of it. She's seen me naked. I've seen her naked. We've made love. And I can't remember it. And I certainly don't feel like doing it again.

I look her over.

Frizzy red hair. Freckles. Too skinny. Too flat-chested. Wide mouth. Nothing, not a spark of attraction.

"How'd we end up married?" I narrow my eyes.

If possible, her blush deepens. "You know. The usual way."

"Actually, I don't know. Enlighten me."

Gran stomps into the room. "You came to the mountain. Took advantage of my granddaughter and then I remedied the situation. How else?"

Jamie coughs into her hand and turns her head away.

Ah. I see.

Apparently Jamie and I had sex, she conceived, and that was that. Makes sense. No wonder I don't feel any attraction. It was a shotgun wedding.

"Why don't I wear a wedding ring?" I stare at my hand. There's not even a tan line on my ring finger.

Jamie sticks her chin in the air and frowns at me. "Some men don't."

I notice she has a dull gold band on her left ring finger.

I shrug and Grandma stomps out of the living room, back to the kitchen, and starts banging pots and pans. She shouts at us, "I'm making poke sallet and cornpone."

What the...?

"Do I have any family?" I'm suddenly desperate to get out of here. To find anywhere else I can stay, anyone else I can talk to.

"Parents? A sister? A...brother?" I feel like I have a brother.

"Well..." Jamie rocks back on her heels and looks at the ceiling.

The smell of bacon frying drifts out of the kitchen.

"Your ma."

I lean forward. "Yes?"

"She died a few years ago. She was a bearded lady in the circus, so we didn't see her much."

What?

Jamie shrugs apologetically. "You never knew your dad. Your ma claimed he was a circus groupie and that he died when an elephant sat on him." She pats my arm. "I'm sorry."

I'm the product of a bearded lady and a circus groupie? Me?

"But what about...siblings?"

"Oh sure. You've got a brother."

My heart skips a beat and then picks up speed. I knew it. I knew I had a brother. "Well let's call him. Where is he?"

Jamie winces. "I mean, we could, but last time you talked to him, he threatened to chop off your..." She wiggles her pointer finger. "He still has another fifteen years in the state penitentiary for that armed robbery spree he went on. Anger management issues." She winces and shakes her head. "But we could make a call. He might talk to you."

My skin goes cold, and the tiny, cluttered living room spins. The smoke and grease smell is getting to me. It's hot and stagnant in the house.

"Hey." Jamie sets her hand on my arm. "Don't fret. You've got us."

I stare at her, my face bloodless.

"I'll show you 'round. See if anything jogs your memory." She nods at the living room, the broken down, stained couch, the busted up coffee table, and the toys littered across the floor. "Living room. You sleep on the couch."

"I do?" I look askance at the sagging, dog hair-covered piece of furniture.

"You snore. You said years ago you didn't want to disturb my rest. You're real kind like that."

I narrow my eyes, not certain I believe her.

She waves at me to follow. We step into a bedroom with a lumpy queen bed, covered in an old-fashioned blue quilt.

"This is where I sleep. Bathroom is through there."

She points out a tiny bathroom with a hard-water-stained shower stall, toilet, and porcelain sink with a mirror above it. I look at myself in the mirror and wince. I'm still not used to seeing my own reflection. It's strange not recognizing yourself, and it's even stranger being covered in purple and yellow-green bruises.

"Your clothes are in the closet."

I walk over to the wall closet and brush my hands over the clothes. There are a lot of flannels, t-shirts, suspenders, and wide-legged blue jeans. They're smothered in the smell of mothballs and pipe tobacco.

"Why do I dress like an old man?" I pluck at a shirt. It has to have been made at least twenty years ago. I sniff again. "I smoke?" It's strange, I haven't had any cravings.

"Huh? Well...you quit."

"Really?"

Jamie looks toward the kitchen, her eyes narrowed. She shrugs. "Anyway. You like vintage. It's your style."

I hold a pair of pants up to my waist. "It's my style to wear pants three sizes too big in the waist?"

She scowls at me. "You lost weight. Happened when you got worms. Don't worry, you'll be back to your old size in no time."

I shove the pants back in the closet. "What do you mean I got worms?"

She shrugs. "Guess you weren't careful at work. Picked parasites up from the poo. Come on then."

I don't want to, but I follow her out. I'm treated to a tour of the kitchen, with Granny glaring at me over the cast iron skillet, a view of the kids' bedroom up the ladder in the loft area, and a walk around the yard, where I meet the chickens.

"You named the rooster after me?" I stare at the ugly, one-eyed rooster, completely astounded.

Jamie's eyes light up and I get the feeling that I'm missing a joke. I'm about to ask, when Tanner and Elijah run over.

Elijah grabs Jamie's hand. "Gran says dinner's ready."

"Alright. Alright." She laughs at the kids pulling her

along. The sun is setting and the dusky light hits her so that once again I'm stunned by the lavender blue of her eyes. They really are unaccountably pretty.

Maybe that's what drew me to her.

The hellions run in front of us and the little one crawls on all fours, meowing like a cat. I'm not sure that one talks. They stop at the back door.

Elijah gestures at the door handle. "You go first, Dad."

I'm distracted by him saying "Dad." It does something weird to me. I frown, not able to place the feeling, then shrug it off. I turn the handle and step over the threshold.

"No!" Jamie's yell comes too late.

Egg after egg rains down from a basket and cracks open on my head, on my shoulders, at my feet. And if I thought Scooter's gas was bad, it's nothing compared to the rotten smell coming off these eggs.

"It worked!" Tanner shouts. He jumps up and down with glee.

"That was awesome." Elijah claps his hands together, his face full of delight.

I blink egg white from my eyes. The sticky, stinky goo drips down my cheek. I run my hand over my face and fling the slime to the side.

Jamie looks like she's trying to be mad, but there's a smile twitching at the edge of her lips.

"Did you see that, Mom?" Tanner beams at her.

"Are those all the eggs the hens have been hiding? Where'd you find them?"

I can't believe they're having a conversation while I'm covered in the slime of two dozen rotten, sulfur-scented eggs. I can't believe the boys booby-trapped the door and walked me through it like a lamb to slaughter. I can't believe I nearly died, lost my memory, and my welcome home present is getting *egged*.

"We found a whole pile of 'em under the—"

My headache, learning that I'm Billy Sutton, that I live here, like this, it's all too much. Anger, sharp and hot boils up. "Trevor. Apologize."

Trevor stops short. Jamie lifts an eyebrow.

"His name is Tanner." Elijah glares at me. Then he grabs his brother's hand and pulls him into the house. The little girl sniffs at my shirt like a cat, wrinkles her nose and slips past.

Jamie frowns. "You can wash up at the hose."

She points to a rolled up green garden hose near the chicken coop.

"They need to apologize." I grit my teeth and try not to taste the sulfur-y egg on my lips. It's probably full of salmonella. Or just my luck I'll pick up another parasite.

Jamie tilts her head and studies the goop slipping down my jaw. I get the feeling, even though she's being perfectly cordial, that she doesn't like me very much.

I almost think that's ridiculous, we're married, she should love me. But plenty of people are married and not in love, or even in like.

"I'll talk to them." She starts to slip past me. I hold out my hand and touch her arm. She pauses on her way by.

"Jamie?"

She keeps her eyes ahead, not looking at me. "Hmm?"

The spot where my hand rests on her arm is warm and my fingers tingle.

I ask in a low, quiet voice, "Do we like each other?"

She stiffens and I think maybe I've offended her.

I clear my throat, the sulfur tickling my nose. "I mean... I can't remember. We're married, but do we get along? Do we like each other?"

She licks her lips and my eyes follow the trail of her tongue over her lush mouth. I'm busy staring at her lips when she says, "You're here, aren't you?"

I'm left staring after her like a fool, until I manage to shake out of my haze, and rinse off with the garden hose. It's only later that night, when I'm lying on the most uncomfortable couch on the planet, with a smelly dog cutting off the circulation in my legs, that I realize Jamie didn't actually answer my question.

11

Jamie

The house is finally quiet. It's two in the morning, the kids fell asleep long ago, and Gavin drifted off about five minutes ago. The mumbling, cursing and tossing and turning has stopped, and I can hear his even breathing under Scooter's snores. I push the quilt to the side and carefully slip out of the bed. The mattress springs squeak and I hold still, waiting to make sure that I didn't wake Gavin.

When I hear a soft snore, I step off the bed and tiptoe to the living room. The moonlight filters in through the window and bathes the room in soft light. Even tiptoeing, my steps still make the floor creak. Scooter is sprawled over Gavin's legs, and when the floor groans, Scooter opens one eye and looks at me. I hold my finger up to my mouth.

"Shhh."

He blows out a breath and closes his eye.

Scooter sure does stink. He didn't just eat the chicken poo, I think he rolled in it too. I'll have to give him a bath tomorrow. I swear, hounds are some of the nastiest-smelling dogs in the world. They're also bed hogs. Right now, Scooter takes up so much of the couch, I think Gavin will fall off if Scooter rolls over. But maybe not. Gavin has a tight grip on the old thin blanket I gave him. It's wrapped around him and pulled up to his chin. Probably because it's cold tonight and the cedar walls let in a nasty draft when the winds blow.

I curl my toes on the cold floor and take a good long look at Gavin Williams.

Even wearing Grandpa's pajamas, with a purple bruise that covers half his face, and a swollen eye, he still makes my insides twist. He's that good-looking.

Before Gran left, I know she sensed what I'm feeling because she pulled me aside and hissed, "Lay down with dogs, come up with fleas."

Apparently, I can pretend Gavin's my husband, but I can't "lay" with him. Not that I was going to. No way, no how. He's an awful, selfish bully who thinks he can walk all over people. He can't. Not on this mountain.

That's how Gran described it to the kids. She kept it simple. "Kids, we're going to get a man that did your mom wrong."

"Are we going to send him up the flagpole?" That was Tanner.

"No." Granny said. "He doesn't remember who he is.

He doesn't remember he did wrong. He owes your mom money. We're going to have him work it off. It's like a game of pretend."

"Meow!" That was Shay.

"But what are we going to pretend?" This was from Elijah, who is more cautious and thinks things through before doing them.

Granny smiled. "We're going to pretend he's your pa. He's going to live and work here. He's going to learn that you can't just stomp all over people and get away with it."

"But I don't want another pa." Elijah crossed his arms and stuck out his lower lip.

"I do." This was from Tanner.

"Meow!"

I pulled all three close. "It's just for a short time. He'll work off what he owes me. He'll learn his lesson and then we'll send him on his way."

And that was that. Growing up here, the kids already knew the rule of the mountain. Never, ever show weakness. Never let anyone get away with taking advantage. Always give as good as you get. If someone hurts one of your own, hurt them back. And always stick together.

The kids understood. This was just another Cody Thorn situation. We're taking care of it in our own way.

I tiptoe close to Gavin and lean in near enough to see the stubble on his jaw, the smile lines at the corner of his eyes, and the softness of his hair falling over his bruised forehead. This close I can smell the tang of the bar soap he used in the shower.

There's a hollow feeling in my chest, one that takes me a moment to recognize. But when I do, I draw in a sharp breath. My mouth twists in self-derision, because that's yearning I feel. And there's no reason I should be feeling yearning for this man.

I reach up, about to brush his hair from his eyes, then stop myself when my fingers are an inch away. I don't have any business touching this man. I don't have any business wanting him.

"Do we like each other?" he'd asked me.

I shake my head. "No," I whisper. "Never. Never and not at all."

12

———————

GAVIN

THERE'S A WEIGHT CRUSHING MY CHEST. I WANT TO FALL back asleep, but the weight is squirming and squeaking and I can feel their breath on my face. I pry open my eyes, it feels like my eyeballs were scraped all night with sandpaper, and stare up into wide, hazel eyes, a little button nose, and pursed lips.

It's the little one. The one that pretends to be a cat. "Which one are you again?"

Her fingers curl in my chest, she leans her nose into mine, and then she hisses.

Yeah. That's about how I feel too. This couch is possibly the most uncomfortable thing I've ever slept on. The lumps are as hard as rocks, the center caves down so I'm positioned like the letter V, and I feel like I've been thrown off a cliff and knocked against a rock ledge. The darn dog kept dropping gas bombs, stinking up the room, and snoring so loud I woke up every five minutes. My legs kept falling asleep because the dog wouldn't get off me, and after the second growl, I realized he figured the couch was his and I was merely a poorly tolerated guest. On top of that, the ratty, threadbare blanket my wife tossed me kept me about as warm as a nudist in the Arctic. The plain fact is, I'm exhausted.

The kid tilts her head and tries another hiss.

I stare at her. "Don't you talk?"

She lifts her chin and jumps to the ground, landing surprisingly gracefully on all fours. She crawls to the kitchen.

I shrug. "Guess not."

It looks like I've got a daughter who only speaks cat, and two boys who like to roll around in the mud and drop rotten eggs on their dad. Jeez. What have I been doing all these years? Did I just give up? I look around the living room, at the junk on the floor, and the broken tv in the corner. Yeah. I think I gave up.

I close my eyes and try to rub the sandpaper grit feeling away.

"Good. You're awake."

Even before I open my eyes I can smell her. It's the scent of wood smoke and beeswax and, unfortunately, chicken. Her scent tickles at my memory, and I know I've smelled it before. Which, to be honest, is disappointing. I'd really like it if all this was a hoax and I had a different life somewhere else.

I groan and open my eyes.

She beams at me. "Good morning."

I swing my legs off the couch and groan at the pins and needles in my half-asleep legs. "This is good?"

"Uh huh. Sure is." She's in a fresh pair of overalls and a tank top, and surprisingly chipper for how early it is. The sun is barely past the windowsill and that old nasty rooster is only just starting to crow. His crow is nothing like in the movies. It's more an anemic shriek, like an old lady that smoked her whole life and is yelling at the kids on her lawn.

"You better get up. The kids need breakfast."

I stare at her. "And?"

"You make it. Remember?"

I give her a look. Of course I don't remember.

She walks over and pats my shoulder. "You make them pancakes and you pack their school lunches. Sandwich, chips, carrot sticks, apple sauce? Okay?"

I shake my head, trying to knock loose a memory, because...I don't know how to make pancakes. I don't remember. It's almost like I've never made pancakes in my life. I don't even know where to begin. But the way Jamie is grinning at me, there's no way I'm going to admit it.

"What are you going to do?" I ask suspiciously. Why isn't she making breakfast?

She shrugs and walks toward the bathroom. "I've been up since four, working. I need to shower before work. Don't dawdle, 'kay? The bus is here in twenty minutes. Then Big Tom's picking you up to go pump poo."

Before I can respond to that nugget, she shuts the bathroom door with a firm click.

I drop my head into my hands. Big Tom? Pumping poo? Making pancakes and lunches? What?

Someone tugs on my pajama top. An old cotton button-up shirt that looks as if a ninety year old man wore it in his recliner. I open my eyes. It's the older boy. He stares at me with solemn eyes.

"Elijah?" I say it as a sort of question.

He sighs. "You don't remember how to make pancakes. Do you?"

I consider pretending that I do, but what would be the point?

"No." I shrug. "Do you?"

He nods, his hair sticking up in a cowlick. "Come on."

I follow him to the kitchen, and then he points out all the ingredients. "A cup of pancake mix. Two eggs. A spoonful of oil. A cup of water. Put it in the blender."

I scratch my chin and consider him. "That's it?"

"Yup. That's it."

Huh. Well, that's easier than I thought it'd be. Elijah grabs the ingredients and I dump them in the blender. While I do, the other two, Tanner and...what's her name, dang it, what's her name, file in and stand at the kitchen entry watching me.

"Now you push blend." Elijah nods at the button on the blender.

I consider the kids. Elijah is a serious kid, that much is obvious. I wonder where he got that from? Maybe I'm serious? His mom doesn't seem to be. He watches me solemnly and nods at the button. "You push blend."

The other two stand there silently watching. Tanner's freckles are darker this morning, probably from the sun he got playing in the yard last night. He has his bottom lip between his teeth. The little one, her eyes are big and round.

For some reason, my intuition is telling me something's up. I look at the ceiling. There isn't a basket of eggs up there, but still...

"I just push blend?" I ask her. She wasn't involved in the rotten egg trick, so she's probably the most trustworthy.

Slowly, she nods her head, her chin bobbing up and down.

Alright.

I hit blend.

And all hell breaks loose.

Okay. No. I'm not foolish enough to fall for the blender without a lid trick. I lost my memory not my intelligence. But these kids are on a whole other level.

When I hit the blender button, the motor whirs, a fishing line that I hadn't noticed twangs, it snaps tight, there's a pulley, there's gears, there's chaos.

The microwave turns on. It starts popping and sparking like the Fourth of July, there's a ball of tinfoil in there. I rush toward the microwave and yank open the door. When I do, I realize too late, that there was a bowl perched on the microwave top. It flips, hits me, and a gallon worth of chicken crap lands on my old man pajamas. The stench makes me gag. I swing around.

All the kids are staring with wide, amazed eyes, like they can't believe their little trick actually worked.

"Again?" I shout. "Is this a daily occurrence? Is this my life?"

I lunge toward the sink and yank the faucet. When I do, the water spurts out the side in a geyser and smacks me in the face. I cough and sputter, swinging my arms trying to turn the darn thing off.

There's a giggle behind me. It's the little one. She's laughing.

I swing around.

I cannot believe this. I'm going to...I just tripped over another bit of fishing line.

I stop at the clicking noise. A fan on the counter turns on and then a cloud of flour and chicken feathers sprays onto me. The flour dust and feathers swirl like a dust storm and I sneeze at them tickling my nose.

The little one giggles again.

I cross my arms and glare at my three kids. Feathers and flour stick to my chicken crap coated skin.

So help me...these kids aren't mine. They're the spawn of the devil.

"Billy! What're you doing messing around in here? Don't you know the kids have to get to school?" Jamie pushes into the kitchen. "Darnit the floor's all gaumed up. If you're going to mess around, do it outside."

I stare at her, my mouth falling open in stupefaction. Then I spit out a feather that slips in.

"Kids. Get to the table. You'll have to have mushmellon and toast. Billy, pack the lunches. No, never mind. You stink again, go wash off at the hose."

The hose? The hose again? What am I, a dog?

I'm about to argue. To reprimand the kids. To say *something*, but then a long, blaring horn interrupts my thoughts.

It sounds again. Beeping out an annoying honking melody.

I glare at Jamie, who somehow looks clean and well-rested and happy. I scowl, ill-tempered and angry. "What is that noise?"

Jamie peeks out the window, then turns back and smiles at me. I notice a dimple in her right cheek, and then I get irritated that I'm noticing things like dimples at a time like this.

"That's Big Tom. You better get dressed, you're late for work." She waves her hands, shooing me out the kitchen. "Get going then. You can hose off when you get back."

I grit my jaw and sweep my eyes over my wife, my kids.

Jamie smiles at me, and her expression reminds me of the saying *sweet as a cherry pie.* Her lips are bright red and glossy, and I grow irritated at how sweet they look. I wonder how long it's been since we kissed.

The horn blares again.

Dang it.

I point a finger at the kids, sitting at the table. "Be good at school."

They all stare at me, identical wide-eyed expressions on their faces.

As I rush to throw on some clothes, I hear Jamie in the kitchen, "Everwho did this is in a heap of trouble."

I smile to myself. I guess she's not so bad, that little red-haired wife of mine.

I throw on an old flannel, cheap jeans that hang off me, and suspenders to hold them up. My boots are too big, and I wonder if losing weight makes your feet smaller. Guess so.

As I yell goodbye and slam out the front door, I feel gleeful, like I'm escaping. Whatever happens at work today, it won't be half as bad as what I have to deal with at home.

13

GAVIN

I WAS WRONG. I WAS SO, SO WRONG.

After twelve hours of pumping crap, hauling crap, dumping crap I've decided that my life is one long miserable stinking pile of...crap.

Big Tom doesn't talk. It's not that he's short with his words. No. He literally doesn't talk. He showed me what to do—how to deliver the port-a-johns, how to service and clean them, how to work the vacuum to suck the port-a-john waste tank dry, how to consolidate the waste and transport it to the treatment plant—he showed me all this with a series of grunts, sighs, and impatient scowls.

I'm certain he can speak. Sometimes I think I hear him muttering under his breath. But when I look at him, his mouth is shut. He's a short, bearded man that reminds me of some hairy nocturnal creature accidentally caught in the daylight.

We spent most of our day traveling from construction sites to parks, to...wherever they need portable toilets delivered, cleaned, sucked, or sanitized. At first, while we drove between locations, I kept my window rolled down, but after a few hours I stopped bothering. My hands, my hair, my clothes, everything smelled like sewage. I swear it's stuck in my nostrils and I'll never be able to get the smell out.

For the first part of the day I tried to make conversation. But Big Tom never responded.

When I asked him how long I'd been working for him, he shook his head and sighed.

When I asked him if we were friends, he grunted. I'm not sure if that was a yes or a no.

When I asked him when I got my paycheck, he snorted.

When I asked how well he knew my wife and kids, he slapped my back and gave me a sympathetic look. Not sure what that was about.

When I asked when lunchbreak was, he opened the glove box and threw a smashed up white bread tuna fish sandwich at me.

I ate it.

I missed breakfast after all.

Now, the sun is nearly down, I'm exhausted, sore, and stinking, and the sight of the big pine trees lining my house's drive makes me want to weep. I'm actually glad to be home. God help me.

Big Tom shifts gears, yanks on the brake, and the truck lurches to a stop. I open the door, ready to head inside. "I'll see you tomorrow?"

Tom lets out a sigh, which if I'm reading things right, means, "why me?"

I shrug. I didn't think I did all that bad, considering I didn't remember anything about my job. Plus, I only tipped over one waste tank and the spill only took two hours to clean up.

"Right. See you tomorrow. Thanks for the sandwich."

I slam the truck door and jog up the drive as Tom pulls away.

At the front door, I pause and look through the window. The boys are in the kitchen, sitting at the table, heads bent over homework. The warm yellow light glows over them. The little one is at the stove, holding onto Jamie's legs. Jamie's stirring something in a pot, and her red hair glows in the light. She looks down at the girl and laughs. I can hear her laugh all the way outside, it rings clear and bright, and the sound hits me hard, right in the gut.

I lose my breath.

That. That right there.

That's why I fell in love with her.

I'm sure of it.

Suddenly I'm hungry for her. I want to hear her laugh again, I want to be the one to make her smile, and then I want to take her mouth, and taste her laughter.

I exhale, long and hard.

She might not be beautiful. She might not be what I thought my taste was. But looking at this scene, my wife at the stove, kids at the table, all in a warm, homey kitchen, smiling and laughing, it hits something buried deep inside me, and I feel like maybe this isn't the first time I've been standing outside, looking in on something I wish I had.

But this...I do have this.

It's mine, isn't it?

All I have to do is go inside.

"I'm home," I call, stepping in the front door. The warmth and the smell of spicy chili and cornbread hits me.

Jamie steps out of the kitchen, a wooden spoon in her hand. Her eyes crinkle when she sees me. "You're back."

Strange thing, she almost looks surprised.

She blushes, and I wonder if we usually kiss when I come home. I stare at her mouth.

"What?" She wipes at her lip and frowns at me.

I clear my throat and realize even over the chili and cornbread I can still smell sewage and yes, chicken poop from this morning. I nod toward the bath. "I'll go shower off."

Is it just me, or are her eyes going dark and warm? I can almost touch the awareness between us, expanding like a soap bubble. If I speak, will it pop?

I stay quiet, holding my breath.

But she shakes her head and the bubble pops anyway. "Dinner's ready in five."

"Alright. Thank you."

She gives me a surprised smile, then waves me off and hurries back to the kitchen.

In the bathroom, I strip down, throw my dirty clothes in the laundry basket, and let the hot water run over my tired muscles. I scrub myself with the soap bar, dragging it over every inch, twice, then three times. I keep scrubbing until the water runs clear and all I can smell is fresh, soap-scented water. The shower water drums against me and echoes in the small stall. It feels so good. I lower my eyes and wonder if Jamie and I ever had sex in this shower. Then I shake my head. I'm not sure what's wrong with me.

It has to be that we've had sex but I can't *remember* having sex. The imagining and the wondering is driving me crazy. We have all this history and I don't remember any of it. I shake my head, flinging the water away.

I want to know everything. I want to know what I like, what I don't like. Why we live here. Why I work at the job I do. What my dreams are. What our dreams are.

The only thing I really know about myself is that I hate small, enclosed spaces. I hate feeling trapped. When I went in that first port-a-john today I nearly lost my mind. My heart slammed against my chest, my throat constricted, and I slammed out of it so fast that Big Tom looked at me like I was crazy. Maybe I am. I don't know what happened.

I rinse off the last of the soap and turn off the water. When I do, there's a quiet knock on the door.

"Yes?"

"I brought you a clean towel." Jamie holds a towel out to me, keeping behind the closed door so she doesn't see me naked. I frown. Is that the kind of relationship we have?

I grab the towel and wrap it around my waist. "Thanks."

"Sure thing. I'll be in the kitch—"

I swing open the door and her eyes go wide, taking in my bare chest, the water dripping down my abdomen.

"—en." A bright flush spreads over her cheeks, and it's like she can't help herself. Her eyes cling to my chest, follow the line down, down to where the towel's starting to tent.

When she sees that, her eyes fly up to mine, as shocked as if I'd struck her with a bolt of lightning.

I smile and shrug. "Looks like somebody remembers."

She coughs, hits her chest, and then backs up. "Uh. Ummm."

I lift my eyebrows. "I mean, I know I'm covered in bruises and scrapes, but it's not like you haven't seen…" I narrow my eyes when she trips over the bed.

She scrambles up. "Sorry. Sorry, the chili's burning. Gotta go."

I frown as she dashes from the bedroom.

What was that about?

I get the feeling there's something my wife isn't telling me.

Was our marriage falling apart before I lost my memory?

Yesterday I got the feeling my wife doesn't like me much.

Now I'm getting the feeling we don't have sex.

We don't even sleep in the same bed, for crying out loud.

Worse, I sleep with the dog.

I drag a hand over my face. It seems like I have a whole lot to fix in my life. The thing is, though, I'm not sure what to fix, because I don't know where I went wrong.

14

———

"THIS CORNBREAD IS DELICIOUS." I SMILE AT JAMIE, grabbing my third piece. It takes like honey, and butter, and has a crisp crust and a fluffy center that melts in my mouth. It's addictive. It's delicious. "Do I usually like your cornbread this much?"

Jamie flushes, which is something I've noticed she does a lot when I talk to her. I thought she was stubborn, and maybe had a temper, but I'm beginning to adjust my opinion.

"I reckon you like it the most of anything you've tasted that I've made," she says, looking down into her chili bowl.

"Huh." I take another bite. Maybe I should save some for tomorrow. I'd rather have this for lunch then another tuna sandwich.

I take a long look at Jamie. She has her hair up in a high ponytail. I noticed she doesn't wear make-up or nail polish or anything like that. Her usual outfit is overalls, but tonight she's wearing jeans and a t-shirt. I wonder what she did all day. I wonder what we usually do at night after the kids are in bed.

I wonder...

I take another bite of the cornbread.

I've decided that the only way to fix whatever problems I don't know I have is by going on a fact-finding mission. I'm going to find out as much about my life, my wife, and my kids as possible. Starting now.

"What'd you do in school today?" I raise an eyebrow at Elijah. He's been dipping his spoon in his bowl and then watching the chili fall back with a splat as he dumps it back in. Not hungry, I guess. Although he should eat, the kid's as skinny as a rail.

Elijah's eyes fly up to mine, he looks surprised that I'm talking to him.

"Nothing." He starts scooping and dumping his chili again.

Tanner bounces in his seat. "Elijah got top score on the math test."

When he says this, Elijah elbows him, like he didn't want me to know. I'm not sure why me knowing I have a smart kid is a problem. Something tickles at the back of my mind, like I knew somebody else that was good at math as a kid. Maybe it was me.

Jamie gets up, her chair scraping over the kitchen floor, and gives Elijah's shoulders a squeeze.

"That's great. I knew all that studying would pay off." Elijah looks embarrassed, but I get the feeling he's also proud.

Tanner waves his hand in the air. "I still got the worst grade. Ms. Crum said I'm hopeless and all the kids laughed, so I'm thinking of a new contraption—"

Jamie shakes her finger. "No more contraptions. You remember what Ms. Crum said."

Tanner's shoulders droop.

Quiet falls over the table, and suddenly everyone seems very serious. Jamie sits back down and picks up her spoon.

"What did she say?" I look between them all.

Suddenly Tanner finds his chili as interesting as Elijah.

"Who is Ms. Crum?"

"Meow!"

I look at the little girl. Dang it, why can't I remember her name? Sharon? Shan? Shanti?

She looks like she's bursting to tell me what happened. I think her name is...

"Shayne...you know what happened?"

Elijah slams his spoon against the table. "Her name is Shay. His name is Tanner. You're supposed to be our dad, how hard is it to remember our names?" He shoves his chair out and stands up, chest heaving.

Shoot. I...dang it.

In all this I never thought about how hard this has to be on the kids. How their own father not remembering them must feel. By the look on Elijah's face, it must feel horrible.

I'm about to say I'm sorry, when he runs from the kitchen, his feet pounding on the floor. In a few seconds the front door slams so loud the plates in the cupboards rattle.

Shay looks around the table with big eyes.

"Rawr." Which sounds a lot like the kitten version of *wow*.

Jamie stands. "I'll go…"

I hold up my hand. "No. It's okay. I'll go see him."

I hurry outside. The brisk evening air hits me, and I look around the yard, trying to find where Elijah ran off to. Dusk makes the shadows darker and longer. Birds swoop overhead, catching bugs, and the hens cluck in the coop. I walk through the tall grass. It brushes against my legs, letting off a sweet smell. I pass a pile of what I thought of yesterday as junk, and now I see that it's old gears, pulleys, wires, wheels, spokes and handlebars, all the things a budding mechanical engineer would need to make "contraptions" to his heart's content. I remember that Andy Warhol loved junk and junkyards and then I wonder how I can remember a fact about Andy Warhol's life, but nothing about my own.

I step past the pile and then I see Elijah in the coop. He's sitting cross-legged on the ground, a hen in his lap. He strokes the hen's feathers and when I come close he turns his head away.

"Mind if I come in?"

Elijah shrugs and lets the hen loose, it flutters off and joins the other chickens mingling on the other side of the coop, looking to roost. I duck through the fence door and close it behind me. There's Billy, the old, one-eyed rooster, glaring at me, making sure I don't bother his ladies.

I ignore him. I'm not here to bother him, I'm here to talk with my kid.

I sit down in the dirt next to Elijah. The ground is cold, and the coop smells like chicken feathers, dirt and the pleasant scent of birdseed held in your hand. The bugs start up, letting us know night is here. The sound is comforting and I get the feeling that I've often sat outside at night, listening to bugs sing.

Elijah doesn't seem like he's going to break the silence. He's just scratching at the dirt with his finger, ignoring me.

I study his face. He has brown hair, a shade darker than mine, and large hazel eyes. I get the feeling that of the two brothers, Elijah takes things more to heart.

"I'm sorry," I begin.

Elijah's shoulders stiffen, but he keeps scratching at the dirt.

I shift on the hard, hen-scratched ground. "I'm sorry I forgot your names. And I'm really sorry that I don't remember you."

Elijah turns his face away and wipes at his eyes. "It's not that you don't remember. I don't care about that."

"Then what is it?"

He turns back to me and my breath catches. I want to tug him close, he looks so lost.

"I'm scared I'll forget. What if I don't remember? You forgot. What if I forget? Nobody will remember then, not Tanner, not Shay, nobody." A tear slips from his eye and he angrily swipes at it with the back of his hand. "I can't forget." He stares at me, as if he's challenging me to tell him otherwise.

I shake my head. "You won't. Don't worry about that."

"I'm not worried." He glares at me then scrubs at his face.

I nod. "I was thinking. I don't know much anymore about what you like or how to be a dad. But you remember what you like, and you know how to be a son. So I was thinking, you might be patient with me, forgive my mistakes, and help me out? You could remind me what we used to do, you could help me be a good dad? How's that sound?" I hold my breath waiting for him to answer. I'm more nervous than I think I've ever been. I dig my hands into the dirt and wait for his response.

Elijah stays quiet, sniffs once, then twice, then he looks up at me with clear hazel eyes. "You want me to teach you how to be our dad?"

I let my breath out, then give a solemn nod. "I thought you might remind me what we like to do?"

He gives me a thoughtful look, then a slow smile spreads over his face.

"We like to play outside."

My chest tightens. "Really?"

"Uh huh. Tanner makes contraptions and I help. Granny says he has a mechanical brain." His brow wrinkles. "You like to help too."

"I do?"

"Uh huh."

I hold back a smile. "What else?"

"I like baseball and you're always up for playing catch or being the pitcher."

"I am?"

He nods quickly. "Uh huh. Also, you never mind when we get into trouble at school and you treat mom real nice, cause she's a good mom, and she works hard and sometimes she gets sad."

My smile turns down, and my brow wrinkles. Elijah's eyes widen then he closes his mouth tight, like he shouldn't be traveling down that road.

The urge to ask my ten-year-old why his mom gets sad is almost unbearable. But I'm not, repeat, I'm not going to go there with a kid. I'll ask Jamie.

I nod then stand and hold out my hand to Elijah. He looks at me in surprise, then takes my hand and stands. His small hand is warm in mine, and he grips me tight.

I look down at him. "Are you sure I never mind when you get in trouble at school?"

Elijah grins at me, bold as brass, and says, "'Course. You don't mind at all."

I cover my smile by rubbing my hand over my jaw. "I see. Well. Let's go back in and finish dinner."

When we come back into the warm, cornbread and chili-scented kitchen, my eyes go immediately to Jamie. Does she look sad? Does she look tired?

I can't tell. I don't know what she usually looks like. All I can see is a bit of worry in her eyes that fades when I smile at her.

She squints at us. "Everything okay?"

I sit down and reach across the table, brushing my fingers over her hand.

"'Course," I say, echoing Elijah.

But it isn't. Because when my fingers touch her bare skin, a raging river, one with a wild current, rushes through me and nearly pulls me under. It's hard to breathe. It's impossible to pull my hand away.

Is this what I feel every time I touch her?

Her eyes fly to mine, sparks lighting in the lavender blue, like fireflies at dusk.

Her mouth parts and she draws in a sharp breath.

My word.

If it feels like this when I touch her hand, what does it feel like when we make love? Suddenly, it seems impossible that we only have three kids.

How is it I'm sleeping on the couch?

How is it we haven't kissed since she came for me?

How is it we haven't touched?

I don't know. But I'm going to find out.

15

———

Jamie

THE DISHES ARE DONE, THE CHICKENS ARE FED AND THE coop is closed, the kids had their bath and are sound asleep, and Gavin is standing in the door of the bedroom looking at me like he has a whole lot on his mind.

When I agreed with Diedre and Gran that I was going to teach Gavin Williams a lesson he'd never forget (even with amnesia), I didn't think the whole thing through. Clearly. I never pictured him in my shower, sleeping on my couch, eating at my table, and I definitely didn't picture him looking at me the way he's looking right now.

Mainly, like he wants to back me up three steps, push me down on the bed, and devour me. My legs go wobbly, and suddenly, I really need to sit down. I grab the old blanket at the foot of the bed and hold it in front of myself like a shield.

"You bedding down?" My voice comes out in a squeak.

Gavin shakes his head. He's leaning against the doorframe, blocking my way out of the bedroom. I can't slip past him without touching him, and after what happened when he brushed my hand at supper, I don't know that I'll be able to handle touching him again.

"No. I'm not tired." He smiles at me and my cheeks burn. Why oh why did I have to be born a redhead? Why do I have to have my feelings painted all over my face?

He lifts an eyebrow and I know he's taking in my pink cheeks.

Yes. You're a good-looking man. We both know this.

Yes. I find you attractive. We both know this too.

I squeeze my eyes shut.

Clearly, clearly I didn't think things through.

I believed Gavin was a selfish, narcissistic, rude, thieving, dream-killing peckerwood. Four days ago, he was. And maybe if and when he gets his memories back, he'll be that man again. The one who tells me I'm ugly and ignorant and that me and my artwork aren't worth anything. But without his memories, the ones that shaped him and made him into that selfish prick, well...he's actually...this is hard to admit...but he seems...decent.

He slept on the couch with Scooter slobbering on him all night and he didn't complain. He got egged and covered in chicken poop and feathers by the kids and he didn't lose his temper. He worked all day with Big Tom, and by his stench when he came home, he worked hard, but he didn't make a fuss. Instead, he showered off then complimented me on my subpar (I admit, I'm not a great cook) cornbread. And then, then, when Elijah got upset, he went after him, and by the way Elijah asked him to read the bedtime story for the kids, I think he and Elijah came to a truce. Which means, no more egging. And it means that he's won my dog over, my kids over, and that maybe, while Gavin Williams was a peckerwood, this other man, he's not.

Does that make me the bad guy?

I have a horrible, sinking feeling that it does.

Gavin's been studying me, his eyes running over my face, my lips, my pajama shirt and my bare legs. It's only nine o'clock, but I've been up since four, and I'm ready for bed.

Gavin pushes off the doorframe and sends me a small smile that makes my heart stutter. "So. What do we usually do after the kids are in bed?"

The image of him taking three steps into the room and pushing me down to the bed flashes through my mind. My mouth goes dry.

It's been too long. Too many years. I should've realized that a six-year spell of nothing meant that when feelings came back, they'd come in like a flash flood.

"We...uh...well..." I lick my lips and Gavin's eyes grow hooded as he watches me. My mind short-circuits. Sex. He's thinking about sex. "You...uh...you do the crosswords."

Oh boy. I give him a bright smile.

He shakes his head. "The what?"

"Well, see. You're tired at the end of the day, so you like

to go outside, sit with the chickens, smoke a pipe, except you don't smoke anymore, and do the crosswords."

I send up a prayer for forgiveness. If Gavin had his memories, he'd be enraged. I'm sure.

"The crosswords? A pipe?" He plucks at his suspenders, holding up his too-large pants. "What am I, ninety?"

I shrug. "You like exercising your brain. Learning big words. Facts about the world."

Oh jeez, I can't believe he's buying this.

He studies me skeptically. Okay, maybe he's not buying it.

"What else do I like?" He narrows his eyes.

He's thinking about sex again. I use the blanket I'm holding to fan myself.

"You're hot?" He frowns, then nods at the front door. "Let's sit on the porch."

He turns and walks away before I can tell him I'd rather go to bed. Or heck, I'd rather have my eyes pecked out by Billy when he's on one of his rooster rampages.

I fidget as I follow Gavin out to the porch, the screen door creaking as it shuts behind me. Gavin sits down on the steps and pats the wood next to him. The crickets are loud, and I feel like this is one of those moments when in movies, the characters are silent, and the crickets start chirping, because it's so, so awkward.

Gavin shakes his head. "What is it? Did we get in a fight before I lost my memory? Is that why I get the feeling you're not happy with me? You have to help me out. I don't know up from down."

I look at the first stars just starting to light up the sky and breathe in the night air perfumed with pine and moss and mountain stone. The crickets are loud tonight, so loud they almost cover the sound of the wind rustling through the trees.

This is the perfect moment to tell Gavin that the reason he doesn't know up from down is that I lied to him. That he's actually wealthy, owns a million-dollar cabin up the mountain, has a beautiful former fiancée, and a life that includes traveling the world, and doing hundreds of other things I know nothing about.

That I'm sorry for tricking him, but before it goes too far, he should know…

Gavin smiles ruefully. "You look pretty tonight."

My hand flies up to my hair, pulled back in a bun. "What?"

He nods. "I didn't see it at first. I didn't know why I married you. But I'm beginning to figure it out."

It's suddenly hard to breathe.

He nods and leans back. "I think you're like this mountain. When we pulled up, I didn't think much of this place. Most people would keep driving, not notice it, and if they did they'd turn up their noses. But after only a day, I'm already noticing all the things that were hidden." He smiles at me. "It's a subtle beauty. One that not many people would take the time to notice. I'm grateful my past self was smart enough to take the time to look."

I drag in a shaky breath. Even in the fresh air, the night feels hot.

He frowns at my expression. "What is it? Did I say something wrong?"

Suddenly, I wish he were still that jerk from before. The world is easier when everything is black and white. He's waiting for my response, so I say, "No. It's okay. It's just been a long time since anyone ever told me they liked the way I look."

In fact, only a few days ago this same man told me that I was drab and ugly.

"Well, I'll change that then." He frowns at the crickets singing loud. "I told Elijah he needed to remind me how to be a good dad. Maybe you could remind me how to be a husband."

It feels like he's punched me. Why does he have to be nice? "I don't want you to do anything. Just go to work. Fix the kids breakfast. I don't need anything else."

"Huh." He frowns and rubs his hand down his face.

After a minute of staring up at the stars, I figure I'm clear to head back inside and bury my head under my pillow, but Gavin pats the steps again. "Come on. I thought you might tell me about myself."

I sigh. But I can't refuse when he's looking at me like he likes me, and he wants to hear what I have to say. I lower to the wooden stairs. They groan as I sit next to Gavin.

A chilly breeze blows past and I wrap my arms around myself. "What do you want to know?"

Gavin peers at me and I shiver. He shakes his head, puts his arm around my shoulder and pulls me into his side. It's like a rockslide of sensation crashing over me. I'm buried beneath it. I have the strongest urge to crawl in his lap, take his face with my hands, and kiss and kiss.

"Better?"

I nod, swallowing down all the feelings coursing through me at the heat of his body pressed to mine.

He smiles. "I was wondering, what's our marriage like?"

Oh boy. "I...it's a normal marriage. The usual."

He runs his hand up and down my arm, warming me, and my brain melts, like glass in a furnace.

"Do we fight?"

"Mmm. Sometimes."

He considers this for a moment. "Is that why I'm sleeping on the couch?"

"No! No. 'Course not."

"Why don't I believe you?"

I look out at the pines, the warmth of his arm around me, lighting me up like fire. "Well, I suppose, we did fight right before your accident."

His hand pauses and I feel his attention. "What was it about?"

I shrug. "It's not important."

"I'd still like to hear about it."

I think about the day we met and my glass shattered around me. I point at the stone barn. "See that barn?"

He nods. "Sure."

"That's my studio. I'm a glassblower. We had a fight and you told me my work was..." I shrug.

"What?" He frowns at me.

"Uninspired. Drab. Ugly."

He cusses and I lift my eyebrows.

"Was I always such a dick?" he asks incredulously.

I can't help it, I grin at him. "I don't know. You tell me."

He scoffs, then his eyes sober. "Does it count if I say I'm sorry, even though I don't remember?"

My stomach lurches, and I have no idea what to say to this. "I…"

He reaches up and touches my cheek. "I'm sorry."

I nod and try to wave away the feelings I'm having at his finger dragging over my skin. "What else do you want to know?"

He pulls his hand away and shrugs. "Everything. Why do I work with Big Tom? Do I like my job?"

I bite my lip and try to keep from fidgeting. He works with Big Tom because Gran thought he deserved a taste of difficult, dirty work, and Diedre used her charm to convince Tom to bring him on. But I can't really say that.

"Well, you needed a job and Tom was hiring."

Gavin stares at me. "That's it?"

I nod. "Pretty much. It's a good job. You work hard, you make honest money, you get to come home at the end of the day. It's not a glamorous job, nothing to brag about, but being able to provide for people you love, that's what makes doing the job worth it."

In the end, I'm not talking about Gavin. I'm talking about all the jobs I take on, the housecleaning, the taxiing, picking up waitressing shifts at the bar, selling my glass. But at my words Gavin squeezes me closer.

"You're right. A man wants to take care of his family. I'll do whatever I can. You don't have to worry. I might not remember my job, but I'll work hard."

I close my eyes and try not to breathe in the reassuring scent of clean soap clinging to his skin.

"I'm not worried," I tell him, even though I am.

"Good. So tell me more. What do I like? What are my dreams? What do you like? What do you want?"

I shake my head. "Tell you the story of the world in five minutes?"

"Pretty much." He smiles and I have the urge to reach up and run my hands through his hair.

"Hmm. Well." I tap my chin with my finger and think about what I know. "You like the outdoors and hiking."

He considers this. "I thought so."

"You're well-read, you know a lot about the world. You have the accent you do because you traveled the country with your mom in the circus."

"Do I ever talk about traveling? Finding another job? Do I ever dream about us picking up and going somewhere else?"

I look right into Gavin's clear blue eyes and say, "No. You like your job. You love it here. You said you never wanted to leave."

His eyes flicker down to my mouth and then back up to my eyes. "I think you're right. All that traveling as a kid must've made me appreciate staying still. Right now, I think I could happily spend the rest of my life right here."

I stare at him, eyes wide, but he's not looking at me, he's looking at my lips. The crickets are still going, but now, my heart's pounding louder than they're chirping. My lips tingle.

"Jamie, one more question."

"Hmm?" I sway toward him.

His eyes glow in the starlight when he asks, "How long has it been since we kissed?"

I don't answer, because he leans forward, reaches up, drags his hands through my hair, and pulls my mouth to his.

I gasp at the sensation of his warm lips on mine and when I do he runs his tongue over my bottom lip. His hands grip the back of my head, pressing me to him, and he devours my mouth. He tastes like honey and cornbread and I realize he's biting my lips, licking me like he's relishing the most delicious meal he's ever had. When he groans, low and urgent, a flood of warmth travels through me. My hips fall open and when he slips his tongue in my mouth there's an answering pulse down low. I suck on him and he groans again, tugging me closer.

"Jamie," he whispers against my mouth.

I whimper, mindless except for the sensation of his lips against mine. The slick feel of his tongue running over my lips, the invasion of him in my mouth. I dig my fingers into his shoulders. I can't think when he's kissing me like this. It's like the six years without a kiss or a touch has made my kindling so dry that I combust into mindless lust at one touch. Just like someone who has lost their tolerance for alcohol, I'm drunk on him.

He pushes me down to the planks of the deck. The wood digs into my back, but then Gavin settles on top of me and I'm not thinking about wood planks or splinters or anything but him pressing into me. Right there.

He tugs on my hair and I open my mouth wider. He

groans and his tongue tangles with mine. I wrap my arms around him and then he reaches down, lifts up my pajama shirt and brushes his fingers over me.

My eyes fly open and I see stars. Not the stars in the sky, but stars from the sensation of him petting me. He makes a noise when he feels how wet I am.

"All that from our kiss?" He stares down at me, completely dumbfounded.

Then he decides that he's done talking, because he puts his mouth back to mine and circles his finger over me. I'd like to say that I'm rational, that I'm thinking. But I'm not. I'm just feeling. I'm running on pure instinct and right now my instinct is telling me that if I don't touch every bit of Gavin, if I don't keep kissing him, or feeling his hands on me, that I'll regret it. I'll regret it forever.

So when his fingers find my entrance, I grip his shoulders and open to him. He swears when he feels me tighten around him. I'm a bundle of sensation, I'm a flaming, vibrating ball of need. And when he sticks two fingers inside me and flicks my clit, that's all it takes. I convulse around him. He makes a shocked noise, realizes I'm already there. Then he keeps pumping his fingers, wringing more and more out of me. He sucks on my mouth, captures my cries like he's greedy for them. And keeps petting me and stroking me until he's wrung every last drop of feeling out of me. Until I finally fall from the stars and back down to earth, to land, out of breath, in his arms.

I blink and stare up at him. He smiles, pulls my shirt

back down, and kisses me on the lips. "You're beautiful when you come."

I flush, and when he sees it, even in the dark, he smiles. "Is it like that every time we kiss?"

I blink and try to shake out of the drunken stupor his lips put me in. "It's...uh...it's...like that every time we've done it."

He smirks, looking extraordinarily proud. He kisses the edge of my mouth. "Thank you."

A cold feeling trickles over me. "For what?"

"I figure you're worried about being intimate when I don't remember our past. Thank you for trusting me." He kisses the other side of my mouth.

I turn my head and stare out at the woods. That's the problem. I don't trust him. And he definitely shouldn't trust me.

But goodness, every time we touch, we're like a furnace burning at three thousand degrees.

"Jamie?"

I look back up. He gives a half-smile and rubs his fingers through my hair. "You didn't say. Are you happy staying here with me? What about your dreams?"

I try and shut out the ache that grows in my chest, but it's nearly impossible.

"I just dream about the kids being happy. Having everything they want. That's all."

He frowns. "What about your art? What I said..."

I shake my head. "That's not a dream. It's an impossibility."

He looks over at the stone barn, considering my words. "Maybe later you'll show me what you do?"

I swallow down a lump as big and heavy as a glass paperweight. "Maybe."

"Alright." He nods, then helps me sit up. It's cold now, and since he's not holding me anymore, I shiver from the chill.

"We should head in. It's an early morning."

Gavin nods, and he doesn't protest when I hand him the blanket for the couch and tell him goodnight.

16

Jamie

I burst into Gran's kitchen, my chest heaving, out of breath, just like I have been since last night. The kitchen is cluttered with all of Grandpa's old implements—toasters, coffee grinders, electric sandwich presses, microwaves. He loved his gadgets, and Gran hasn't gotten rid of a single one, it's like a flea market in here. Stacked in between the 1980s kitchen gadgets, Gran also manages to shove her cast iron collection and the big old iron cauldron that they used to do laundry and make lye soap in when Gran was a kid. Someday, this kitchen is going to burst, but today's not the day.

The screen door slams behind me, and Diedre and Gran look up from where they're sitting at the table.

Gran has a bowl of shelling beans in front of her. She

has a mountain of beans piled high in a bright red bowl, and her hands work fast snapping and stripping the shells. She lifts an eyebrow at my flushed cheeks and sweat-lined brow.

Diedre gives me a happy grin. She's my Gran's number one fan and was pleased as pie to be invited over. But this isn't a friendly get-together. No.

I wave my hand in the air, making a chopping motion. "I can't do it. I'm done. I'm going to tell him everything. I can't do it."

It's late afternoon. I rushed through cleaning houses and called Diedre and Gran so we could have this chat.

Gran tosses the bean she's shelling into the bowl. "Now why would you go and do a thing like that?"

Diedre narrows her eyes on me and I flush. "I... uh...well..."

Gavin's mouth on mine flashes through my mind, the way he touched me, the way he looked at me, what he said.

Diedre gasps. "You had sex with him."

Gran snaps her long, fat shelling bean in half, and I flinch at the violent motion, because if there was ever a woman imagining snapping a man's willy in half, that was it.

"Jamie Lynn."

"I did not!" I deny, but then I go and ruin it because I can feel my face growing hotter.

Gran shakes her finger at me. "Look at you wiggling like a worm in ashes."

I hold still and stop shifting my feet on the old tile floor.

Diedre grins. She loves Gran's old sayings. "Good one, Granny Allwright."

Granny doesn't have time for nonsense. "You hush, child. Jamie Lynn, you listen to me." She points at the pile of shelling beans. "But while you're listening, shell these. I've a truckload of them to get done."

I pull out a wooden chair, the one with the old cross-stitched chair pad with a whisk and the phrase "Don't be afraid to take whisks." I scowl at it.

I grab a handful of beans and start snapping. "Gran. Diedre. I'm having second thoughts. We thought Gavin was a terrible person, but it turns out, he's not. He's really not. I don't feel right—"

"Listen here," Gran interrupts. "Did he insult you?"

"Well, yes, but—"

"Did he sign a contract, have you slave on a project for months, and then renege, taking nine thousand dollars rightly owed to you?"

"I mean, yes, but—"

"And did he cause you to fall and shatter the work you could've sold to someone else, robbing you of even that income?"

"Okay, yes, but—"

"And did he then walk out and tell you he would never pay and that your art, your life, and you were ugly and uninspired?"

"But Gran, I don't think he meant it."

Gran gives me a pitying look. "He meant it."

Diedre sighs. She has a small pile of shells in front of

her that she's shredding into fine strips. By the look of the pile, I don't think she's ever shelled a bean in her life.

"I agree with Granny Allwright. I know a lot about men." She opens her eyes wide. "A lot. Just the other day, one of those repressed city boys messaged me and..." She looks over at Granny Allwright, then thinks better about what she was about to say. "Well, needless to say, a man never speaks the truth when he's trying to...err...make whoopie."

Gran snaps another shell and I flinch.

Diedre widens her eyes at me and nods meaningfully. "I can guarantee, if a man is trying to...make whoopie..."

"Diedre, for crying out loud, just say sex. I'm eighty-seven years old. I was doing the deed long before your daddy was even old enough to wank his own stick."

Diedre coughs into her hand and I grin at her. Diedre's dad was a legendary ladies man in his day, and everybody on the mountain knows it.

Finally, Diedre gets her coughing under control. She clears her throat. "That's all well and good, but my point was, if a man wants to have sex with you, then he'll say and do anything. If he doesn't want to have sex with you, his true colors come out. Before Gavin lost his memory, he didn't want to have sex with you, so he showed his real self. Now, he's like a bear, chained to a tree, and you're the only honey pot he can access. Of course he's going to treat you nice. Of course he's going to be charming. He's being nice, right?" She narrows her eyes.

I nod. "Yeah. Real nice."

Gran snaps another bean.

Diedre gives a satisfied smile. "I thought so. It's not that he's changed. It's that he thinks you're the honey pot. Don't let his charm the honey pot routine distract you from your goal."

I look at her forlornly. "What's my goal again?"

Gran clicks her tongue. "Just desserts, Jamie. Getting what's coming. And what's coming is not a biddable wife and dancing in the sheets."

Diedre coughs. "Uh, thought we were saying sex?"

I block out the image of Gavin and me rolling on my bed, the sheets wrapped around us.

"Shush. I'm serious here. Repeat after me." Gran stares me down like a general preparing her troops for battle.

I nod. "Okay."

"Gavin Williams is a no-good, selfish, horrible man."

I flinch, but say, "Gavin Williams is a no-good, selfish, horrible man."

Gran nods. "I will not be swayed by sweet words, handsome looks, or"—she glares—"rampant sex appeal."

Diedre snorts and covers her mouth with her hand.

I sigh. "Gran..."

"Jamie Lynn." She crosses her bony arms over her chest.

I look up to heaven. She's right. Diedre's right. To use a cliché, a leopard can't change its spots, it can only shave them off, but the fur always grows back. Gavin might seem different, but he's only being nice because he thinks I'm the honey pot. He's still the same man underneath.

I firm my jaw and look at Gran and Diedre.

"Okay." I nod. My resolve is back. "I will not be swayed by sweet words, handsome looks, or rampant sex appeal."

Diedre grins at me. "There's my best friend. Go get 'em, tiger."

I take a deep breath and blow it out. The kitchen smells sweet and earthy, the bean shells pungent. My panic is gone, my confusion is gone, and it feels like I can take a normal breath again.

But there's one more thing. "I think…I'm worried the kids will get too attached."

I touch my necklace, the glass sliver in the locket. I saw how Elijah was looking at Gavin during story time. Tanner too. Even Shay curled up beside him, like a cat on a rug.

Gran scoffs. "No chance. Your kids are smart and tough. They know what's what. Remember how long it took them to warm up to Regal Miller?"

Regal was the last person that moved to Hollow Creek. He's the cashier at the five and dime.

I nod. "Nearly a year. And he's nice as punch and gives them bubblegum to boot."

"That's right." Gran nods. "Gavin will be gone in a few weeks, lesson learned. And the kids'll forget all about him."

I press my hand to my necklace. I realize that maybe that's what I'm afraid of. I don't want another man in their lives that they'll forget.

Gran reaches over and pats my hand. "Don't fash yourself. The Lord works in mysterious ways and me—"

"—and him are real good friends." Diedre grins at Gran and Gran scoffs and waves her off.

"All better?" Gran studies me. "You'll send him on his way soon. Or he'll remember and he'll send himself on his own way. But until then, keep on the good path."

Diedre tosses a bit of shell at me. "No kissing. No sheet dancing."

I resolve to follow their advice. No more touching, no more kissing, no more softening toward Gavin. That's what's making this complicated. As long as I keep it about just desserts, then I won't feel so confused.

"Okay. No kissing. No sheet dancing."

Gran nods. "Remember Jamie Lynn, he isn't a good man. Roses don't grow in a bed of manure."

And that is all there is to say about that.

17

———

Gavin

The motor of the vacuum chugs along as I pump the waste from our fifth port-a-john stop of the day. The sun beats down on the plastic, heating the stagnant air. A fly buzzes overhead, and I swat it away. The stench is still all-consuming, even with the sanitizer I spray and the deodorizer I put down.

You'd think that would've turned me off years ago from doing this job, but like Jamie said, I'm providing for my family, doing honest work, and there's no shame in that.

I think about the kids, and figure, I loved them, and even if I don't remember them being born, or playing catch with them, or teaching them to ride their bikes, that doesn't mean that I won't remember it again. Someday soon, I'll have my memories back, and I'm sure I'll be ashamed of myself if I don't keep caring for them as best I can.

A twinge pesters me, like the fly buzzing overhead, and I realize it's that the doctor said I might never remember. But that doesn't seem so terrifying anymore. They're good kids. Jamie is...I like the way we fit. Who am I kidding? I love the way we fit.

There's a part of me that almost doesn't want to remember. Because there's an itch inside that tells me there's a reason that Jamie looks at me like I'm a feral dog that might bite. And there's a reason the kids egged me. And there's a reason my grandma in-law doesn't like me. I'm almost afraid to learn those reasons.

I shake my head and wipe the sweat from my brow. I'm almost done pumping, I'm crowded into the tight walls of the port-a-john.

Thankfully, stepping into the claustrophobic space isn't as terrifying as it was yesterday. Mostly, I admit, because I'm distracted with thoughts of Jamie. As soon as my throat starts to go tight and my mind yells, run, run, run, I just have to picture her lavender eyes regarding me with that dazed, just-been-kissed expression, and the desire to run flees. I guess I'm claustrophobic, and even though I've forgotten everything about myself, apparently my subconscious hasn't.

I shrug and turn off the vacuum, pulling it from the john. Big Tom's at the truck, working on the paperwork for our next stop. I load the waste into the tank and hop into the rumbling truck cab. Tom doesn't spare me a glance.

He's just as talkative as he was yesterday. Meaning he's grunted, sighed, shrugged and thrown another tuna sandwich at me. I was kind enough to share some of my cornbread.

"Tom. I've been meaning to ask you." I wait until he looks up. I turn down the country music crackling over the radio. Then, "In all the time you've known me, have I ever talked about my wife?"

He gives me a flat look.

I rub my chin and look out the window at the carpet of dark green grass and the thickly leafed trees shading the roadside park. "I mean to say, did I like being married?"

He grunts, turns the radio back up and puts the truck into gear. We pull onto the twisting mountain road, heading for our next stop. Apparently, Tom thinks the conversation is over. But we have five minutes until we hit the next park, and I still have more questions.

The leaf-scented breeze from the open window rolls over me and I watch the trees fly by. "So, did that grunt mean yes or no?"

He scratches his beard. Okay.

"I think I'm a friendly guy," I continue. "I like people. I think I'm happy. And when I look at my wife..." I draw in a breath, gazing out over the lush forest and the craggy mountain boulders. "I can't describe it, but when I look at her." I shake my head. "Never mind."

Big Tom nods, his furry beard not big enough to hide the reddening of his cheeks, I take that as encouragement to keep going.

"Alright. So it's like this. When I first saw her at the

hospital, I thought there was no way that I was married to her. Couldn't see it. I didn't believe anything she said about my life. But it's only been two days, and now I can't see my life any other way." I peer at Big Tom to make sure he's listening. He grabs a handful of sunflower seeds, pops them in his mouth and then nods, so I figure he's still with me. "When I'm near her, I feel...I feel like a raft, being tugged down the current toward a waterfall, I can't pull away, and I really want to go over that cliff." I rub my head. That sounded stupid. Big Tom spits his sunflower shells out the window.

I sigh. "Here's the deal. I can't stop looking at my wife. Last night, I caught myself counting the freckles on her cheeks. There are thirty-seven of them, in case you were wondering."

Tom grunts. He wasn't wondering.

"I've decided her eyes are the shade between a morning sky and lavender just blooming. And she does this thing, where if she finds something funny but shouldn't laugh, the left side of her mouth twitches. When I compliment her, her face turns pink, and all those thirty-seven freckles pop and I want to..." I clear my throat, thinking about what I want to do. "Do you see? Was I always this poetic about my wife? I don't think I'm a poetic person. Am I?"

Tom spits more sunflower shells out the window. I guess I'm not. I frown. "I think I like my wife. I think I loved her." There's an aching flutter in my chest, like my heart's beating against a closed door, in a dark, lonely room. "I loved her, didn't I?"

I think about this morning. She came into the kitchen when I was stirring the oatmeal. She stopped with a surprised look, and I grabbed her hand, pulled her close, and dropped a kiss on her lips. She tasted like mint toothpaste and cherry lip gloss, and I could feel her pulse racing as I rubbed my thumb over her wrist.

Lust, wild, raging lust shot through me and I wanted to drop the oatmeal spoon and tug her to the bedroom for a repeat of last night. But Scooter snorted at me from the floor, and I could hear the kids in the loft, getting dressed.

"Morning," I'd said instead, tucking a strand of hair behind her ear.

Jamie flushed and stared with wide, shocked eyes, like she'd never gotten a morning kiss before in her entire life.

That was odd. Really odd. Didn't I ever kiss my wife?

I look over at Tom and he lifts an eyebrow, like he's asking why I can't tell whether or not I loved my own wife.

"You're right. I should know better than anyone else." I consider this. "I think I may have hurt her in the past. Maybe I wasn't always good to her. I'm not sure what she thinks of me." I give him a sidelong glance. Tom confirms what I was thinking by putting a calloused hand on my shoulder and giving me a hard pat.

So there's that. Apparently, I was a dick.

I nod. "Thanks. Good talk."

We pull into the next roadside park, a U-turn drive with a scenic view over the blue-green valley and a wooden picnic table. I hop out of the truck, the birds are singing, and even though apparently I've not always been the best man, I think I've been given an opportunity to be better.

Like I told Jamie, there isn't anywhere else I'd rather be. Looking out over the sloping mountainside, the wide open valley, and the blue, blue sky, it feels like the world goes on forever and ever, and I'm standing in its center.

18

———

Gavin

The sun slides down the sky slowly, lazily. It's as if the sun is a kid, trying to push his bedtime back as far as possible, because it knows the early nights of winter are coming. Not that I'm complaining. The longer daylight means that I can be outside, playing a game of baseball with Elijah, Tanner, and Shay.

Surprisingly, a girl pretending to be a cat is really good at fielding a ball. Elijah has a mean right arm, and nearly every time Tanner swings, he hits the ball to the outfield. The "outfield" being the grass past the stone barn.

I spin the baseball in my hand, the stitching rubbing over my fingers, as I eye Elijah's stance. He's swinging the bat, his tongue sticking out of the side of his mouth in concentration. Tanner's on second base and Shay's in the outfield.

"Come on, Elijah!" Tanner shouts, jumping up and down. If he hits it and Tanner makes it to home plate, then I'm clearing the table and doing dishes tonight. That's a big deal, since apparently Tanner has been working for months on a robotic arm dish scrubber to no avail. Maybe I can blow his mind someday and bring home an actual dishwasher.

I blow on the ball and wind up my arm.

Elijah's eyes grow wide and then I let loose a pitch straight down the middle.

"Hit it!" shouts Tanner.

Elijah cranks his arm back then swings for all he's worth. A loud crack sounds as his bat smacks the ball. Tanner shouts in triumph. Elijah drops the bat and stares open-mouthed at the ball flying through the air.

"Run! Run!" Tanner waves his arms.

Elijah realizes he's going to have to wash dishes if we tag him out, so he snaps out of it and sprints toward first base.

I try to hold in my laughter. Tanner's arms pump wildly as he jumps through the grass, heading toward the pile of gears and motors we dubbed third base. Elijah sprints toward the chicken coop, aka first base. And the ball finally hits the ground. It lands ten feet from Shay. She looks at me in surprise and I can see her mouth go "meow!" Then she pounces through the grass like a cat on a hunt.

I can't hold it in anymore, I laugh as I run toward her.

"Get it!" I wave at the ball. She somersaults through the grass.

She grasps the ball and thrusts it in the air, a triumphant smile on her face. Tanner is nearly to home plate and Elijah is rounding into second.

"Come on. Let's get 'em." I grab her, pop her on my shoulders and then run toward home plate.

"Run, Elijah! They're coming!" Tanner jumps up and down at home plate, waving his arms.

Shay grabs my shoulders and shrieks with laughter. Elijah sees us coming and kicks it into high gear, there's no way that kid's doing dishes tonight. He slides through the grass, dirt flying up in the air, and lands at home plate.

"Yeah!" Tanner jumps on him to celebrate, and I get to the plate seconds behind. I drop to my knees and pretend exhaustion. Shay rolls off my shoulders and I fall over.

"You win. How could you win?" I land in the grass, and then all the kids are tumbling and wrestling and laughing.

I look over at Elijah. He's smeared in grass and dirt and his eyes are lit up. I remember the first time I saw the kids. They were dirt-covered then too. I thought it was because they were unkempt. Now I know better. The dirtier you are, the more fun you're having.

I look at him, as if to ask, am I doing okay?

His chin dips and he gives me a nod.

My heart swells as I take in the sound of laughter, the dandelion fluff floating through the air from us rolling over the seed heads, and the smell of crushed grass and mud. I'm glad I woke up to this. I can't imagine what it would've been like if I'd woken up alone, without a wife and a family. Miserable, I'd think.

There's a sharp peck on my leg. I sit up and there's my namesake, Billy the darn cock, pecking at my calf. I narrow my eyes. "You darn bird."

The kids laugh.

Tanner points. "Mom calls him 'drumstick.'"

"And 'soup stock' or 'pot pie.'" Elijah adds.

I grin at them. I can see why. I'd like to call him a few things too.

I grab my namesake, his wings flapping, his beady eye glaring.

"I'm putting you back where you belong." He gives my hand a sharp peck and I curse. "Hold still, will you?"

I'm walking across the yard, toward the chicken run, when I hear the sound of a car rumbling up the drive. By the groaning and backfiring, I'd say it's the station wagon. I smile. My wife's home.

I shove Billy back in the chicken run, closing the gate. Sure enough, it's Jamie. She pulls under the carport, then climbs out of the wagon.

The kids are running around the yard. I walk past them, my eyes on my wife. She looks tired, her eyes have bags under them and her shoulders are slumped. She leans against the car door and gives a slight smile at the kids, but when she sees me coming her smile fades.

I pause a few feet from her, taking her in, breathing in her beeswax smell, watching her eyes shift from want to determined resistance.

"You're here," she says, and I huff, because every time she sees me here, she seems surprised that I'm still around.

"Where else would I be?" I watch her face flush.

She shrugs. "Thank you for being here when the kids got home."

I reach forward and wipe a streak of dust from her cheek.

"Of course." She called Big Tom's cell at three, saying she still had another house to clean, and could I make it back in time. I could. I did. "It's my job, isn't it?"

"Hmm."

Dang. I can't take it anymore. I lean forward, cup her cheek, I want to kiss her again. She shakes her head, my lips an inch from hers.

"What?"

She clears her throat and looks up at me with wavering eyes. "I don't think we should…kiss."

I frown. Her saying that makes a queasy feeling start in my stomach. "Why not?"

She turns her face to the side, and I drop my hand from her warm skin.

"I think…I think we should wait to do things until you have your memory back."

I frown. What she's saying makes sense, except, "What if I never get my memory back?"

She jerks back toward me, her cheeks flushing.

"Well." She clears her throat. "Gran always says, weddin' without courtin' is like vittles without salt."

I let out a shocked laugh. I'll bet she does. I decide to point out the obvious.

"But we're already wed."

Jamie drops her chin, acknowledging my point. "Except we don't know each other. We should take the time to learn each other before doing...that."

That right there is worse than sitting shut in a dark, locked room. Which, apparently, is my worst nightmare. Touching her is like touching starlight. She lights up the dark. And no kisses...

I'd like to see how serious she is about this rule. I shake my head and give a grumpy frown. "No deal."

She coughs and then lifts her eyebrows angrily.

"No deal?" She sounds like she's about to unleash a whole world of hurt on me.

I grin. There's that stubborn, intractable woman I thought she was when she came for me at the hospital.

I lift an eyebrow and plow on. "I like kissing you. When we kiss, it feels like I'm getting to know you better. Don't you feel that too? Doesn't kissing count toward learning each other?"

She presses her lips together and glares at me.

I grin. I wonder if I rile her up enough, whether she'll throw something at me, or chase me around with a cast iron pan, then we can make up by kissing. I study her expression. Or not.

I frown. "You really don't want to kiss?"

"I really don't want to kiss."

I breathe in the mountain air and inwardly curse. Going without her kisses will be like going without air.

"Is it because I don't remember and you're afraid of being hurt, or is it because you're already hurt and I'm an ass?" I study her expression. "Or are you afraid I'll remember our past and then you'll get hurt?"

Across the grass, the kids laugh and sprint around the coop, Scooter runs after them, barking excitedly.

"Yes." Jamie pushes past me and stalks toward the house.

"Yes to which one?" I call after her.

She waves her hand in the air. I jog after her, catching up. "Does that mean all three?"

"That means no kisses."

I look up at the darkening sky, at the birds swooping around, picking their dinner out of the air. "Alright. Deal."

She stops and gives me a surprised look. Then, she seems to realize she's showing her cards so she sticks her chin in the air and gives me a superior look.

"Good. If you want to feed the chickens and close them in for the night, I'll get to supper."

She turns to go and I catch her wrist. She stops and looks over her shoulder at me, and seemingly against her better judgment, her eyes turn warm and hazy. Her skin is warm and smooth and her pulse flutters under my hand.

I smile at her. "Even without kisses, I still want you. I'm going to like getting to know you again."

I let go of her wrist and she practically runs to the house.

I watch her go and let out a long sigh. The logical side of my brain agrees with her, getting to know each other again is smart. But the other part of me, the part that's hard and straining for her right now, it's telling me that there's going to be many, many cold showers in my future.

19

———

Jamie

It's only been three days since I implemented the no kisses rule and already I feel like a piece of glass glowing red hot, looping and bending in the heat, responding to every single thing Gavin does.

He smiles, I ache. He laughs, I shiver. He speaks, I go warm and flushed. He walks by me, not even touching me, but the air currents shifting feel like him stroking me and I...*goodness*. It's torture.

When he reads to the kids at night, my heart melts and I can imagine a sculpture, a raspberry red heart blooming like honeysuckle, opening wide. I'd call it *Gavin, you dog, why do you have to make me feel this way?*

I slam the chess pie onto the counter and glare out the kitchen window. Gavin's chasing the kids around the bases, in some strange version of baseball I've never seen before. His bright, happy laugh squeezes my insides and winds me so tight I think I might explode from wanting. His laugh pets me and covers me in need.

"I can't take it anymore." I blow my hair out of my eyes and turn to Gran and Diedre.

"Careful with that pie, you'll ruin the custard." Gran walks over and pokes at the sugary innards. She grunts in approval when she sees I didn't destroy the glistening custard. I wouldn't. Chess pie is a lot like glass. The eggs and sugar and butter melt together to form a glossy, smooth surface that melts and molds to form a beautiful piece of art. Mmm. Pie.

Diedre looks out the window. She frowns at Big Tom. He's currently at the pitcher's mound, winding up a throw for Elijah. Then Diedre fluffs her bottle-blonde hair, poofing up the big fat curls she ironed in and tugs down her crop top to show a little more cleavage. I narrow my eyes. Maybe she isn't as indifferent to Tom as I thought.

"The pie's fine."

I jiggle it to make sure it's done. Yup, cooked through. It's Sunday dinner. We always have Sunday dinner at our place and invite Gran down.

This weekend Gavin said we should ask Big Tom over since he doesn't have family, and then I suggested Diedre come along too. So, we've got pan fried chicken going, Gran's minding it at the stove and the meaty, salty steam crackles and pops. I made cornbread this morning, and when Gavin gave me a sly smile and stole a chunk while it was on the cooling rack, I merely wagged my finger at him.

Then my stomach dipped, because he looked at my lips and I knew if I didn't have that rule in place he'd be kissing me. Instead, he popped the cornbread in his mouth and winked.

Diedre finished up the turnip greens and tossed them in a bright yellow enamel bowl, and now she's mashing the potatoes, stirring in enough butter to float a city. The iced tea is ready, flavored with fresh peaches, honey, and sugar.

We have a picnic table set up outside, with a red checkered cloth and flowers in the center that Shay and Gavin picked this morning and popped into an antique soda bottle. The laughter from outside, the Sunday dinner smells, the sun shining on the table and the food piling up in baskets and bowls, it looks like a dream life.

Except, none of it's real.

I shake my head, staring at Gavin as he swoops Shay up and settles her on his shoulders. He grins up at her, his hair falling over his brow. I groan. "I can't take it."

"He still being nice?" Diedre frowns at the heap of potatoes then adds another half stick of butter.

I nod. "Too nice."

Gran smacks her spoon against the side of the cast iron pan. "No such thing as too nice."

I stare at Gavin, and somehow, he sees me looking at the window. He smiles at me and gives a cheerful wave. My stomach flips and I lift my hand and wave back. I turn back to Gran and Diedre. "He isn't only going to his job with Big Tom though. He also fixes the kids breakfast. Then when he gets home at night, he helps them with their homework so they can play outside before bed. After dinner, he helps with the dishes. And"—I point at the sink—"he fixes. He putters."

"Putters?" Diedre frowns. "What do you mean, putters?"

That first night, after I told Gavin we wouldn't be kissing, I thought he'd sulk. But he didn't. Instead, he found the toolbox and went around the house finding things to fix. All those things that I've wanted repaired for years but never could find the time to do, he's getting to them, without me even letting him know they need done.

I point at the sink. "He fixed the faucet. It doesn't spray you anymore when you turn it too far to the left."

Diedre gives the faucet the stink eye. It's hit her more than once. "Thank goodness for that."

"He also tightened all the loose knobs on the kitchen cupboards. He mended the torn screens on the windows. He changed the lightbulb on the porch and patched up the chicken coop so Billy can't escape and varmint can't get in."

"He's still after the honey pot then." Diedre nods knowingly, then she glances at Tom and sets to whipping the mashed potatoes with a whole lot of pent-up frustration.

I recognize that emotion for exactly what it is.

I pull a stack of eight plates from the cupboard, then grab silverware.

"I don't know. I think...he said he doesn't like to sit still. He likes taking care of us and he's surprised he didn't keep things up before."

I look down at the strawberry and vine patterned

plates. When Gavin asked why he hadn't fixed the broken hinge on the front door, or mended the screens, I didn't have an answer. I could only think about how Bobby had always made time to fix things, and with three jobs, I never seemed to have the energy or the time.

Gavin saw the look on my face, and I think he thought I was remembering that he'd never helped out before, because he'd nodded and said, "Forget I asked. I'm here now. Okay?"

Gran whistles and spoons the pan fried chicken onto a big ceramic platter. "That boy sure is trying his darnedest."

I rub my finger over a chip in the edge of the top plate and frown. The thing is, I'm not so sure Gran and Diedre are right. I don't think he's trying for the honey pot. I just think he's trying to be happy in the life that he believes is his.

"How much longer 'til he pays his debt? 'Til you cut him loose?" Diedre studies me with a frown, like she knows what I'm thinking.

I shrug. "Big Tom paid him on Friday. By what he earned and his help around the house, I'd say in two months we'll be square."

"Make it one." Gran frowns at me. Clearly she doesn't think I'll be able to resist Gavin longer than a month.

"Alright. One month."

It's not like a month is long enough to change a life, or fall in love, or do anything that you'll regret.

We set the table and bring out all the dishes. The kids swarm the table, and Gran smacks their hands away from the chess pie. Somehow Billy has escaped the chicken run, and I shout after him as he runs away, "That's your brethren on the table. You better behave!"

Gavin laughs as I run after Billy and I get a happy feeling in my chest when I hear him chuckling.

When we're all seated and grace is said, everyone scoops the potatoes, greens, cornbread and chicken onto their plates like we're starving and this is our last meal.

"Slow down," Gran chides.

Gavin's next to me, his thigh plastered against mine. Seating is tight—there's eight of us after all. His foot tangles with mine in the tall grass and a zing sparks up my calf, lighting up my whole body. I look over at him quickly, my eyes wide, knowing a bright blush is covering my cheeks. But he doesn't acknowledge me, he just keeps rubbing his foot up and down my calf, a small smile on his face as he picks up his cornbread.

Well.

I can't eat with him touching me. It's not possible. His foot tangles around my leg and he pulls me even closer. The tingle on my leg travels up and starts up a throb in my core. I grab my glass of iced tea, condensation already running down the glass, and swallow a long gulp.

Gavin gives me a satisfied look and takes another bite of cornbread.

I kick his shin.

He coughs, choking a bit on the cornbread and then hits his chest.

"What is it?" Gran scowls at him. "Don't you like my cornbread recipe?"

She looks like Billy the rooster when he's about to start a fight, all puffed up and chin out.

Gavin shakes his head and aims a charming smile at Gran. "Not at all. In fact, I was wondering where Jamie learned to cook. Now I know, she learned from the best."

Gran levels a disbelieving look at him and then snorts. She shoots Gavin an *I'm watching you* look. "I hear you're fixin' the house."

Gavin nods. "Yes, ma'am."

She narrows her eyes on him, her scrawniness only drawing out her extreme hardheadedness.

"From what I've seen, you're not worth the salt that goes in your butter. My Jamie's too good for you." She taps her head. "Forget anything else, but remember that."

Gavin watches Gran, and I get the feeling he's taking everything she says to heart. I shake my head. "Gran, he doesn't—"

Gavin brushes his hand over my thigh and I cut off.

"It's alright." He turns to Gran and nods. "I'll do my best to be a good husband."

The table goes silent, even the kids look wide-eyed between Gran and Gavin. Elijah has a chicken leg halfway to his mouth and Tanner pauses mid-reach for another piece of cornbread. The crickets chirp around us as Gavin and Gran stare each other down. I think Gran's silently telling Gavin to watch himself or she'll bury him under the mountain, and Gavin is telling Gran that he's my husband and he's doing his best to prove he's a good man.

A lump of juicy chicken that I was working on

swallowing suddenly goes dry and sticks in my throat. I cough and try to get it down.

Big Tom looks between us all, lets out a long sigh and sets down his silverware. He frowns at us, then says chidingly in a deep, deep voice, "Oh what a tangled web we weave, when first we practice to deceive. A Palmer too! No wonder why I felt rebuked beneath his eye."

Someone drops their silverware. I hear it clatter against a plate. Big Tom spoke. He spoke in rhyme, in a booming, deep voice, and he's...

"You're Scottish?" Diedre glares at him. "What the heck? How are you Scottish?"

Gavin lifts his eyebrows and gives me a look. I shrug. I didn't know. I've never heard Tom speak. He's got a Scottish burr a mile wide though.

Big Tom shifts uncomfortably on the picnic bench and frowns down at his plate.

"You are so odd." Diedre smacks at a fly buzzing over her chicken and scowls at Tom.

"What's Scottish?" Tanner asks, finally grabbing the cornbread.

Gavin leans forward and ruffles his hair. "It's a country. Scotland. They've got great mountains there, the Munros. There are two hundred and eighty-two of them, the highest is Ben Nevis and if you climb them all it's called bagging the Munros."

When he's done talking, his eyes go wide and he turns to me with a confused, stunned expression. "How do I know that?"

I bite my tongue. "Umm." Think...think...think.

A strange light enters his eyes. "Name another country."

Elijah bounces on his seat. "New Zealand!"

Gavin looks up at the sky and then snaps his fingers. "It has the world's highest cliff jump, in Queenstown."

Big Tom grunts in appreciation.

Diedre's eyes light up. "How about Bali?"

Gavin grins at her, like a kid who has just learned how to whistle and thinks it's the neatest trick in the world.

"They have great diving, like the wreck of the *USAT Liberty* and the coral garden. Ask another."

"Cambodia," Big Tom says, and for a man who never talks, he sure has chosen the worst things to say and the worst day to say them.

Gavin's hand brushes over my thigh, making my blood feel warm and viscous, like the sugary, sweet syrup of the chess pie. He grins at me.

"Easy. There's the Tonlé San River, a tributary of the Mekong."

I swallow painfully, thinking about the first email he sent, asking me to create a glass wave the color of the sky filtering through jungle leaves, falling on the Tonlé San River. Then I remember the cerulean glass, shattered around my feet.

"There are ancient lava fields that cooled in sloping rivulets and honeycombed footpaths crisscrossing the jungle. You can sail down the river toward Laos and stop at a temple along the way. There are fisherman pulling up nets alongside their small boats, mountains in the distance, sand bars to swim at, and food stands along the bank that smell like stir-fried rice noodles, spring onions, chives, and fresh fish." The hypnotic rhythm of his voice makes me feel like I'm in Cambodia with him, sailing down the river too. "The sky is lapis lazuli blue, and the clouds reflect on the water. I..." He stops, stares at me. "How do I know that?"

I blink, Gavin watches me, his brow furrowed. "You, uh..." I lick my dry lips. "You do the crosswords, remember? They've got all sorts of trivia. And you like to watch documentaries and read and learn about faraway places." I shrug. "You always have done."

He frowns at this, but then Elijah tugs on his sleeve. "Someday can we go there? Can we sail that river, can we go snorkeling, and climb mountains in Scotland? Can we do that?"

"Meow, meow!" Shay says through a mouthful of chicken.

Gavin looks at the kids, their hopeful faces, and then he looks at the yard, the house and the rickety porch, the run-down station wagon, then he smiles at the kids.

"We could...but why would we want to go anywhere when we already live in the most beautiful place in the world? The only thing traveling can do is make you see how much you love home. But we already know that, don't we?"

He squeezes my thigh, and at those words, I realize that I'm fighting a losing battle. Because while I thought he was seeing the wear and tear and the drab ugliness that he'd said the mountain was before, he was actually looking around seeing someplace he loves.

"Well. Who's for pie?" Granny claps her hands together and I jump.

"I am!" Tanner waves his arms.

I'm grateful to Gran, because her interruption gives me a minute to wipe the lovestruck expression off my face. So, when I finally turn to Gavin and hand him a plate of pie, I'm able to give him a cordial smile, completely free of all the wanting I'm feeling.

Thirty minutes later, the kids are tumbling in the field with Big Tom. Gran and Diedre volunteered to do dishes, and Gavin and I are sitting in the grass leaning against the cool rough stones of the barn.

Gavin sits close enough that if he wanted to, all he'd have to do is move a hairsbreadth my way and we'd be touching.

I concentrate on the kids and smile at Big Tom lumbering around pretending to be Bigfoot. The clouds fly swiftly overhead and I close my eyes when they move past the sun and a ray of warmth falls on me. I feel Gavin's eyes on me before he speaks.

"Your Gran doesn't like me much, does she?"

I sigh and open my eyes. "She's protective of me."

He frowns. The shadow of his stubble makes him seem softer and more down to earth than the first time I saw him, when he was clean shaven, remote, and as unreachable and untouchable as a movie star on the big screen.

"Why does she have to be protective?"

His eyes lock with mine and I think about reaching up and running my fingers over his jaw. I wonder if his stubble feels as rough as it looks, or if it'll be soft against my fingertips. "She doesn't want me to get hurt."

He looks down at my mouth and I take in a sharp breath of the pine-scented air.

"I won't hurt you. I won't ever hurt you." It's a promise, and he means it, but it's a promise he can't keep.

His blue eyes darken as he watches my expression. "I already did, didn't I?"

I shake my head and reach over, pressing my fingers into his arm, the only part of him that I'll let myself touch.

"No. You didn't." Pressure stings the back of my eyes and my locket feels heavy around my neck. "Sometimes, though, people don't have a choice about whether they hurt others or not. You know?"

"Not really."

I smile at him and stroke my fingers over his forearm. His skin is hot and the hair on his arm is silky smooth.

He watches my finger wander over his skin a look of longing in his eyes. My heartbeat thrums loudly in my ears. I imagine I'm stroking him in other places, quieter places. I press my fingers into his muscles and tendons. Suddenly, he stands.

I look up at him, dazed by his abruptness.

"I..." He clears his throat. "I just remembered I promised to fix the...ladder. There's a rung loose."

I frown at him. His jaw is tight and there's a strange light in his eyes.

"Now?"

He nods. "Now."

Before I can say anything else, he's gone. I watch him

stride across the grass, seeds and dandelion fluff flying in the air as he passes.

Funny enough, as he walks away, I feel as if I'm tethered to him by an invisible band and it's stretching, and stretching, but soon, it's going to snap and yank us back together. And then...the force of it is going to knock me off my feet.

20

GAVIN

Ten days.

Ten days of bliss, mixed with pure torture. I still don't remember my past. I don't remember anything about my life from before. But that doesn't matter. The desire to remember has faded along with the purple bruise on my face. It's gone. And I'm happy. Somehow, I expect I've never been happier in my entire life.

Jamie was right. Working with Big Tom is a good job. Bringing home a paycheck for my family is rewarding. I only wish I made more, because I see how tired Jamie is when she comes home from cleaning houses all day, and shuttling people around in the station wagon, and picking up waitressing shifts at the bar. More than that, every morning, I hear her alarm at four, and then I pretend to still be asleep when she tiptoes out to the barn to work on her art.

When she's out in her studio, I wander through the house, finding things to repair, and then start on making the kids' breakfast and sack lunches. Tanner has trouble with math, so I've started writing math problems on his napkin, and when we play baseball I have him run stats and keep score. I think when I was a kid I must've had trouble with math too, because having him jump and run and throw a ball while reciting his math facts comes naturally to me. I try to figure out ways to help him learn, and I try to think of ways I can earn more money so Elijah can be on that little league team he told me about. Maybe I can also figure a way to help Jamie.

She still hasn't shown me her studio or her glass. I must've really hurt her. But I want to help her dreams come true.

She hasn't opened up about her art, but she's shared other things. Every night, after the kids are asleep, we sit in the kitchen and I ask her questions. It's like that old game, twenty questions, but the answers always lead to me wanting to make love to her.

What's my favorite food?

Cornbread.

Yours?

Peach pie with loads of vanilla ice cream. At that I imagined her licking melted ice cream from her lips.

What's my favorite song?

"Foggy Mountain Breakdown." She said this with a devious smile, so I think she was joking.

Yours?

Gymnopédie Number One. It reminds me of fog rolling over the mountains, it's pretty like that.

I resisted the urge to kiss her pert mouth and asked, *what's my favorite color?*

Cerulean. To that, I said I had a revised favorite color, that it was now lavender blue.

She smiled, and I asked, *what's my favorite thing about you?*

Kissing me. She blushed bright red at that.

Your favorite thing about me?

She unconsciously stroked her fingers over her lips as she thought about her answer.

And just like every other night, I ended our conversation abruptly by excusing myself to take a shower before bed. A very, very cold shower.

Ice cold.

In fact, in the past ten days I've taken an ice-cold shower every single morning, specifically because hearing Jamie rustling in her sheets, sighing in the dark, and creaking in the bed makes me so hard that I'm out of my mind imagining what it'll be like making love with her.

Then in the afternoon, when I get off work, I take another freezing cold shower, because seeing her after being away for twelve hours sends a shot of lust straight through me. All the fatigue from the day is gone and I'm ready to take her behind the stone barn and make love against the wall.

But that's not all. After dinner, once we've cleaned the dishes and put the kids to bed, we talk. And the intimacy of sitting in the kitchen, her low voice stroking over me, her lavender blue eyes turning dark and needy, talking about anything and everything, it makes me harder than the handle of a cast iron pot. And right when I think I'm about to lift her onto the table and make love to her like I'm certain I've done hundreds of times before, I say goodnight and go stand under an icicle shower.

It's been bliss and it's been torture.

I hope soon she says we know each other well enough to make love again. I'm nearly out of my mind with wanting her. I imagine it almost every second of every day. It seems to me that I've already connected with her in every way possible except that last one. I don't know how much longer I'll have to wait. But for her, I'll wait as long as it takes. Even forever.

I'M IN THE LOFT READING A BOOK TO THE KIDS WHEN I HEAR Jamie pull in. It's later than usual, she had an extra house to clean that wasn't on the schedule. I'm nearly done with the book. Tanner and Elijah are tossing a softball back and forth, listening to the story, and Shay is rolled up on the pillow next to me.

"The cat had a..." I point at the word. "What word is that?"

Shay looks at the page and frowns.

"Huhhh." I make the H sound. "Sound it out."

She shakes her head no, her pigtails swinging.

Elijah stops tossing the ball. "Shay doesn't read. She just started kindergarten."

I look from the book to Shay. Her lower lip quivers and she wrinkles her brow. "You don't know this word?"

I point to the word *hat*.

"Rawr."

Tanner lets out a big sigh, then looks at the door to make sure Jamie hasn't come in yet. He leans forward like he's telling a secret. "Ms. Crum said Shay is undisciplined and ignorant."

Elijah scowls. "No she didn't. She said we all are undisciplined. She said Shay refused to know her letters or to read and she was going to flunk her."

There's a spark of irritation in my chest, about to ignite into a big ball of anger. "Who is Ms. Crum?"

Shay drops her head to my shoulder and looks up at me with mournful eyes. I wrap my arm around her and squeeze.

Elijah gives me a loaded look. "She's the principal. She doesn't like us."

I frown and chew on that information for a minute. "Why not?"

Tanner grins. "Because I make contraptions, and Shay pretends to be animals, and Elijah can't sit still. We're troublemakers."

I narrow my eyes. "You are not. You're good kids." I'm feeling incredibly protective of them, and I'm not sure I like Ms. Crum telling my daughter she's going to flunk kindergarten or telling my sons they're troublemakers.

"We don't like sitting still. It's boring."

I nod. There's something deep inside me that tells me I was exactly the same. "I was just the same as a kid."

Elijah's eyes widen. "You were?"

I scratch my jaw and consider. "I can't remember being a kid, but I'm certain. Yes. I'm certain. I could never sit still."

"Wow," Tanner breathes. He grins at me like I'm his hero.

I shake my head. "You still need to learn. You can't dump rotten eggs on your teachers or—"

"We don't do that," Elijah promises.

Tanner nods. "We only pay bullies back for picking on Shay, or test out devices to open windows, or once, I played some music over the loudspeaker system because I wanted to see if I could."

I fight a grin, then when I can't hold it in, I hide it behind my hand. Finally, I say, "I think...hmmm...I think you boys better promise me you'll try to behave during school hours. Then afterwards, we can do all the things you like. Building, running, playing."

Tanner jumps up. "Can we go on a canoe trip down the river and go camping?"

All of them stare at me, like kids with their noses pressed against a toy store window, waiting for my response. The hope and expectation on their faces is almost too much for my heart to hold. I reach out and tug on Tanner's red hair, so much like his mom's. "Tell you what. If you boys get a good report on your next report card, we'll take the best camping trip you've ever had."

Tanner's eyes go huge. "Can we have a campfire too? And roast hotdogs?"

"And go hiking?" Elijah asks.

"And stay up late and tell spooky stories around the fire?"

I nod. "All of the above."

The boys whoop and high five each other. I grin, then I feel a small hand tugging at my sleeve. Shay looks up at me, an impatient expression on her face.

"What is it?"

She frowns, her little nose wrinkling. I lean in, expecting a meow or a rawr, but instead she juts out her chin and points at the book.

I frown. "What?"

She points again.

"You want me to keep reading?"

She shakes her head, her pigtails swishing. Then she cuddles up against my arm and whispers, "I want you to teach me that word."

I stare at Shay, completely stunned. She spoke. Shay spoke, and she has the cutest voice, with a lisp from a missing front tooth, and the sweetest, lilting accent. I look at her like a flower that just opened up for the first time, and I'm finally seeing what it looks like.

Tanner and Elijah quit hopping around and turn to watch Shay.

"She's not a cat anymore," Tanner says.

Elijah nods. "Huh. Guess not."

Then Shay frowns and tugs my sleeve again, so I wipe

the dumbfounded expression from my face and say, "You want me to teach you?"

"Uh huh."

I grin and then point to the letters. "That's an 'h,' it says hhhh. Here's an 'a,' it says aaaa. That's a 't,' it says teh. Put them all together, hhhh-aaaa---ttt. It says—"

"Hat." She smiles up at me, her eyes dancing.

"Hat," I agree.

Then she climbs in my lap and turns the page. I'm too stunned to notice the writing on the next page, until Shay elbows me in the stomach. I grunt and then start to read again, helping her sound out the words.

Downstairs the front door shuts and Jamie calls, "I'm home!"

Elijah and Tanner rush down the ladder, sliding down the sides, but Shay stays put. "I want to read it."

I nod. "We'll be down in a minute," I call.

Then I lean back against the wall of the loft, sink into the soft braided rug, and finish the book about the cat, the rat, and the hat.

When it's done, Shay looks up at me, a happy smile on her face.

"I read."

I nod. "You did."

She considers me, and I get the feeling she's weighing her words. So I tilt my head close and give her my full attention.

Finally she asks, "Are you going to leave us?"

I shake my head, confused by the concern in her eyes. "Why would I leave?"

She shrugs her little shoulders. "Sometimes dads leave."

I pull her close and press her in a tight hug. She's right, dads do leave, but I'm not one of them. "I'm not going anywhere."

Her voice is muffled against my shirt when she says, "Promise?"

I ruffle her hair. "Of course I promise."

She grins up at me, her pink tongue sticking through the hole where her front tooth is missing. "Okay. I'm going to play with Scooter."

I nod and let her go. She skips across the room and then climbs down the ladder. Below, I can hear Jamie showering off. Soon she'll start dinner. The boys are outside, and the door slams, Shay running out to join them.

I let out a long breath.

My accident must've really upset Shay. I'm glad I can promise her that I'll be here for her, and I'm glad the boys have a camping trip to look forward to.

I'm looking forward to it too.

Like I said, every day is bliss.

I hear the shower cut off, and I imagine Jamie, stepping out of the shower, naked and toweling dry. I wonder if she has freckles on her breasts, or on her inner thighs. I groan, thinking of it.

Every day is bliss, and every day is torture.

21

———————

Gavin

Jamie's at the stove, stirring the pot of split pea soup. The ham bone makes the soup smell savory and salty. My stomach growls when I step into the kitchen, and Jamie turns and grins at me.

"Hungry?"

I stare at her lips. "You could say that."

She flushes and turns back to the soup, giving the wooden spoon a bang on the edge of the pot.

My mouth kicks up in a half-smile and I go to the cupboard to take down bowls, so I can help set the table. "How was your day?"

Jamie sets down the wooden spoon and reaches for salt to sprinkle in the pot. When she's done she wipes her hands off on the kitchen towel. It's a light blue and yellow checked towel, and something about it niggles at me.

I've been getting that sometimes, twinges at the edge of my mind, like a finger poking me when I'm asleep, trying to wake me up from a dream. "Did we...did we ever fight about kitchen towels? It seems like I remember something..."

Jamie drops the towel to the counter and turns, a strange look on her face. I would almost call it fear, or sharp anxiety, but that can't be right. Her face pales, her freckles standing out. "You remember...towels?"

I frown and stare at the blue and yellow towel crumpled on the counter. It's surrounded by the clutter of the kitchen—pots, dirty dishes, cut-up vegetables, the dish-drying rack. For a moment the towel seemed to stand out from everything, like one of those picture searches where you finally find the object and you're surprised you didn't see it before, but now, it's back to normal. Just an old rag towel.

"Never mind. I can't place it."

Jamie's shoulders sag, and it seems almost as if she's relieved.

"What?" I smile, and step closer, reaching out to smooth a stray strand of hair on her brow. "You don't want me to remember the great kitchen towel incident? Was it that bad?"

"No. Gosh." She waves it off and smiles. "I don't know what you're remembering."

"Huh." I step back and shrug. "Me either."

Jamie glances at the soup pot. "I think it needs taters. Can you go in the tater hole and grab me some?"

I was thinking about kitchen towels and formless memories, but all that evaporates at the mention of tater hole. Jamie looks at me expectantly, so apparently this isn't a joke.

"Did you just say 'tater hole'?" I hold back a horrified smile.

She puts her hands on her hips and nods her head.

I grin. "What kind of dirty talk is that?"

She fights a smile, the left edge of her lip twitching.

I lift an eyebrow. "Hey darling. Bend over, so I can access your tater hole."

She picks up the spoon and shakes it at me.

"Excuse me, ma'am. Can you point me in the direction of your tater hole, I've got a sausage I need to store in it."

She snorts.

"Whatever happens in the tater hole, stays in the tater hole."

Finally she grins. "Awww, are you trying to sweet talk me?"

I nod. "Is it working? Because I wouldn't mind seeing your tater hole." I give her my best, charming smile. I'm certain Jamie likes how I look, I've seen her watching me when she thinks I'm not looking. I use that to my advantage, showing her my dimple.

"Nope." She thrusts her spoon toward the side door. "The tater hole is the cold cellar. Where we store the taters."

I tap her on the nose. "Are you sure that's what it is?"

She smirks. "Go on now."

She shakes her head as I wander outside to the old, rusted cellar doors leading into the ground. The kids are playing around the corner, I can hear them running after Scooter, the old rooster, Billy, crowing in irritation. Through the window, I can see Jamie frowning down at the soup, adding a bit more salt.

Everything is normal. It's a beautiful night.

Except...

I stare at the cellar doors. I knew they were here. How could I not? I walk past them every day. But when I do, I try my best to ignore them, because they give me that feeling a kid gets late at night, when he does his best not to look at the monsters hiding in his closet.

I shake my head. "Pull it together."

The hinges creak, and flakes of rust fall from the doors as I swing them wide. A puff of cold, dirt-scented air whooshes upward. I peer down into the dark. The hair on the back of my neck stands on end, and I look back at Jamie through the window to see if she's laughing or waiting to see my reaction to the cellar. But no. She's at the counter, cutting up a pan of cornbread, completely at ease.

Didn't I ever tell her my phobia?

Is it new?

The cold air from the cellar swirls around my ankles and the darkness makes my chest tight. The dusky light spills over the stone steps, and I can make out an uneven dirt floor. There are potatoes down there, I can smell them.

A trickle of sweat runs down the back of my neck.

What in the world?

"It's not a big deal. It's just a dark, closed-in, creepy tater hole. No big deal." I grit my teeth, and even though my heart pounds against my chest, I listen to my reasoning and step down into the cellar.

The cold wraps around me, and the air is stagnant and filled with the scent of root vegetables. The stone steps are uneven and let out onto the packed dirt. The cellar is only four feet by six feet at most, and my head nearly reaches the ceiling. Wire bins of potatoes, turnips, and carrots line the wall. I've stopped breathing, but it's not a big deal, I'll just grab a handful of potatoes and run up the stairs. I hurry forward and grasp two cold, rough, dirt-covered potatoes.

Then, without warning, my mind splits open. Except that's backwards. Because for a moment, there's light, it's bright, and it illuminates the crack of a door held open. The light floods my mind, and I see the door, a tiny, gray room, and the outline of a man. And then, my mind slams shut, and I'm in the dark, in that room, and I can't get out.

The potatoes fall from my hands, thump, and roll across the dirt. I claw at my neck. I can't breathe, there's no air. I can't see. It's dark. Rushing, pounding, yelling, hopeless dark consumes me. The room smothers me and I can't get out. I can't see anything. The door's closed, there's no light and I can't get out.

Someone closed the cellar door. Someone locked me in. I can't get out.

Spots flash across my eyes and the room goes darker. I can't hear the kids anymore, I can't hear Scooter barking, I can't hear Jamie in the kitchen. They're gone and I can't get out.

I claw at my throat again.

They locked the door. The door's locked.

I can't breathe.

The door's locked.

"Hey. Hey. It's open. Look. It's open. It's just there. Hey." Jamie grabs my arms, her voice penetrating the darkness.

I stare blindly ahead, trying to find her. Her fingers dig into my arms, the pain pulling me back to the present. I still can't breathe, I still can't see. She's here but it's still dark.

"Hey. I'm here. The door's open. You can leave. You can leave anytime you want. Here." She links her fingers through mine. "You can leave. You can get out."

She squeezes my fingers and tugs at my hand. I stumble across the dirt floor. It seems impossible that she's here. In that memory, no one was ever in the room with me.

"I'm here. You can leave." She pulls me up the stairs and I trip over the steps, until finally, she pulls me over the lip of the doors and I'm bathed in the light of dusk.

I yank in a painful breath. The fresh, woodsy air burns my starved lungs and spots swim in front of my eyes. I drag in another breath. My skin is cold and covered in a sheen of sweat. Slowly, the light reaches my mind, and then other sensations, the grass under my feet, the sound of the kids, the ever-present crickets singing, the smell of the pea soup bubbling on the stove, Jamie's hand clasping mine. Her fingers are small but strong. She's gripping me like she'll never let go.

I shiver and look down at our linked hands.

What just happened?

She reaches up and touches my chest, drawing her fingers over my racing heart. "You okay?"

I look into her worried eyes, anchor myself by counting the freckles on her cheeks. "Did you know I'm claustrophobic?"

She frowns, the line between her eyebrows wrinkling. "That's what that was?" She shakes her head. "I've never seen anything like it. You were taking too long, so I came down, and you were shaking, and your eyes were glassy and you were saying you couldn't get out, that the door was locked and..." She trails off. "I didn't know. I'm sorry, I wouldn't have sent you down if I'd known."

My legs shake, and I realize I've felt this before, and in the past whenever I did, I ran. I ran into the woods, or across a field, or anywhere. I ran and the shaking stopped.

"You didn't know?" I frown at her. Maybe it never bothered me when we were married, maybe the head injury made it all come back.

Jamie squeezes my hand, then she reaches out and brushes her cool fingers against my forehead. "I'm sorry. I won't send you down again."

I nod. "It's fine. I had a memory." I give her a sideways look, watching her take this in.

She bites her lip. "What was it?"

I shake my head. "Nothing really. I was in a small room. Maybe a closet. There was a man and he shut me in and locked the door. Then it was dark." My skin runs cold again and I have the urge to run. Run, run, run far away.

Jamie's eyes flicker with something like sorrow or regret. She steps close and rests her cheek against my chest. "You think it was from when you were a kid?"

I nod and rub my hand down her back. Holding her makes me feel steady again, my heart's slowing down and the urge to run fades the longer I have her in my arms.

"I guess I didn't have the best childhood." I smile down at the top of her head and resist the sudden urge to brush my lips over her hair.

She presses closer to me. "I always thought you had a silver spoon in your mouth from infancy on. I thought you had a charmed life."

I laugh, "What? While I was traveling in the circus? I don't think so."

Her hand stills on my back and I look down at her, trying to take in her features, but her face is buried against my chest and I can't make her expression out.

"I think I had the wrong impression of you." Her voice is muffled against my chest.

I rest my chin on her head. "Maybe. You know, I'm not sure I want my memories back. If that's a taste of them, it'd be better if I forgot."

"Are you scared of being locked in? Is that what it felt like?"

"It felt like I was locked in, buried alive, and I'd never be let out. All I wanted to do was run. Run across the world to get away, but then..." I frown over the trees, tilt my head to listen to the kids laughing and Scooter barking. I drift my hand over Jamie's spine, running my fingers over her t-shirt, feeling the warmth of her and the curve of her.

"Then what?"

I smile down at her. "Then you were there. I didn't need to run anymore, because I knew that you and the kids were the ones I'd want to run to anyway."

I thought that realization would make her happy, but instead, it seems to make her unaccountably sad. She drops her head back against my chest and holds me close.

I stand holding her, soaking in the light, and after several long breaths, I say, "Shay talked to me today."

Jamie looks up quickly. "She did?"

I nod. "She wants me to teach her to read."

The sadness filters out of Jamie's eyes, and it's replaced with happiness. "What'd she say?"

"She asked me not to leave." I shake my head. "She said sometimes dads leave. That's not me though. You know that, right? Even though I can't remember, I'm not leaving."

Jamie blinks, and it's not just my imagination, there's the sheen of tears in her eyes.

I smile at her, then chuck her chin. "What's so sad about that? You don't want me sticking around?"

She shakes her head and steps out of my arms. "Let's go have dinner. Forget the taters, the soup's ready. I made you cornbread too."

"Mmm. What else could a man want but a pretty wife, a gaggle of kids, and a plate of cornbread." I wink at her, grab her hand, and follow her into the kitchen.

22

Jamie

The night is still, the quiet solitude is like the space between the stars. They float in the sky together, but they're thousands of light years apart and will never, ever meet. It's three in the morning, and the space between Gavin and I may as well be the distance between two stars.

Before, I always thought the night sky was beautiful and looking at the stars made me feel less alone. Now, though, thinking about how those stars will always gaze at each other but never meet, it makes me horribly lonely.

Bobby used to say that the stars were shards of glass scattered through space, and that someday, they'd all melt, and a new universe would be made. I guess in that scenario, the only time the stars meet is when they're destroyed.

I kick off my quilt and the bedsheets, and glare up at the ceiling fan, lazily rotating, not sending a lick of cool air my way. The bedsprings creak and groan and I wipe at the sweat dripping down my chest. At the creaking noise, I lay still in my bed, and listen.

But no. There's no shifting, no sighs, no noise coming from the living room.

I guess Gavin is asleep.

Why wouldn't he be? He works twelve-hour shifts with Big Tom, he repairs the house, he fixes meals, he plays with the kids and helps with their homework, he talks with me after the kids are asleep, charming me, teasing me, learning me. Of course he sleeps well.

I grasp the wash-worn bedsheet in my fist and twist it into a tight ball.

A picture of Gavin in the cellar, his face white, his eyes glazed, flashes in my mind. When I saw him, my heart nearly exploded from my chest. I thought he'd remembered. I thought he knew what I'd done and he was shocked, stunned, devastated.

But that was my own fear coming to the surface. The truth, though, was worse. Someone hurt him when he was a kid. They hurt him so much that it made a kind, generous, strong man become overrun with fear. He couldn't remember where he was or find his way out.

I want to go back in time and wallop whoever did that to him. I'd like to take Granny's shotgun and deliver a talking-to. But what a goldarn hypocrite I am. I'm running the scam of the century on this man. All for a bit of just desserts.

Granny claims it's never too late to mend. But just like the stars, if I mend things and tell Gavin the truth, the minute we come together and know each other for true, everything we have here will be destroyed.

When I was younger I destroyed a lot of things. I'm not keen to do that again.

I kick at the sheets and tug down my pajama shirt. It's three thirty now, I may as well head out to the studio. I've been working on a new project, one with interlocking spheres. Azure, cerulean, lavender blue, all the colors Gavin loves. It looks like a hundred bubbles floating in the sky. A wish, every single one.

I slip into my overalls and then tiptoe across the cool wood floor. When I pass by the couch, Gavin is a dark, lean form lying on his side. I pause, take in the long line of him, Scooter on his feet. The wall clock ticks the seconds by as I hesitate. I'm only a foot away from him. The moon bathes him in cool silver light, and I have the strongest urge to reach down and run my fingers over his jaw, then kneel down and—

"Looked your fill yet?"

I squeak and jump back. "You're awake."

Slowly, Gavin opens his eyes, then stretches. His lips curl into a sweet smile. "How couldn't I wake up? You're leaning over me like creepy stalker looking to do naughty, nefarious things."

"I was not!" I whisper.

He grins and looks me up and down, his eyes crinkling. "Too bad. I wouldn't have minded naughty and nefarious."

Gosh. It is so, so hard not to like him. I can practically

hear Gran and Diedre yelling, *he wants your honey pot! He's not a good man!* But they're not here, they haven't been living with him, they haven't seen him with the kids, and they didn't see him in the cellar.

They don't know him.

And you do, Jamie Lynn? Gran's voice scolds.

Maybe not.

I sigh and look toward the front door. "I'm going to my studio. You can go back to sleep. Sorry to wake you." I take a step past the couch, but as I do, Gavin reaches out and grasps my wrist.

"Wait." His hand burns on my bare skin, and my pulse pounds in my throat at his touch. It's dark, it's quiet, and he's holding me.

"Hmm?"

His thumb strokes the inside of my wrist. "Can I come with you?"

I don't answer right away. My mouth is dry and my pulse races.

He drops his hand and my brain reconnects.

"I...um..."

Honestly, I've been avoiding him coming out because the last time he saw my work he said it was uninspired and ugly. I'm afraid that if he thinks that again, even without his memories, that it'll be especially true. I doubt he'll say those things, but I'll be able to tell what he thinks by the look on his face. And I'm scared. Because even more than what Gran says, or Diedre, or the kids, or a stranger, for some reason, I really, really care what Gavin thinks.

If he says he doesn't like it, I might not have the

wherewithal to keep believing in my art. It's funny that he could have that much power after only knowing him for two weeks.

"It's okay. Go on then." He nods at the door and gives me an encouraging smile. "I'll see you at breakfast."

I step back toward him, study his earnest expression, and then hold out my hand. "Come on."

He gives me a surprised look that quickly turns happy. "It's my charm, isn't it? You can't resist my smile." He flashes a grin and I let out a quiet huff of delight.

Then he grasps my hand and stands. "I'll get dressed."

I yank my hand away, because I suddenly realize that Gavin sleeps in boxers and nothing else, and he is...

He's just as good-looking as I remember from the peep show I got after his shower. Except now, the bruises are gone and even in the dark I notice even more details. Like the definition in his abs, and the trail of hair leading down to his length, which is currently...hard.

I clear my throat and feel the flush working its way down my neck. "Go ahead." I wave my hands and turn away.

I hear the rustling of clothes, smell the woodsy, soapy scent of him, and try my darndest to get the dizzying lust I'm feeling under control.

"All set." His voice is deep and rumbly and it scratches over my skin and makes me shiver.

I nod and turn back to him. He's in his usual outfit, an old flannel, and too-big jeans, but it doesn't take away from his attractiveness. He smiles at the expression on my face, grabs my hand and leads me out the door.

I let him, avoiding the loose floorboards so the squeaks don't wake the kids. He shuts the door quietly behind us and then pulls me across the grass, like he's been taking me out to the studio for years.

The stars are shining, the night bugs are making a racket, and I can smell dew in the air. Gavin squeezes my hand, "No wonder you come out this early. It's as if we're the only people in the whole world."

"Beautiful, isn't it?" I look up at the sky, strewn with glass stars.

"You can wake me up for this anytime."

I smile at him, then lead him to the old stone barn.

Yesterday, Gavin showed me a bit of himself. He left himself vulnerable and open. I should do the same. I've not told him the truth about who he is, but I can be truthful in other ways. I can tell him the truth about me. Then he can decide what he wants to do with that.

Jamie

Gavin blinks when I turn on the lights and I hold my breath as I watch him take in my studio. I don't have to look around, I'm in here every day, I know what he sees. I'd rather watch him. He holds my hand, and as he takes my work in, he strokes my skin.

I'm waiting for him to smile, to frown, for his brow to furrow or for his shoulders to hitch, really for any reaction, but his face is as smooth and unreadable as melted glass sitting in the crucible.

The longer he stares without saying anything, the more worried I get.

I turn to the open room and judge it as if I were seeing it for the first time. First off, it's an old stone barn. Even though a decade has come and gone without any animal or agriculture passing inside, you can still feel the history, smell the wet stone, and imagine the milking cow lowing as she meandered inside for the night.

The ceiling is low. It might be considered claustrophobic, although I like to imagine it's cozy. A year back, Big Tom installed new lighting, tracks that run along the low wooden beams and illuminate the room in a soft yellow glow.

The furniture is second-hand and mismatched in styles, but I painted them all a pearly white. There's my chunky workbench in the center of the room, my easel where I hang my latest watercolors for project ideas, and the long rows of shelves along either wall holding all my finished glass pieces. Against the stone walls, the white furniture, and the gray concrete floor, the glass, to me, looks like bright rays of hope, colorful and optimistic.

There's a decade's worth of work here. I've given away many pieces, and sold others, but most of what I've created is stored here. It's almost a museum, and if I look at it closely enough, I can tell exactly which year and which season I created a piece.

There are flowers from my early years, the easiest pieces to make. The simple Roman vases and the glass tumblers. Moving all the way to the complex sculptures I create today.

I can point out the early years with Bobby in the carefree abstract designs and the bright primary colors. There's the sunshine yellow and persimmon orange flowers, dozens and dozens of flowers, from when Elijah and Tanner were born, when I was exhausted from having two babies but couldn't stay away from glassblowing. There's the clear, uncolored bowls and tumblers, from after Bobby was gone, when life was so completely without color that I couldn't even put it in my glass.

There's the shelf full of blue wine glasses with thin, fragile stems, a mirror of when I thought I myself might break. Not surprisingly, I wasn't as gentle as I should've been, and many of the glasses broke when I attempted the transfer between the blow pipe and the punty.

I can point out the season when I started seeing color again, when Shay first laughed, and I put the shape and color of her laugh into a pink and gold vase.

There's the Christmas ornaments from when Diedre told me that from now on, we'd be celebrating Christmas together, and that we'd never be on our own. They're green and red, silver and blue, white and gold and full of friendship.

Finally, there's my current work in progress, the spheres that I'm slowly creating, iridescent balls of color, each one a bubble, rising into the sky, with the hope that this one will never burst.

So, to me, my studio is like looking through a kaleidoscope, with the colored glass shifting as you turn, giving a thousand views and a thousand emotions to a single life.

Gavin steps forward into the studio, his warm hand clasping mine. Our footsteps echo on the concrete floor, his heavier, mine hesitant and quiet. He stops in front of my workbench, the most recent spheres laid out.

He reaches out and his fingers stop an inch from the smooth, curved surface.

I lick my dry lips. I can taste my nervousness, a tannic, coppery flavor that's similar to the smell of a heated metal rod.

Gavin squeezes my hand and my shoulders fall. "You don't like it?"

He looks to me quickly, his eyebrows raising. "Not like it?" He shakes his head and stares at me as if he's never seen me before. As if I'm an entirely different person than the one he's known.

I take a shaky breath. "You aren't...you aren't saying anything."

He stares at my mouth, and my lips tingle as his gaze roves over them. His hand tightens on mine.

"I have no words." He shakes his head and gestures around the studio. "I didn't know. I knew you were beautiful but I had no idea that you could make all that beauty come to life like this."

I stare at him, not quite understanding what he's saying. "You..."

He gives me a self-deprecating smile. "Don't you know how much I want you?"

I feel short of breath, like I'm breathing through the blow pipe and can't get enough air.

He touches my cheek, running his fingers over my skin, like I'm as fragile as that wine glass stem. I lean into his touch and his eyes warm.

"Why aren't you sharing your art with the world? Not that I don't mind keeping you to myself, but why is all this here, hidden from view? Am I the reason? Is it my fault?"

I shake my head, like I'm trying to dispel air bubbles from glass. I can't think when he's looking at me like I'm the most beautiful thing he's ever seen.

It's all a lie, Gran's voice warns, but it's far off and muffled, and I can barely hear the warning over the sound of my pounding heart.

I step back and reluctantly let go of his hand. Even though I'm not touching him, the heat of his palm is still imprinted on mine.

"It's not your fault."

He frowns, looks at the studio full of glass. "Then what? You should be selling in museums, galleries, in stores and online. Why are you working three jobs? Why am I not doing everything I can to make the whole world see your work?"

I shake my head. "It's not that simple." I reach out and run my hand over a cerulean blue sphere. "Do you know why I started glassblowing?"

I look over at him and then realize how silly my question is.

He smiles. "Maybe I once did."

I shake my head. Then I walk across the concrete floor to the farthest shelf. Gavin follows, his footsteps whispering behind mine. I can feel him, his warm presence comforting and solid, and I want to lean into him. Instead, I reach out and pick up a clear flower. It's lopsided, varying thickness, the petals uneven, it's clearly the work of a beginner.

"This is the first piece I ever made." I hold it out to him and when he opens his hand I set the flower in his palm. "It's not pretty. Not anything special."

He nods.

"Mr. Garza, he was my mentor, he always claimed glassblowing is Gradus Ad Parnassum."

"Right. The steps to Parnassus."

I lift my eyebrows and Gavin stares back at me. "I speak Latin? Why do I know Latin?"

I lick my lips nervously. He watches my mouth and says. "Nitimur in vetitum. We strive for the forbidden." Then he looks down at the flower and gives a wistful smile. When he looks up he shakes his head. "I'm sorry. Tell me more about your mentor."

I glance at the flower and take a deep breath. "Mr. Garza. He started the glassblowing studio in Hollow Creek. It's still there, that's where I do all my work."

"Not here?" Gavin looks around the barn.

"No. You need your furnaces, glory holes, annealers, benches...what?"

Gavin grins. "You and your holes. I'd really like to see this glory hole."

"Maybe I'll take you down. Help you make your first flower. You can stick your punty in the glory hole—"

"That's in the cards?"

"Hmm."

We stand there for a moment, just grinning at each other. Then I shake myself out of the moment and say, "You need a lot of space, insurance, fire codes in place. Mr. Garza left the studio to the town, and it's run by a group of volunteers. I keep my supplies and my batches there. But I work out my ideas and bring my finished products here."

"So, when do you find time to blow?" He lifts an eyebrow and I get the feeling he's trying really hard not to add innuendo.

"I go between jobs, when the kids are at school. An hour here or there."

Gavin carefully sets the glass flower back on the shelf. Then he wanders down the row, looking closely at every piece. I follow, biting at my lip, watching his reactions.

"So, Gradus Ad Parnassum?"

I push my hair behind my ears, suddenly feeling hot at his close proximity. "Right. Mr. Garza said glassblowing is just like the steps to Parnassus. There are mountains in central Greece, and you walk each one, getting higher and higher as you go, until finally you can climb the highest, Parnassus, where Apollo and the nine muses live. Nobody can reach Parnassus at the beginning, but if you work hard, and practice, then you'll eventually get there."

He looks back to the shelf. "So you start with a flower."

"And you end with elaborate, technically difficult works of art inspired by the muses. Parnassus. It's a long road though."

He frowns. "So you aren't selling these because they aren't Parnassus? Don't you believe in yourself? Didn't I believe in you too?"

I shake my head. "That's not it. I mean, I sell some. I give away some. It's more..." I look up at the low ceiling pushing down on me. I always told Gran that when I didn't have to take care of the kids I'd start taking care of myself, chasing my own dreams, but until then, my dreams had to be put on hold. To which she responded *"Can't never could do nothing."*

"What? What is it?"

I step closer to Gavin, and when I do he pulls me into his chest and wraps his arms around me. "When I was sixteen, my dad died of a heart attack in his sleep. He was there one day and then the next he was gone."

Gavin's arms tighten around me, like he's holding me up or if he'd been there he would've held me together. He brushes his mouth over my hair, and my chest squeezes tight. It's a kiss, and we said we wouldn't kiss, but it's also not a kiss, it's just Gavin letting me know he's here.

I fit myself against him and continue, "My dad was my best friend. My mom was a stay-at-home mom, she never graduated high school, so to earn money she started waitressing at the bar."

"The one you take shifts at?"

I nod. "Yeah. She was never around after my dad died. Things were rough. I got lonely. I got angry. I got...I got in trouble. I vandalized cars. I smashed headlights. I broke the windows of the school gymnasium. Every time I did something I figured I wouldn't get caught and I prayed that I would. I was so angry."

Gavin strokes my arms, his fingers gently rubbing me. I can feel his warm breaths falling across my cheek and tickling my hair.

I set my head against his shoulder. "One night my mom and I got in a fight. Lots of yelling, lots of blaming, broken dishes, broken everything. I ran off to town, took a stick, and smashed all the windows of Mr. Garza's studio. He was new on the mountain then. He'd come from Charlotte and set up shop, put stained glass windows in and displayed all his art. I smashed those windows. Every single one. I remember how good it felt to destroy something so beautiful. I had so much rage that it felt like all that beauty was mocking me. Because how could something so fragile be beautiful? It deserved to be destroyed." I shake my head and Gavin presses another kiss to my temple.

"What happened?"

"Daryl the sheriff came. My mom. Mr. Garza. It was clear that repaying Mr. Garza and any court action was enough to land me in trouble for years. My mom too. She'd lose the house if she tried to help me out of the mess I'd made. But Mr. Garza, he just frowned at the busted glass and said, 'Any creature can destroy and tear things down, are you human enough to create?' I cussed him out and said yes, of course I can create. He demanded I prove it. That very night I cleaned up the mess I made, and the next day he started teaching me glassblowing."

Gavin gathers me to him, and I breathe in the solid feel of him and the warmth of his chest.

"Did Mr. Garza ever see who you became?"

I bite back a smile. "He died three years ago. He always said if I took my rashness away, my glass would turn out better, but then he said, if I took my rashness away, what made my work unique would also disappear."

"Hmm. You're rash? I didn't know."

I look at him, tilting my head to meet his considering

eyes. "Rashness may be my worst quality. I rush into situations and then regret the tangle I've made when I can't find a way out without breaking everything or everyone. With glass you can always stick the piece back in the crucible, heat it, and smooth it out. In life—"

"We have crucibles too. Isn't that the definition of crucible? Severe personal trial that forges something new?" He smiles at me. "Huh. I guess I really do like crosswords. So random."

I swallow down the lump in my throat. It's as sticky as a ball of hot coating gather stuck on the tip of a metal rod.

"I guess I never thought of life that way. Hard times being the heat forming people new. Maybe me rushing into situations is me trying to plunge back into the fire. Smooth my life out. That's a generous way of looking at it though. Mr. Garza just thought I always let my emotions get the better of me."

Gavin strokes his hands over my arms and hums a response. "That's not always a bad thing." Then, "I was wondering. In your opinion, what's my worst quality? You know me well. What do you think?"

I frown. Before I would've said he was selfish, arrogant, unkind. His fiancée didn't seem to care for him either. She thought he was irresponsible and didn't have the ability to love anyone but himself. I can't see that though. I don't see any of those things in him.

"I think..." I frown as I consider. "I think your worst quality is that you love too freely. In my experience, people who love too freely get hurt and turn bitter. And when they're hurt they say horrible things and take their pain out on other people."

"I see." His hands still and he lets out a long breath. "You know, I've been going back and forth between whether or not I want to remember my past. I've finally decided, even if my past is full of things I regret doing or saying, I wish I could remember it, because I'd really, really like to relive the first time we made love."

My breath catches, and the room suddenly feels as if I've opened a furnace door and am being blasted with two thousand degrees of heat. Gavin's hands lick over me like flame and everywhere he touches, sparks ignite.

"Jamie?"

I shake my head no.

I can't.

Not because Gran and Diedre said he's after the honey pot and his just desserts don't include a dance in the sheets, but because I know someday, maybe someday soon, if Gavin and I have sex, he's going to hate me. Well, he might hate me anyway, but he'll especially hate me if we have sex.

His hands stroke down my arms, and then he gathers me close. He's hard. At the feel of him against me, there's a throb so sudden and so strong that I nearly lose my breath.

"I wish I could remember. It twists me up thinking about it. I keep imagining how it was. But I know I'm not getting it right." His eyes are a darker shade of blue and they shine, like the light of the fire glowing through a piece of blue cut glass.

Every single cell in my body has attuned itself to his

voice, and they're all vibrating, sending jolts of pleasure through me.

"You're not ready. But maybe…" His eyelids lower and his mouth softens. "Maybe you can describe our first time?"

I'm wrapped in his heat, and I feel almost as if I'm being dipped in the crucible. Maybe Gavin's right. I was jagged before, maybe he's smoothing out all my rough edges.

We never had a first time. We're not married. We never had sex. I know as much about our first time as Gavin does. But that doesn't mean I haven't also imagined it. I can tell him my fantasy of our first time, and in that, I'll be telling him the truth. We'll have a first time together.

I nod, my head swimming like jelly. I want to touch him, I want to kiss him, I want to take him inside me. All that need I experienced when I first saw him is back, but a thousand times more, because I know him now.

His eyes light up and he whispers, "Thank goodness. I don't know how many more cold showers I can take."

I fight a smile. "No touching though."

His forehead wrinkles, and he frowns in thought. "What if…what if when you describe it, you touch yourself remembering me, and I'll do the same?"

Holy.

Holy.

Mountain top of flame.

I let out a shaky breath. The image I have in my mind is enough to make me nearly come undone right here and right now.

"Okay. Yes."

"Yes?" His grip on my arms tightens and he focuses on me so completely that I feel devoured by his stare.

"Yes."

He lets me go and takes a step back. "Good. I'm...okay. Dang, was I this nervous the first time too? I feel like a sixteen-year-old about to grope my girlfriend under the bleachers." He grins at me. "Are you nervous?"

I nod. "A little."

A lot.

I flush at the widening of his smile. "Tell me what happened."

I clear my throat and glance around the silent studio, all the memories of the past have receded and I'm only left with me and Gavin standing in the middle of the room, in this moment.

My voice comes out low and scratchy as I start. "You were twenty-one and I was eighteen."

"Mmm. Younger woman." He winks.

I repress a smile. "You were traveling through the mountains and you stopped for the night at a rental cabin. When you arrived I still hadn't finished...cleaning."

He watches my mouth, paying close attention to every word. "I found you in my cabin?"

I take a step back. "You did. I was on my knees. On the floor."

He groans. "I wish I could remember that."

Everything up until this moment almost happened, there was a cabin, and I was cleaning, sort of. But this is where my fantasy deviates from reality.

"You saw me, I jumped to my feet, and you said, 'I don't know your name, but I do know I've never felt this way about anyone before.'"

"A bit forward, wasn't I? Did that line work?"

"No. I said, 'Nice try, city boy.'"

He nods. "Figures. Then what?"

"You smiled like I was a delight and I saw your dimples."

"And then you fell for me?" He shows me said dimples.

"No. Then you said, 'Let me take you to dinner.' And I said no, and I grabbed my bucket full of cleaning supplies and went to leave."

"This is our first time having sex?"

I nod. "Yes. Patience, young grasshopper."

He shakes his head. "I've never had patience."

True. That's another fault, I suppose. But really. I like his impatience.

"Well, as I passed you, I brushed against you. And when we touched for the first time, I felt it."

Gavin nods. "Like you've finally found the light to balance the dark. It feels like starlight."

My chest squeezes tight. He's felt it too. He's felt the same thing I have. "When we first touched, I stopped, I couldn't keep walking away. You said, 'Don't tell me you didn't feel that.' And I couldn't."

"Then what?"

I bite my lip, the studio is quiet, as if it's holding its breath waiting for my response.

"Then I took your hand in mine and I placed it over my

breast, so you could feel how hard my heart was pounding."

His eyes darken. "Show me."

Slowly, I lift my hand to my breast and stroke my hand over my nipple. Gavin watches my nipple bead in response.

"When you stroked me, my breasts felt heavy, and achy, and my bra felt tight and constricting. So I arched my back and you drew my t-shirt up over my head."

Gavin nods, his eyes demanding. "Do it."

I grasp the hem of my t-shirt in my hand and carefully tug it over my head. The fabric scratches over my sensitized skin and my hair fans out as it falls away, sending out the scent of my orange blossom shampoo. My skin prickles against the wash of cold air and I shiver as Gavin's eyes light over my body. This is his first time seeing me without a shirt on. His hands clench and his jaw hardens, as if he's holding himself back.

"Then what?"

I lift my hands behind me and unclasp my bra, letting it fall to the floor. My breasts release and the weight of them falling free is a blessed relief.

"You took my breasts in your hands and you kissed them."

He stares at them, rubbing a hand over his jaw. "I would've been a fool not to."

The look in his eyes makes my nipples harden, and I move my fingers across my breasts, pretending that my touch is his mouth feasting on me.

"Go on." His voice is strained and harsh. A vibrant

pulse ricochets down from my breasts and coats the rests of me in warmth and need. I stare at him, still clothed, so I say, "Then, I took your shirt and pulled it off."

He smiles, then keeps his eyes on me as he unbuttons his shirt and tosses it aside. His chest is defined and ruggedly muscled. His abs flex as he takes in a harsh breath at the look on my face.

"Then I kissed down your chest, unbuttoned your pants."

He lets out a shuddering breath. "Dang."

"But then, you captured my hand, set it aside, and licked down my stomach, ran your hands over my hips, and teased me, until I was on fire. Then you unbuttoned my jeans and slid them down my legs."

He stares at my pants, his eyes hot and fevered. "Did I kiss you?"

I nod, my blood sparking with need. "You kissed me everywhere."

He smiles. "I thought so."

Then I slide my jeans over my legs, letting the rough fabric run over my skin, imagining it's his hands touching me that gently.

"Look at you," he breathes. His eyes are glazed and his expression is awe-filled. "Just look at you."

Everywhere his eyes touch feels as if he's lighting it on fire. I'm burning under his gaze.

"Then you took off my panties. And touched me."

He swallows, his Adam's apple bobbing. And the look he gives me is raw with need. "Show me. Show me what I did."

I step out of my panties and reach down, running my finger over myself, until I find my clit. And when I touch myself, the studio spins, and I clench my legs at the throbbing ache. I'm swollen and wet.

"You're wet, aren't you?"

I nod and he swears, long and low.

"Then what?" He watches my hand circling my clit, a hungry light in his eyes.

"Then you pushed me down to the floor."

"Yes."

"And I'm climbing higher and higher, and your fingers are working magic." I stroke myself, imagining his fingers playing over me. "Then I open up your fly, push down your jeans, letting you free."

"You've always been generous."

I watch hungrily as he unzips his fly and springs free. The length of him, the hard thickness. My goodness. He's gorgeous. He's so beautiful. The jutting length of him strains toward me and I pulse, wanting him so much it hurts.

"Tell me," he says, voice raw.

"I wrapped my hand around you."

"Thank you." He watches me as he slowly wraps his fingers around his length.

"I stroked you, slowly, up and down."

"My word." His eyelashes flutter as his hand works up and down his length, and he lets out a low, urgent moan. But then, he regains focus and his eyes find mine, pinning me in place.

"I'm still touching you, aren't I?"

I nod, resuming the rhythmic circling, letting the electric pulse build and build and build.

"Then what?"

I lick my dry lips. I'm still captured by his gaze, by the silence except for our breathing, and the sound of his hand sliding up and down his length. My legs are shaky and the room pulses in time with the rhythm of my finger rubbing down my clit.

"Then you spread my legs apart, you took my mouth, and you thrust inside me."

His hand jerks and he lets out a low, strangled sound.

"Put your finger inside yourself," he demands.

I watch him as I slip a finger inside, feeling my wetness and the ache there.

He shakes his head. "Two."

I do, stretching around my fingers.

"Are you imagining it's me?"

I feel the roughness of his voice run over me, and the tingling in my spine is so intense that I'm nearly undone.

"Are you?" His jaw is tight and his eyes are desperate.

"Yes." Of course I'm imagining it's him. Of course.

"How do I feel?" He strokes himself again, running his hand up over the tip and then pulling back down.

"You feel like two stars coming together. You feel like heaven."

He holds my gaze. "That's what I thought."

Then he's stroking himself harder, faster, and I quicken my pace too. Imagining his weight on top of me, his woodsy scent surrounding me, his length thrusting deeper and deeper.

And then I'm coming, coming, coming. I cry out, stay captured by his gaze, because it's the only way, the only place we're connected.

"Jamie." Gavin grips himself tighter, faster, and then he's coming too.

And I'm pulsing around my fingers, and crying out, keeping ahold of his gaze, until I realize that's not the only place we're connected, because I can feel him in my heart, right in the center of my soul.

When the sparks fade, and I take my hands from myself, Gavin and I stare at each other, breathing heavily, taking in the enormity of what just happened.

Our bodies didn't touch, but our souls did.

Gavin steps forward, drags a finger over my jaw. He looks down at me, an open, awe-filled expression on his face. "My Jamie. Did you know? I really, really love you."

With that, all the happy, dizzy, floating feelings fall like glass whacked off a punty and shatter on the concrete floor. I reach up and put my fingers over his.

This moment was truth. I won't stop telling the truth now.

So even though it breaks my heart to say it, I whisper, "I really, really love you too."

24

———

Gavin

The bed is just as warm and comfortable as I thought it'd be. The mattress is soft and worn-in and rolls toward the middle, so that even if we didn't want to, Jamie and I would still end up touching.

Not that I mind. I don't mind at all.

She's asleep, her breathing soft and even and puffing out over my chest. Her head rests in the crook of my shoulder, her arm is thrown across me, and her legs are tangled over mine. She fell asleep almost right away, and even though she started out on the other side of the bed, she soon rolled to the middle and wrapped herself around me.

I brush my hand through her hair and smooth the strands. I wouldn't be able to sleep even if my life depended on it. I want to savor this moment, live in it, luxuriate in it, never forget it. We're in our bed, Jamie's in my arms, and we just made love.

Fine, we didn't actually touch, but it felt like we made love, so that's what I'm going to call it.

The feeling I have right now, I don't know that I've ever felt it before. I must've since I'm married to Jamie, but it feels new. Like a revelation. As if I'd been running my whole life, and I was exhausted, my body and soul tired, and now, I've finally reached home and I'm allowed to rest. My body is warm and content, and my heart, it's as if my heart has found the place where it would be happy to reside for the rest of forever.

I brush my hand over Jamie's hair, it's smooth, soft, it looks as hot as fire, as if a touch could burn. It's no wonder she was drawn to a profession with furnaces and fire. She has so much passion and love to give.

I wonder, over the eleven years we've been together, how much of that passion we've shared. If it's remained hot and malleable. Or if over time, our love cooled, and became hard, brittle and as fragile as the glass windows Jamie once shattered. Is love as beautiful but as breakable as glass? Or is that only a human being?

When Jamie told me how she lost her dad, I wasn't ignorant to the fact that her breaking windows was the same as life breaking her dad. I wanted to hold her. I don't remember what it's like to lose a parent, but I do feel that I've lost someone. There's still a thread inside me that tells me there's someone there, that I loved, that I don't remember. That hollow feeling, I think, is a sliver of what she felt.

I imagine, since she only has her grandmother and the kids, that her mom is gone too.

It's lucky we have each other.

I pull her closer, the softness of her bare legs slide over mine, and she buries her face into my chest, her lips running over my skin. I concentrate on the ceiling fan overhead, counting the slow rotations, and try to squelch the desire to wake Jamie and make love. Press my lips to her wet core. Slip inside her.

I'm ready. Obviously I'm ready.

But she trusts me.

I'll save it for cold showers and save up for all the days and nights in the future.

I smile and shift Jamie closer. Her hair falls over her cheek and lets off a flowery, orange scent. It's a new shampoo. She got it only a week ago, I think, for me, since I told her that I've decided my favorite fruit is orange.

I've also decided, or I suppose, my heart decided for me, that I love Jamie. Before, I believed I had. Now, I know I do. I'm going to stay with her, with the kids, for the rest of forever. No matter what I remember, if I remember, I'm going to stay.

Two weeks ago, I saw Jamie in the hospital and thought my life must be hell. Now I know, it's actually heaven.

I love her.

I love her enough to stay in a small mountain town that I'm not from.

I love her enough to work servicing port-a-johns day in and day out.

But...honestly, it has nothing to do with loving enough. Loving enough makes it sound like there's a limit to love. By the feeling in my chest when I see Jamie smile, or hear the kids laugh, there isn't a limit. Loving her is easy.

I've figured out what I'm going to do. I don't know why I didn't see it before. Maybe I became too accustomed to the status quo. But that doesn't work for me anymore.

When I asked Jamie what her dreams were, she told me selling her glass, showing it in galleries wasn't a dream, it was an impossibility. I don't agree. And as her husband, I may not be able to give her a ton of money, or a big house, or that trip around the world the kids wanted, but I can help her with her dreams.

In the studio earlier, Jamie wanted to work the rest of the night away, but when she smothered a yawn, I gathered her in my arms, brought her back to the house, and climbed into bed next to her.

She gave me a wary expression, her forehead creasing.

I tucked the old worn quilt around her.

"I reckon you're not sleeping on the couch anymore," she'd said.

I'd smiled and whispered, *"Go to sleep."*

And she did. Only minutes after she drifted off, she migrated over the bed, wrapped herself around me like the morning glory vine twisting around the base of the oak tree in the back yard, and she hasn't let go since.

I listen to her soft breathing, feel the warmth of her in my arms, smell her sweet orange scent, look around the small, cluttered bedroom, with creaky old furniture and chipped paint, and decide, yes, this is what happiness feels like. This right here.

Grandma Allwright's house is two miles up the mountain, an old square log cabin that looks like it was tossed down in the middle of a waterfall of boulders. The morning shadows fall over the rocks and make them look like weary sentinels surrounding a fort. Somehow, the thicker forest and the nearness to the river makes the air smell like uncharted wilderness. At the edge of her cabin there's a vegetable patch full of beans, corn, and squash circling the rocks, eating up any tillable soil.

Her home is exactly as I imagined it would be, a rough-hewn, carved-out-of-the-earth, rustic place. The exterior looks just like she does, a bare-bones essential home in rocky, inhospitable terrain. But the inside of her house, maybe that's like her too.

I glance around the kitchen that she reluctantly invited Tom, Diedre and me into. It's stacked full of kitsch, rooster salt and pepper shakers, cross-stitched chair pads, I'm sitting on a cross-stitched pot that says *simmer down*. There are dozens of retro kitchen gadgets on the counters and on the kitchen shelves. There's a pile of corn that she's in the middle of shucking. Glossy ears with fat kernels rest in one metal pail, and light yellow corn silk and dark green husks in another.

"Make yourself useful," she says, gesturing at the ears of corn. "I'm canning today."

Then Grandma Allwright frowns at me, Tom and Diedre all sitting at her kitchen table. "I'll bet you want tea."

Diedre is in the middle of hiding a yawn behind her hand, but when tea is mentioned she perks up. "You're the best, Granny."

Tom perches in the chair next to Diedre, and when she smiles he watches Diedre like a kid staring out the classroom window, wishing he was outside, playing at the playground.

"Thank you." I nod at Grandma Allwright and then grab an ear of corn.

She narrows her eyes and watches me for a moment to make sure I know how to shuck. Apparently, I do. I pull down the husk. It makes a squeaky creaky noise, and a burst of sweet, sugary corn smell fans out. I strip off the silk. It's soft under my fingers. I'm careful not to leave any strands behind. Finally, Grandma Allwright is satisfied. She grunts approval and then turns to the counter.

Diedre and Tom don't bother to reach for the corn. Diedre's nails are long and painted with sequins and stripes. I don't think shucking is in her future. Now that Tom has gotten over looking at Diedre, he's staring down at his thick, calloused hands.

Gran walks over and sets four glasses on the table with a hard click. They're glass tumblers with swirls of color and I realize immediately that Jamie made them. Gran pours iced tea into each one, the ice cubes kaplunking against the glass.

When she's done she plops into the last wooden chair and narrows her eyes on me. "I've made you tea. Now what do you want?"

I smile. You can say one thing for Grandma Allwright, she's definitely consistent. She hasn't liked me from the moment I walked out of the hospital. I imagine she didn't like me before that, and she won't like me long after this. But that's fine, I don't need her to like me, I just need her help.

"I asked you all here because we have something in common."

Grandma snorts. "Not likely." She points at the pail. "Reach me that corn."

I hand her a cob and she quickly yanks the husk like she's imagining it's my head, or another bit of anatomy.

Oh well.

"What do you mean?" Diedre asks, eyeing me skeptically.

Tom stays silent, which is what I expected.

Diedre picks up her glass and takes a swallow of the iced tea.

"I mean we all love Jamie."

Diedre spits her iced tea, coughing on it and spraying it back into her glass. She coughs and chokes and Tom stands and hits her on the back, his face flushed.

Gran doesn't notice. She just stares at me and then snaps the ear of corn in her hand, right in half. She holds the two mangled ends and looks at me like she's about to beat me over the head with them.

"Ice...sorry...choked on ice cube..." Diedre coughs and Tom keeps hitting her back. She smacks her hands at him. "Stop...stop whacking me. I'm fine."

Her eyes water and a bit of eye makeup runs, making her look like a startled raccoon. Tom sits back down in the chair next to her, his face flaming beneath his beard. Diedre scowls at him.

"Strong, aren't you? Your pats are like a bear pounding on a log trying to find grubs."

He clears his throat. "Hmmph."

I grin at him. Someday, I think he's going to have to tell Diedre he's in love with her.

Yeah. I recognize the symptoms.

I look back to Grandma. She's tossed her corn into the pail, and she's peeling the husk off another, deliberately stripping the silk away, frowning at me as she does, like she's watching a venomous snake sneaking through the jungle. You should always be wary of venomous snakes... I frown and scratch my chin, because for some reason I feel like I've had close-up personal experience with them.

I shrug. I probably read it in a book or saw a documentary.

I turn to Diedre. "Jamie told me you've volunteered to create an online store for her, taking photos of her art, putting it online, helping with marketing. Were you serious? Will you do that?"

Diedre sits up straight and gives me a considering look. "Are you kidding? I've been wanting to do that for years.

Years. Are you going to help her?" A slow, expectant smile spreads across her face.

I nod. "I want to."

"Wow. You're really something." Diedre's eyes crinkle, and I grin at her smudged makeup and her happy look.

"Diedre. Don't forget the honey." Gran frowns and throws her stripped ear of corn into the pail.

"Aww Granny. I don't need honey. I'm through talking about that. I actually think Jamie might be right. You don't like honey, do you?"

Diedre lifts an eyebrow, directing the question at me. Granny turns to me, her gaze beady, her face as wrinkled as the bark on a walnut tree.

"Uhh. Umm, well. I don't need honey to enjoy tea. It's perfect without it." I nod and lift my glass, taking an appreciative sip. "See? I like it."

Diedre nods. "Okay, Granny? He doesn't need honey. He's not asking for it." She smiles at Grandma's humph.

I guess the sweetness of tea is a big deal. Who knew?

"Okay, good." I smile at Diedre, glad that Jamie has a friend like her. "I wanted to ask before I told Jamie my ideas. If you can set up everything online, get photos up, get an online storefront, a bio, start networking—"

"I've been dreaming of this. I'm ready. Just give the word."

"Good." I nod. "Thank you."

"Don't thank me. Thank all those repressed city boys that gave me oodles of experience earning a living online."

I clear my throat and look quickly at Tom. He's glowering at a magenta toaster on the far counter. I thought Diedre was a model. Not a...whatever it is that earns money off repressed men online. Huh.

"Tom."

He turns to me and tries to hide his scowl.

"I want to build a storefront, but I don't know much about carpentry. Can you help with the plans, the building? We could either have the store in the barn at our place, or if it works, we might find something in town. At the studio or another location?"

He crosses his arms and considers my question. Then after a silent moment he gives a nod. He'll do it.

Amazing.

"Well? What do you need me for? Looks like you've got it all figured out." Grandma Allwright frowns at me, managing to look affronted and annoyed at the same time.

I don't smile at her. I level her with an earnest look that I hope shows my intentions. "Jamie respects you and loves you. If you support this idea, I think it'll mean the world to her."

Gran crosses her bony arms over her chest and scowls. "Of course I support it. I've been telling the Lord she needs help getting her work out for years now."

"Well, Gran," Diedre says. "Maybe the Lord just sent the help you've been asking for." She jerks her head at me and puts a meaningful look on her face.

Grandma Allwright chews on Diedre's statement and for a minute she looks stunned, but then her hard as nails expression comes back. "Fine. You want my help. You've got it. What do you need?"

I can't help but smile. Even though she isn't showing it,

I think I just won Grandma Allwright over. "When Jamie and I are busy planning, building, and starting this business, we'll need help watching the kids. I don't want them to feel left out or left behind."

Granny manages to look upset and pleased all at once. "Who do you think I am? Of course I'll spend time with my great-grandkids. Don't I already?" She smiles at me, it's a twist of her lips, and I think it's the first time I've seen her send a smile my way. "I'm glad you're thinking of them."

I shake my head. "Of course. I want them to be happy."

The kitchen falls quiet and I look at everyone. "Thanks for your help."

Diedre smiles.

Tom grunts.

Granny stands and pushes back her chair with a loud scrape. "Good. Now go on. You're not laying out of work today."

I stand and so does Tom.

Before we go, Gran says, "By the way, if you hurt Jamie, I've got a shotgun with your name on it."

I grin at her and she scowls. But behind the scowl is a smile.

I get the feeling that Grandma Allwright might just have paid me a compliment.

25

———————

Jamie

When Gavin puts his mind to something, there isn't anything that can stop him. After we spent the night together in the studio, he had a chat with Gran, Diedre, and Tom. Then after supper he asked me, point blank, would I be willing to let him help make my dreams come true?

At first I thought he was asking if I'd be willing to spend the rest of my life with him. Then I realized he already thought we were doing that. No, he was asking if he could help spread my glass art around the world.

From the second I said yes, he's been on a mission. We've spent every spare minute after the kids are in bed, and before they're awake, writing the business plan, applying for a business license, working out how to run a business with no start-up cash, sorting what pieces I can sell, deciding on pricing, working out the plans for converting the barn to a storefront gallery.

In two weeks Gavin built display shelves, tables, and a counter, all from donated lumber (thank you, Tom). Granny helped us price everything. Diedre has the website up and running, and she wouldn't hear of me giving any money to pay for her time.

It's like a dream. For years I imagined what it would be like if I could ever really, truly sell my art and make a living. I thought that when Gavin contacted me by email inquiry through the studio in town, I'd gotten my big break.

I hadn't.

And I see that what I'd been doing for years was stalling and hiding and making excuses. Because in two weeks Gavin has managed to create what I'd been dreaming of doing for ten years. It's extraordinary actually.

He went at it with single-minded passion. Getting up early, going to work, spending time with the kids until their bedtime, then going back at it again until he collapsed in exhaustion. Only to start up again the next day.

I was right next to him the whole time. Working just as hard and just as much. Driving myself to do this if not for me, then for Gavin. Because he believes in me.

I also worked to exhaustion so I didn't have to think about the fact that we still aren't kissing, still aren't doing...that.

When he was building, I'd bring him sweet tea, the

glass dripping with condensation. He'd smile a thanks, brush his hands over mine as he took the glass, and I'd shiver, like water drops vibrating. Then he'd tilt his head and swallow long gulps of the tea, and I'd watch his throat work, sweat running down his neck, and I'd find myself touching my neck, my mouth, imagining it was him, drinking me.

When I'd walk past him in the studio, organizing my glass pieces, working out stock and prices, he'd cross my path, and sometimes his fingers would stroke low across my back or my hips, his touch as subtle as the breeze over a leaf of grass.

I'd look over my shoulder at him, and he'd smile happily, then get back to work.

But me, every time he did that, it'd take minutes for me to come down from the honeyed imprint of his hand running over my spine, wrapping around my legs, and pulsing through me.

Not to mention that we're sharing a bed now. If I wasn't drop-dead tired every night, I don't know what I'd do. Still, every morning when I wake up, somehow I find myself tangled around him, or tucked into his arms, and I have to very, very carefully extricate myself without waking him. Because if he were awake, I swear, the temptation would be too much.

It's nearly been a month with Gavin. And I told Gran and Diedre weeks ago that Gavin would've repaid his debt in a month's time. Honestly, if I could go back in time, I'd acknowledge there was no debt. There never was.

In fact, now I owe him more than I can ever repay. Not in a month, not in a lifetime.

I'm in the studio, walking through the area that Gavin and Tom renovated, running my hands over my glass, the smooth shelves, smelling the smell of recently sanded wood. Gran put out handwritten labels on ivory cardstock for each piece. The kids put up white Christmas lights on the beamed ceiling. Gavin put in old speakers he found in Gran's kitchen to play soft music. Everything is set.

I have the twinkle lights on, the music playing, Gymnopédie Number One, my favorite, and I'm taking it all in. I'm in awe. How did he manage to change my life so much in only a month?

The door to the studio clicks open, and like I conjured him from my thoughts, Gavin strides in.

My heart pounds at the smile on his face, the warmth in his eyes, the love I see so clearly written there.

"I came out to congratulate you. You made your first online sale." His eyes light up, he reaches out, tugs me to him. "You're official now."

I look up at him, captured in his arms, my mind going blank. "I'm...what?"

He grins down at me, his dimple showing. "Twenty Christmas ornaments, to be shipped all the way to California. You did it, Jamie, you did it."

Twenty? Twenty ornaments? They're thirty dollars each. That's...huge. I can put it towards next year's little league, or Shay's treehouse, or Tanner's canoe trip. A laugh bubbles up. I can't hold it in.

Gavin laughs too, then he lifts me up and spins me around in his arms.

I feel like the blow pipe, spinning as I'm blowing a piece of glass, and I'm formless and free, and all the rough edges of the past are smoothing out. I hang on to Gavin's shoulders and laugh more, with relief and happiness and gratitude.

Finally Gavin stops, the studio tilts and spins as he lets me down, dragging me down the front of his body. My breasts press against his chest, and my legs mold against his. I grip his shoulders and hang on as sensations rush over me.

He looks down at me and his eyes turn from happy to yearning. "We did it."

"We did."

I don't turn away as Gavin leans down, takes the back of my head in his hands, and presses his mouth to mine. No, I don't turn away. Instead, I stand on my tiptoes and invite his kiss.

A conflagration ignites inside me, and I whimper against his mouth. His hands tighten in my hair, tugging on my scalp, and he groans in response. I open my mouth to him and he plunges in, tangling his tongue with mine, licking my lips, thrusting in and out. He tastes sweet, like oranges and honeyed tea. I press into him and feel his length hardening. He groans again and then nibbles at my lower lip, kissing me and tasting me.

I dig my nails into him and run my tongue over his lip, the one I've been dreaming about tasting for the past twenty-nine days.

He makes a desperate sound and then grasps my hips, lifts me up, and wraps my legs around his middle so that I'm situated right on his length. Exactly where I need to be. He lets out a curse word as I rub myself along him.

I'm in jeans. He's in jeans. Why are we still in jeans?

He breaks free from my mouth. "I want to love you so much. Let me love you."

I start to nod, then a bit of lucidity penetrates. We can't. I can't.

I shake my head and then cut off a moan as I slide down his hard length.

"I can't."

His breath comes out uneven.

"Hell." He rubs his hands down his face. "You're still waiting? I'm not remembering, Jamie. It's not happening." He looks at me with frustration stamped on his face and in the way he's holding himself. "If you're scared that I won't want you after I remember, it's not a possibility, not even a remote possibility."

I nod, my lip quivering as I fight the tears pressing at the back of my eyes.

He gives me an intent look. "You know, I was thinking, why do we only have three kids? We should have another. Maybe two more. I hate that I don't remember the kids being born, learning to walk. I want to experience that again. Wouldn't you like that? We should have another."

Oh.

Oh no.

I...I want that too, and I know that it's never, ever going to happen.

"What? What's wrong? Three is fine. Three is great. We don't have to."

My limbs start to shake and I swallow down the glass shards of fear and self-loathing scraping at my throat. "No. It's not...I can't...I...I have something I have to tell you."

My heart pounds furiously.

At my words, he frowns and his brow furrows. "Did something happen? Can we not have any more kids?"

"No. That's not it. I..." I can't say it.

Gavin takes a step back, his face solemn. "Why do I get the feeling I'm not going to like this?"

I shake my head. It's nearly impossible to speak past the pain in my throat and the yelling in my brain. It's screaming, *don't tell him, you don't have to tell him, you can keep going like this forever! He's happy, the kids are happy, you're happy. You can have kids, a marriage, you can have everything. You don't ever have to tell him.*

But I do.

I do have to.

And if not now, then when?

Every time is a terrible time to break the news.

But I can't, like I said before, I can't be intimate with him under a lie, and we can't keep going like this without being intimate. Clearly.

"Are you married to someone else?" he asks, his voice hard.

"What? No." I shake my head and frown at his relieved look.

"Okay. Were you or are you cheating on me?"

I let out a stunned breath. "No. That's not even possible. No."

He closes his eyes in relief. When he opens them he asks, "Were we planning on divorcing? Did we hate each other?"

A hysterical laugh bubbles in my throat. You can't divorce if you've never been married. "No. We weren't getting a divorce. That's not even a remote possibility."

He lets out a relieved sigh and his lips curve into a smile.

"Are you a felon?" he asks.

"No."

"Am I?"

I shake my head. "I don't think so." I hope not.

"Do we have massive debt?"

"No." I throw up my hands.

"I'm just trying to cover all the bases."

I nod my head, then reach out and link my hand with his. This just might be the last time I touch him. I want to take a moment so I can remember how it feels.

Gavin looks down at our entwined hands and smiles. "Okay then. I'm ready. Anything else you have to say, we can handle together."

Gosh, I wish.

Together is a really, really nice word.

Slowly, I pull my hand free. I don't think he'll want to touch me after I've told him what I've done.

"Okay." I clear my throat, pushing away the sharp pain. I reach up and touch my locket, the glass shard inside. I started all this because of a promise I made to Bobby. I expect he'd want me to tell the truth, because more than anyone, he believed in my ability to do the right thing. "Here's the thing…"

I trail off at the chirping of my phone. I pull it from my pocket, ready to ignore it, when I see it's the school.

Gavin looks at the screen. "What is it?"

"The school. Hang on." I pick up and take a breath to get my emotions under control. "Hello?"

"Jamie. This is Ms. Crum. Your children missed the bus. This behavior is unacceptable. They are in my office—"

"I'll be right there."

I glance at Gavin's concerned expression. It looks like our conversation has to wait.

"What is it?"

I've hung up and am hurrying toward the studio door. "The kids missed the bus. They're in the principal's office. She's the worst sort. I need to get them before there's trouble. There's no telling what Tanner will try."

I look back at Gavin, and funny enough, beneath the concern, he's hiding a grin. Of course. After the egging and the feather bath, Gavin became Tanner's biggest fan. I'm sure he's imagining Ms. Crum covered in rotten eggs.

"I'm coming too."

I don't have time to argue.

Hopefully, when we're there, Ms. Crum doesn't out us all. That would be worse than me telling Gavin myself.

26

Gavin

The school is a collection of double wides shoved to the edge of town, like dust swept to the side of a room waiting for the dust bin. It smells like coming rain. The sky is washed out gray, matching the faded vinyl siding of the trailers. Behind the buildings, a merry-go-round turns in the wind, squeaking shrilly. There's a teeter totter, a jungle gym, swings, a patch of grass. I suppose if I were a kid, I might think it's nice, but looking at the classrooms, with their tiny windows, I doubt it. Not that I can remember, but I get the distinct feeling that school and I didn't get along.

Jamie half walks, half jogs down the sidewalk towards the principal's office. It's the last double wide in the line-up, farthest from the parking lot. Jamie throws a nervous look over her shoulder, her cheeks white and her freckles standing out. Strangely, the feeling I'm getting from her is like the one you'd have walking on a narrow, treacherous mountain trail, one wrong move and you could plunge to your death. So you have to walk very, very, very carefully, because your life depends on it.

I frown at the tightness of her shoulders and the shaky way she draws in her breath.

It doesn't make sense.

I have no idea what she's so scared of, but for some reason I get the feeling it's almost like she's afraid of me. Or my reaction to whatever it is she has to tell me.

I'm not worried though. Maybe in the past we fought, or had differences or troubles. Maybe I did things, or she did things. None of that matters.

It's in the past.

Sometimes life gives you a fresh start. I'd be a fool not to take it.

"Gosh darn it." Jamie picks up her pace, hurrying down the cracked sidewalk. "I can hear her hollering."

I tilt my head. Through the maze of old double wides, twisting sidewalks, and the cawing of a crow, I can hear yelling too.

Forget jogging, I grab Jamie's hand and start to run, pulling her behind me.

I duck into the main office, pushing open the corkboard door, and focus on where the yelling's coming from. Down the narrow hall, Shay backs slowly out of a room. Her shoulders are hunched, her eyes wide, and I get the feeling she's considering being a cat again.

"You are just like your mother! Don't you laugh. Don't you laugh, Tanner Sutton. Failure isn't funny."

I've never known what a shrieking banshee sounds like, now I have a reference. It sounds like a high-pitched teapot, boiling over, whistling in fury, brought to life in Ms. Crum's voice.

I reach Shay and grab her hand. She's surprised to see me, her eyes go wide, and then she lets out a relieved sigh, gripping my hand tighter.

"Tanner's in trouble," she whispers.

I'll say he is.

I take in the scene. Elijah and Tanner stand defiantly in front of Ms. Crum's desk. Elijah's chin is raised in a stubborn, give 'em hell kind of way that I recognize, and Tanner has that joyful devious light in his eyes that tells me he just pulled a prank worthy of a super villain.

I can easily guess what the prank was because Ms. Crum is standing behind her desk, a metal folding chair stuck to her behind. She's twisting, grasping at the legs, trying to yank it off. Unfortunately, it's not budging, it's just stretching out the polyester fabric of her blue dress pants.

Ahhh, superglue.

I can smell the rubbery, chemical scent. I imagine to Tanner, it smells like victory. The little hellion.

Jamie hurries past me, her cheeks flushing. She nearly trips over her own feet when she sees the chair legs sticking out of Ms. Crum's behind.

"What...what?" She turns to Tanner, her eyebrows sky high. "Tanner Robert Sutton. What did you do?"

Elijah winces. "Uh oh, Tanner, she's using your middle name, you're in trouble."

Jamie rounds on Elijah her finger shaking at him. "Don't think you're in the clear."

Ms. Crum smacks her hand down on her metal desk. The sound as sharp as a warning gunshot. "Jamie Sutton!"

Jamie snaps to attention.

Shay squeaks and hides behind my legs, peering out from behind me.

"Ms. Crum...hi...how are you? How did you, uh...find yourself attached to your chair?" Jamie spins her finger in a circle and winces.

I hold back a snort.

Ms. Crum looks like the rusted edge of an old battle-ax —she's old, wrinkled, and still swinging. Jamie was right, this lady isn't someone you want to mess with. I imagine she's been a principal for decades and has crushed hundreds of misbehaving kids like smashing flies under a heavy book. Unfortunately for her, I don't think she's ever come up against anyone like Tanner.

"You know very well how I did." Ms. Crum narrows her eyes on Jamie, her nostrils quivering and her lips folding down. "Your good-for-nothing son can't sit still, can't behave for a minute. He is the definition of a bad seed. I told you the last time you were in here, if you couldn't get your undisciplined, unmotivated, misbehaving children under control I'd have to fail them. It gives me no pleasure to tell you this but your daughter would still rather imagine she's an animal than learn her letters. Your sons, they're constantly disrupting, laughing in class, making jokes, they don't take life seriously. They will never succeed. They will never get anywhere. They'll end up just like you, ruining lives, ruining—"

"Hold on now." I step into the office and move between Jamie, the kids, and Ms. Crum. The more she ranted, the angrier I got. The closed-in, dark little room, the musty, pencil shaving and glue smell, the sterile, institutional desk and chairs, it tears at something inside me. There's an echo deep down telling me this isn't right. That somehow, a long time ago, I was in a similar situation, and I couldn't get out of it, and I couldn't help anyone else. But now I can.

I give Ms. Crum a hard look. "That's enough."

Jamie takes in a sharp breath, and I feel her staring at me in shock.

Ms. Crum narrows her eyes on me. The chair sticking out from her behind looks like a grotesque appendage.

"They're kids." I look at Elijah, his cheeks red and his eyes wide. Tanner stares at me, his mouth hanging open wide. Shay peers at me from behind the door. "They should be imagining. They should be laughing and joking. They should be playing and having fun. Show me a kid who doesn't imagine or dream. That would be the failure. That would be the tragedy. Why would anyone want to make a child sit still and be quiet? I don't know why you're saying they won't be a success, but lady, my idea and your idea of success is vastly different. Because to me, someone who is true to themselves, stands up for others, and is honest, and kind, then that person is a success. You don't have to sit still, be quiet, and do what someone else tells you to do to be a success. I don't know who you think you are, but you aren't the end all and be all when it comes to determining what's right for these kids." I wave my hand at the metal chair. "And sorry about your...chair."

I grab Tanner and Elijah's hands. They both have identical stunned expressions on their faces.

Ms. Crum isn't done. She smacks her hand on her desk again. "Who I am? Who I am? Who in tarnation are you?"

I narrow my eyes on the woman. "I'm their father."

Elijah squeezes my hand and Tanner grins up at me, his eyes full of hero worship, for the dad who apparently just slayed a dragon.

Ms. Crum's coughing, but we don't need to hear any more.

"Have a good night." I nod at Ms. Crum, then march the kids from the room. Jamie's cheeks are flushed bright red. She grabs Shay's hand and we all walk out the narrow, musty old office, to the fresh air.

THE KIDS ARE RIDING HIGH. JAMIE, AS USUAL, TAKES THE curves on the road like she's running a roller coaster at an amusement park, and faster means more fun. After riding with her, Gran Allwright, and Big Tom, I figure it's what comes when you know the curves, hills, and turns as well as you know the nose on your own face.

The radio crackles playing some fast-paced bluegrass medley, adding to the excitement from the kids bouncing in their seats and Tanner giving a play-by-play of the superglue incident.

"And then Shay said she really, really had to go to the bathroom, and then Elijah said he did too. But Ms. Crum said she wouldn't fall for their mischief. And even though Shay was crossing her legs real tight, Ms. Crum said we weren't allowed to take our tushes off our chairs, not for the bathroom, not for boredom, not even if it was raining frogs. She said we had to learn discipline. So then I figured, what's right is right, and if we couldn't leave our chairs, she couldn't either!"

Jamie glances in the rearview mirror, frowning at the kids. Shay is in the middle seat and the boys are buckled in on either side of her. "Shay, do you still have to go? Elijah? Should I stop?"

Shay shakes her head. "I can hold it."

"Me too."

"Fine." Jamie hits the radio, silencing the music, and leaving only the rumbling of the engine and the wind whistling through the gap in the windows that never seals properly. "In that case, Elijah, Tanner, you think you did good?"

She glares at the boys in the rearview mirror, and the elation coming from the backseat takes a quick plummet back to earth. I study Jamie's face. Her cheeks are still white, and her lips are tight, all in all she doesn't look happy. I wonder if what I said back there isn't what she would've done. Maybe she agreed with Ms. Crum, maybe Jamie and I don't agree on how the kids should be raised, maybe this was a problem before.

The boys exchange a glance, and Shay gives a wide-eyed shake of her head. Elijah speaks up, "Welllll, we don't think we didn't do good."

Huh.

Jamie's knuckles tighten on the steering wheel. She glances at me, her eyes just as worried as before when she said she had something to tell me, then she quickly looks away. "Boys. Listen carefully. In life people are going to treat you wrong. That's a fact. People hurt other people. What makes the difference between a good person and not is that when you get wronged you don't seek retribution. You can stand up for yourself, you can say, no that's not right, but if you take an eye for an eye, then pretty soon, every single person is blind. Do you understand? You get to choose. Do you want to be a good person, or do you want to blind the world? Every time someone wrongs you, you get to make that choice again. That choice never ends. Keep up the cycle of hurt or be a good person and forgive."

Jamie turns her face away from me, but even so, I can see that she's upset. Her shoulders are tense, and the line of her body is rigid.

I reach over and touch her arm, letting her know that I support her. I look over my shoulder at the backseat.

The boys are chewing on what Jamie said, frowning at each other.

Shay sniffs and wipes her nose with the back of her hand.

"Your mom's right," I tell them.

If possible Jamie stiffens even further.

I squeeze her arm to let her know it's okay, and then continue, "Elijah, I love how you stand up for your brother and sister and how you look after them. Tanner, I love how inventive you are. Shay, I love your imagination. Each of you is amazing, and I'm always going to be there for you, but like your mom said, trying to get back at someone who wrongs you won't fix your problems, it'll only make them worse. That isn't the way to live. Okay?"

Elijah watches me with a peculiar look in his eyes and Tanner's mouth hangs open a bit. Shay is chewing on her lip and it looks like she's having really big, important thoughts.

"Okay." Elijah nods solemnly.

Tanner snaps his mouth shut. "Deal."

Jamie turns the station wagon into the driveway, and the car starts bumping over the ruts and crunching the gravel.

The last time we were all in the car together, we were coming back from the hospital, I was in the rear with Scooter, and I thought this place was a living hell. Now, I'm telling my kids I love them, and I'm so glad to be home.

Jamie yanks the car to a stop under the carport, the tall grass scraping along the sides. I think, maybe if we save up, I can build an actual garage. That'd be nice. Especially come winter.

Elijah clears his throat. "We got our report cards today."

The front seat creaks as Jamie quickly turns around. "That's right. You did."

Tanner smiles a big, toothy grin. "Remember how you promised if we did good you'd take us camping?"

A warm smile-like feeling comes over me and I nod.

"Did you mean it?"

What? Am I not good to my word? I frown at them, suppressing a smile. "Of course I meant it."

Shay bounces up and down. "That means we're going camping!"

I grin as the kids squeal, yell, shriek and tumble from the car, tossing their backpacks in the air and running and jumping through the tall grass. I figure pretty soon they'll start doing somersaults.

"I guess that means they did good?" I smile at Jamie, expecting her to be just as excited as the kids, but she's looking at me with a whole lot of trepidation. Honestly she looks a little green around the edges, like she's on a boat, tossing in the ocean, and she's about to be sick.

"You okay?"

She nods and presses her hand to her stomach. "Uh huh."

I frown, but Shay is running back toward the car, a huge smile on her face. I step out of the car and bend down to meet Shay. "What is it?"

She reaches up and grabs my shirt to pull me down close.

"What?" I smile at her, at the sheer happiness in her eyes, and the way she's bouncing on her toes.

She stares at me and then smiles her big, missing-front-tooth smile, and says, "I love you."

Then Shay lets me go and runs off, back to chasing her brothers, and Scooter, and the darn rooster.

My chest feels like it's been kicked by a draft horse. I stare after her, completely stunned, and rub the aching spot where my heart pounds against my ribs. I think if it pounds any harder it's going to break my chest right open.

"Love you too," I finally say, even though she's halfway across the yard, tugging on Scooter's tail.

My word.

My word.

Is this what it feels like to have a family? Was it always this way?

Jamie's car door shuts with a loud click. And I look back at her, walking toward me. Her lavender blue eyes are taking me in, taking in everything around us. The low-hanging gray clouds, pregnant with rain, ready to water the earth. The wind flipping the leaves on the trees, and the tall grass bending like waves on some faraway green and blue sea. The air smells like rain and tastes electric and expectant. In fact, expectancy hums in the air around us. Even the old moss-covered house, with only the porch light on, feels as if it's waiting. Waiting for someone to come in and turn on all the lights and bring life and laugher inside.

Jamie walks toward me, the wind bending the grass before her. Her red hair tangles around her face, her cheeks are pink, and I realize that in my whole life, I've never seen anyone as beautiful. And I never will.

I could travel the whole world, visit countless countries, and I'd never find anyone as beautiful as her.

When I saw her in the hospital I only noticed her worn-out, cheap clothing, her thinness, her too-red hair, her accent. Now, those things aren't even in my mind. I just see her.

The real her.

She stops in front of me and I smile. "We're going camping. Just like our honeymoon."

She blinks. "Our...oh."

She shakes her head and I reach out and take her hand. "Have we been since?"

"No. We've never gone camping."

"That's a shame." I tug her closer and look down at the tenseness of her full lips. She's so worried. "Don't worry. Everything's fine. Maybe when we're out in the woods, we can stay up late, after the kids are asleep in their sleeping bags, and we can recreate the last time we were out." She stiffens, and the breeze pulls more of her hair free from her braid. I shrug. "Or we could make a new tradition. We could lay on a blanket near the fire, look up at the stars, listen to the fire crackle and pop, and I could kiss you, probably for hours if you'd let me."

I reach up and touch a finger to her cheek. Her skin is cold and unlike me, she looks like laying out under the stars, making love is the worst thing that she could imagine.

"What's wrong?"

She looks over my shoulder, toward where Tanner is directing Elijah and Shay in a new project at one of the piles of tires and pulleys and gears. She breathes in a long, careful breath and then focuses on me. My heart misses a beat because for some reason it looks as if she's about to tell me...goodbye.

"Thank you for what you said at the school."

I let out a quick exhale, I hadn't realized I was holding

my breath. I'm dizzy with relief. "Of course. I meant what I said."

"I know. I know you did."

Her mouth quivers and I run my finger over her bottom lip. "Jamie. I love you. I love the kids. I'm always going to be here for you."

She closes her eyes. Her eyelashes brush over her skin. I move my finger, rubbing her lip. Then I bend my head and brush my mouth over hers. She tastes like running free, like starlight, like everything I've ever dreamed of.

Her eyes fly open and she draws in a sharp breath.

Slowly, she steps back. The wind draws at her hair again and she pushes it from her eyes. "I had something to tell you."

I nod, ignoring the heavy feeling in my chest. "Go ahead."

She looks toward the barn. "Let's talk in there."

Once inside, we flip on the lights and the silence, free of wind and crackling leaves, surrounds us. The lights shine down on all the glass and the space is so perfect, so wonderful, I can't believe we didn't do this before. The new paint smell leaves me with a content feeling. We did good.

Jamie had her first sale today, the kids are happy, and everything is looking up.

I take Jamie's hands in mine. "What did you have to say?"

Her mouth firms and she nods, like she's gathering up courage. "Remember how I told the kids that you shouldn't try to pay people back for the wrongs they do?"

She looks at me earnestly, so I nod. "Sure. I agree."

"Okay…well…we, I, we…jeez."

I move closer, looking down at her tense face. "Jamie, it's okay. Just tell me."

The longer she takes, and the harder this is for her, the more concerned I get.

She studies my expression, like she's memorizing my features.

"Just tell me. Like ripping off a band-aid. Quick is better."

"Right." She untangles her hands from mine, steps back and lifts her chin. She looks me square in the eyes and says, "You're not Billy."

I stare at her. My mind sort of trips over itself. It was running along, thinking smoothly, and then, when she said "You're not Billy," it stumbled.

"What?"

She twists her hands nervously. "Your name is Gavin."

I lift an eyebrow. That name doesn't sound familiar. Not at all.

"I think my driver's license says otherwise." I pat my pocket. Inside my wallet I have my driver's license, pictures of the kids, a life in which I'm Billy Sutton.

Jamie shakes her head. "It's a fake ID."

I lift my eyebrows. What she's saying is less than believable. It's impossible.

"We only met a month ago. You commissioned me to create a glass sculpture. But when I brought it to you, you said it was awful and you refused to pay for it."

"Uh huh." I'm not buying it.

"It broke and that was that. But then you hit your head

and had amnesia and Gran thought it'd be a good idea to make you pay off the cost of the sculpture by working for Big Tom, being my husband. And I agreed with her. I figured you deserved it. An eye for an eye."

"Right." And Diedre, Big Tom, Grandma, the kids, they all just played along. I'm sure.

She's breathing heavier and her cheeks are flushed. "But like I told the kids, it's not right to pay back wrong for wrong. I've never felt right about this. I can't keep it up. This isn't your house. I'm not your wife. They aren't your kids. This isn't your life."

I'm fighting a smile. Jamie's saying exactly what I was thinking when she was driving me back from the hospital. That this couldn't possibly be my life. But it is.

"You really don't want to have sex yet, do you?"

She jerks back, her eyes flashing. "What?"

That's the only explanation for this crazy story. The second we got intimate, the moment it looked like we were going to make love, she pulled out this crazy tale.

"Jamie, what are you afraid of? Are you that scared of being happy? I'm happy, aren't you?"

"No! I'm trying to tell you, I lied. I can't keep lying to you. I care about you too much."

I step forward and grab her hand, squeeze it. "Hey. It's okay. I don't know what happened between us before. Maybe I hurt you. Maybe I wanted out of our marriage, or out of this town, maybe I said some terrible things. But Jamie, that's not me anymore. I want you. I want the kids. I want our life. You don't have to make up crazy stories to give me an out. I'm not going anywhere."

She stares at me, as if I'm her idea of heaven and her idea of hell. "Gavin."

I shake my head. "Come on, Jamie. We both know what this is about."

"We do?"

I nod. "You're scared about what'll happen when I get my memories back."

Her pulse flutters in her neck and I have the urge to reach out and soothe her.

She shakes her head. "That's not it."

I shrug. "Even if I hated it here. Even if I wanted to leave. Even if you and I weren't in love, none of that matters anymore."

Her face goes pale. "But we're not...you're not..."

I sigh. Enough.

"Alright. There's an easy way to solve this."

"There is?"

I grab her hand and pull her out of the door of the barn. The wind bites at us, and a few misty droplets are falling. I tug her toward the kids, putting together some sort of pulley lever basket system.

Tanner sees us, and when he does, he grins and runs over the grass toward us. When Elijah and Shay see where he's going they hurry after him.

"You'll never believe what we're building." Tanner points back at the pile.

"Bet we won't." I smile at him. "But first things first. I've got a question for you."

Elijah and Shay come up next to Tanner, they nod their heads, listening.

"Okay," Elijah says, sensing the seriousness in my tone.

"Your mom was telling me that my name isn't Billy, it's Gavin. And that before you picked me up at the hospital you'd never seen me before. That this has been one big ol' prank. Is that true?"

I watch them carefully. Tanner frowns and looks between Jamie and me. Elijah's face is solemn. Shay just stares at me, like she did when she was hugging me and telling me she loved me.

Jamie pulls her hand from mine. "Tell the truth, kids."

Tanner and Elijah look at each other, the brother-to-brother communication passing between them. Then Elijah nods and turns back to me.

"Okay."

I lift an eyebrow. "Okay what?"

"We did pull a prank."

Jamie looks down at her feet. My heart skips a beat. "What do you mean?"

Tanner lifts his chin. "We're sorry about dumping rotten eggs on you, and about blowing the chicken poop and the feathers all over you. We were mad 'cause you were mean before, so we were paying you back. But like you said, we won't do that anymore."

I smile at Tanner. "Good."

He looks up at me with an earnest expression. "I'm real sorry, Dad."

Elijah nods. "Sorry, Dad."

Jamie's head snaps up, "What did you say?"

Tanner lifts his chin. "We said we're sorry."

"I said tell the truth."

"We are telling the truth, we didn't pull any other pranks." Elijah crosses his arms over his chest and glares at Jamie.

There's a battle of wills going on between them.

Tanner shrugs. "Well, maybe we did rub Scooter in chicken poo 'cause we knew he was sleeping with Dad."

I grin at him and he smiles back.

Then, Shay runs forward and throws her arms around my waist. "I love you, Dad."

I squeeze her close. "Love you too, kid."

Shay grins up at me, her eyes squinting and her pigtails swinging in the misty wind.

"Can we go finish our build now?" Tanner asks, impatient to be off.

"Go on then." I wave as they all take off, then I turn to Jamie. "Are you ready to admit you're just scared?"

She shakes her head, then points down the drive. "Gran's coming. She'll tell you."

I turn, and sure enough, Grandma Allwright is bouncing down the drive in her old, rusted car, banjos ripping from her speakers, and smoke backfiring from her engine.

I shrug and head toward the driveway. When Grandma Allwright turns off the engine and hops out of the front seat, she looks between Jamie and me and frowns. "What now?"

"Gran." Jamie nods her head and speaks very slowly. "I've told Gavin."

I frown at Jamie.

Gran lifts an eyebrow and crosses her skinny arms. "Who's Gavin?"

I smile at her. "Exactly."

"I told him that he's not my husband, this isn't his life, that we tricked him so he'd have just desserts for not paying me for the sculpture."

Gran looks over Jamie like she just said the craziest thing she's ever heard.

"Jamie Lynn, don't go telling stories. Why would you do that to your husband? What's wrong with you?"

I put my thumbs in my pockets and nod.

"That's what the kids said," I tell Gran.

"'Course they said that. You're their dad, aren't you?"

I level a look on Jamie. She looks like she's about to explode, her face is red, and she's working herself up, like Billy right before he lets out a loud crow.

I nod at Gran. "Exactly."

"Gran. Tell him! This has gone on long enough. It's not right."

The wrinkles on Grans face deepen and she steps toward Jamie. "You're right. It has gone on long enough. It's time for you to stop hanging on the past and start living in the present. Let go of what happened. Forgive and forget, that's what the Lord says. From my eyes, you've got a husband who loves you, a good life, and there isn't any reason to toss it aside. Billy here is a good husband. Now what you need to be doing is getting busy making me another grandkid."

Now that sounds like an excellent idea.

I smile at the old woman, once my greatest detractor, now apparently, my biggest supporter. "Thank you."

She winks at me and my smile spreads into a wide grin.

Jamie glares at her. "Gran, we're going to burn in hell for this and you're just tossing logs on the fire."

Grandma Allwright scoffs and waves her hand. "Nonsense. Your wood's been wet too long. It's about time somebody lit it. What's wrong with a little baby-making? Besides, me and the Lord are good—"

"Friends." Jamie finishes, glaring at her grandma.

"Exactly. Now, I came down because I'm old and lonely."

I lift an eyebrow. The day that Grandma Allwright is actually old or lonely is the day this mountain crumbles. She winks at me.

"I'm going inside to make some chicken and cornbread. Why are we all standing out in this drizzle?" She puts her fingers in her lips and whistles, then, "Come on, kids. Help me make supper." She points a gnarled finger at Jamie. "Apologize to your husband. Billy doesn't deserve your nonsense. Then come inside and help me cook."

She heads toward the house, the kids see her going, and take off after her. Then Scooter, I'm sure in hopes of dropped food scraps, lopes after them.

Jamie sighs and her shoulders drop. She looks completely drained.

"So..." I reach out and touch her hand.

She looks up and her lips shake.

"You didn't get rid of me."

She shakes her head, her cheeks wet. I'm not sure if it's rain or tears.

"Why would you want to? Was I really that bad?"

She sniffs, the tip of her nose pink. "No. I wouldn't want to. That's just it. I never want you to go. I love you too much. That's the problem."

Even in the cold drizzle, a happy warmth settles over me.

"That does sound like a problem." I step forward and wrap my arms around her. "But if you have that problem, then I have it too."

She lifts her chin and stares into my eyes. "You're going to hate me someday."

I look at her lips. "I doubt it."

Her tongue darts out, licking her bottom lip.

"I'm going to kiss you. That's what we're supposed to do right? Kiss and make up?" I smile at her, and finally her lips soften.

"If you forget everything else," she says in a ragged voice, "I hope you never forget that I love you."

I span my hands around her ribs and pull her close. I give her my promise when I kiss her beneath the gray, drizzling, wide open sky.

27

JAMIE

I spent the night wrapped in Gavin's arms. Warm beneath the old quilt, settled in the soft mattress, tucked against his side. We kissed. We kissed a lot.

He's under the distinct impression that I was trying to give him an out of our marriage. That before his accident we were unhappy and I'm fabricating stories so he can leave and not feel guilty. He spent hours of the night coaxing me with his mouth and his hands. Kissing and kissing and kissing.

I don't think I'll ever look at kissing the same way again.

His mouth was a promise, a gift, a revelation. It hurt as much as it exalted.

Finally, I fell asleep, warm and feeling as though I've

been smoothed out and all my hurts, and rough edges, and pains are gone.

When I wake, Gavin's sitting on the edge of the bed, staring down at a piece of paper. I rub at my blurry eyes and shift on the creaky mattress. The dim morning light shines through the window, spraying over us. From the kitchen, I smell buttermilk biscuits, eggs, and crispy bacon. Gran must've already come down for a Saturday morning breakfast. I bet because of yesterday, she's keeping an extra watchful eye on things. It looks like she's decided this fake marriage is going to stick, and if necessary she's going to use her shotgun to make it work. This time, though, she'll be pointing the shotgun at the bride and not the groom.

When I shift, Gavin looks over his shoulder, the light falls on his sandy brown hair and his unshaven jaw. His eyes land on my lips, still swollen from last night, and he gives me a heated look.

"Morning."

I sit up in bed and pull the blanket over my chest. "Morning." My voice is scratchy and my lips tingle under his gaze.

I glance to the paper in his hands. He holds it out. "I was looking over our marriage license."

My heart kicks up speed, knocking around my chest. He's figured it out. I don't know whether I'm relieved or...depressed.

"It's our wedding anniversary today."

What?

"It is?"

He laughs and holds out the paper. I take it and look

down at the date. Sure enough, Diedre put today, eleven years ago, as the day of our fictitious wedding.

"Don't we celebrate?"

I shake my head, unable to say anything.

"Well, we're going to today." Gavin reaches over and plucks the paper from my hands. "I spent the last few hours going through all our photos, looking at this license, looking around the house. I don't remember any of it. It seems like you don't want to remember any of it. So I want this anniversary to be like our first. The day we begin again."

"You do?"

He nods. "I thought we could start by going to the studio in town. You can show me around, let me see what you do, what you love. I want to learn."

My heart flutters, opens like a glass flower pulled from the heat.

"I called your gran down. She's going to watch the kids while we're there. Okay?"

Slowly, I nod and Gavin's eyes warm, like a bright summer sky.

He leans forward and presses a kiss to my mouth. The only thing that stops us from continuing is Gran banging a spoon against the cast iron pot and calling that breakfast is on the table.

Gavin stands next to me taking in the studio, the furnaces, the bright orange of the melted glass. The studio smells of beeswax and burnt cherry wood and the acrid taste of smoke lingers on my tongue. Gavin has a small smile on his face, he's been watching me with this secret expression the whole while I've been showing him around. It's making me short of breath and unsteady. When he runs his fingers along my back I hold myself back from melting into him.

He wants to make a glass flower. He says he wants it to be his anniversary gift to me. When he said it might not look good, but it'll be made with love, I couldn't say no.

"First you take the punty." I hold the long metal rod out to him. I've already gone through all the safety precautions and described the equipment.

Gavin reaches out, brushes his fingers over mine and takes ahold of the punty. I shiver at his touch and let go. The heat from the furnace licks at me, nearly as hot as the flame arching between us. Inside the furnace, the orange glow is bright, blinding.

"You dip the tip of the punty into the crucible. Gentle now. Start with just a little glass. Gather it just like you would spinning honey onto a honey dipper, spin it round and coat it evenly."

Gavin spins the punty in the melted glass. "Like this?"

He holds up the punty. I peer at the rounded bit of glass he's gathered and nod. "Good."

He smiles at me, his lips quirking in a proud smile, and I bite back an answering grin. "Now gather on top more glass."

He dips the punty into the crucible again.

"Good. That's good."

He pulls it out and I nod toward the bench. "Now we head to the bench. We'll flatten the glass with the pincers."

Gavin and I walk to the bench and I take the pincers and show him how to pull on the glass, flattening it out. "Like this," I say, handing him the tool.

He nods, his brow wrinkling in concentration. He flattens the glass, and I watch him carefully, making sure he isn't going to burn himself.

"Now pull at a forty-five degree angle. That'll make the petals." I show him again, standing so close that my breast presses against his arm. I pull a petal out, and he nods, flashing a look at me.

"Got it." He takes the pincers and shapes the petals, the soft glass bending. His hands are strong, his fingers long, and as he shapes the glass, his hands steady, his face a study of concentration, I imagine that this is exactly what he'd look like making love, running his hands over me, moving with me. I wonder if he'd be as gentle with me, if I'd bend as easily.

I realize I make a small noise when he looks up at me, his eyes as warm and fiery as the glass. "Is this okay?"

I nod. It's more than okay, it's...oh, he means the flower.

I study it, the petals are rounded and curved, delicate, it looks like a rare orchid, something exotic, something you'd never, ever find here, on the mountain.

"Now what?"

"Here." I take the punty and let the glass flow down, so I can make a constriction. "Now we just break it free."

He frowns at the flower, "Just like that? Won't it shatter?"

I shake my head no. "No, it wants to be free. If you do it right, it won't break."

My heart skitters and I turn my face away so he doesn't see how much saying that affected me. Quickly and firmly I break the flower free, and it falls onto the fireproof blankets. Unbroken.

Gavin and I stare at the flower. Finally, he looks up at me.

The edge of his lip lifts into a smile. "We did it."

I watch his eyes light up. He pushes back the hair that fell over his forehead and grins at me. His enthusiasm catches me and I smile back. "You did it."

He nods. "I guess I'm a pro now. Move on over, you have competition."

I laugh. "Watch it."

His smile falls away and he reaches out, running a hand over my braid. "Your hair is the exact color of melted glass. It's extraordinary."

I stand still, unable to move beneath the burning warmth of his touch.

He strokes a long strand of my hair between two fingers. "So soft."

His eyes go unfocused and I know exactly what he's imagining, because I'm imagining it too. I lean toward him and he cups my cheek in his hand. His eyes reflect the light of the furnace and I can almost, almost see a future for us. One that's full of passion and love, family and home, but then he shifts and the reflection disappears. Because for those things you need truth and trust. And just like glass, trust is easily broken, and once it shatters, what you had is gone forever.

Gavin watches me then pulls his hand away. "I'd be worried about the look on your face, but I finally got to stick my rod in your glory hole, so I figure, things can't be that bad."

I let out a stunned laugh.

"Was it as good for you as it was for me?" He gives me a leering smirk and I laugh, shaking my head.

"I can't say that I noticed your rod."

"Oh. That hurts. That really hurts."

I grin at him, then nod at the flower. "Let me take care of that. It has to cool."

He nods, glowing with what I'd call happiness, if I had to name it.

I wonder for a moment, why can't I just reach out and take happiness too? It's right there in front of me. Except, in glassblowing, and in life, sometimes if you reach out without a thought for protecting yourself, you get burned.

I take care of clean-up and making sure everything is set while Gavin walks around the studio, studying me from the corner of his eye, keeping track of my movements. I feel his gaze on me, as soft as a morning kiss, the entire time.

When I'm done, he nods at the door. "We should head home for lunch."

I bite my lip, hard, dissuading myself from kissing him. "Thank you for the flower. It's the best present I could've ever asked for."

"I'm not sure it's all that nice looking, I was distracted by my instructor."

"Really?"

He grabs my hand. "Yeah. I kept thinking about how much I loved her."

I stop walking just short of the door. He looks down at me and raises his eyebrows. "What?"

That's it.

I'm done fighting this.

Gavin wants to stay.

The kids want him to stay.

Even Gran wants him to stay.

And me, I want him too.

No, even more than that, I love him.

So, I'm going to reach out and try to break away from the past, like glass from the punty. And if I do it right, we won't break, and neither of us will get burned.

Gavin said we should start over, we should believe that this is our first anniversary, so that's what I'm going to do.

"What is it?" he asks again with a small smile on his face.

I shake my head. "I was just thinking, I feel the same."

As we head out the door, I send up a prayer: please, please don't let this shatter into a million pieces.

28

GAVIN

THIS IS ONE OF THE BEST DAYS OF MY LIFE. I'M SURE OF IT. I hold Jamie's hand as she pulls into the drive. I watch her, while trying not to let her know I'm watching. I don't want to miss her reaction.

We may not have much money, I can't take Jamie to New York or Paris to see the museums and the galleries for our anniversary, but I can give her something else she loves. Her family and her friends. The sunlight flickers through the tall, shaggy evergreens and splashes across her face. I smile at her.

She takes her eyes off the drive, looking at my smile. "What?"

I shrug. "I'm just happy."

She squeezes my hand. "Me too."

Then we've rounded the last curve of the gravel drive, and right before us is the surprise that I planned. Everyone is outside, in the afternoon sun. Elijah and Tanner are dressed in matching blue dress shirts with khakis, pulled from the back of their closets. Easter Sunday clothes, they'd said. And Shay, she's wearing a light yellow dress, all poufy and wide, it makes her look like a dandelion dancing in the green grass of the yard.

The kids are filling mason jars with flowers on the picnic table, wild ones picked from the field, the little blue ones with the ragged edges, the white ones that look like lace, the yellow daisies.

Grandma Allwright is bringing out a pie to set on the picnic table. The table is crowded with all the foods that Jamie told me she loved, crispy-skinned Sunday chicken, iced tea with sugar, sweet corn slathered in butter, greens with bacon, and desserts, lots of desserts. Peach pie loaded with peaches, lemon meringue pie with meringue that's as high as the clouds, strawberry shortcake, piled with fresh strawberries and cream. It's all there. I'll admit, those nights we sat in the kitchen and I asked her about her favorite things...I didn't forget a single one.

Diedre and Tom are here too. They've hung red streamers on the front porch and Diedre is pointing out where to tack a bunch of white balloons. When she hears us coming down the drive, she elbows Tom and points our way.

The kids shove the last of the flowers into the mason jars, hop off the picnic table benches and run toward the station wagon. Grandma sets down the pie, wipes her hands on her "That ain't burnt, that's flavor" apron, and watches us pull in with a satisfied smile on her face.

I'll admit, when I called her at six this morning, she was happier to help than I thought she'd be. She enlisted Diedre and Big Tom, and the kids to help. Everybody pitched in.

Jamie looks at the kids running our way, at all the food stacked on the table, the decorations and flowers, and her lips tremble. I can't tell whether she's stunned with happiness or if she's going to cry.

"What is all this?"

"Happy anniversary." I smile at her and brush a kiss over her mouth, then the kids are yanking open the doors and shouting and pulling us across the grass.

"You should see all the food Gran and Diedre made." Tanner jumps up and down, dragging Jamie behind him. "Dad told them to make all your favorites. Crispy chicken, corn, peach pie, and lemon meringue and strawberry shortcake. I'm gonna eat dessert first!"

I grin over at Jamie. There's no way he's eating dessert first. But I don't think she heard him. Instead she's looking at me as if I just reached up, grabbed the moon, and handed it to her.

"You made me my dream meal?"

Suddenly, I'm embarrassed. I didn't think it'd make her cry. She takes a hurried step forward and then throws her arms around me. I let out a whoosh of breath when she hits me, then I wrap my arms around her and hold her close.

"Thank you. Thank you, thank you. You have no idea."

I shake my head. The kids seem to realize we're having a married moment, so they take off, running across the grass back to the picnic table.

"Everyone pitched in."

Jamie's not listening, she's holding me so tight I don't know if she'll ever let go. That's alright, she fits in my arms just fine.

I breathe in her orange blossom-scented hair, and the lingering cherry smoke from the glassblowing studio. She's small, I always forget how short and how small until I'm holding her in my arms. The grass blows against our legs, and the kids are shouting to Diedre and Tom that they can come to the table, because it's finally time to eat.

Gran tells the kids they're as cute as speckled pups, and Diedre tells Tom he better learn to speak up if he ever wants an anniversary party of his own, and I smile and press my lips against Jamie's temple.

"You're happy?"

She sniffs and nods. "The happiest I've been in years."

Somehow, I think the same is true for me.

I unwrap my arms from her and take her hand, "Come on. We have a party to attend."

Jamie smiles at me, and her lavender blue eyes, her glass flame hair, her freckles, they all hit me, and I imagine I could spend the rest of my life looking at her, finding all the different ways she's beautiful.

We walk through the tall grass, hand in hand. I pat Scooter as he hurries by, heading for the plate of chicken no doubt. The kids are seated already, and Gran's pouring iced tea in all the cups. Tom and Diedre are arguing about something, well, more like Diedre is arguing and Tom is silently letting her.

It's a picture that I hope I get to see many more times in my life. I'm just about to tell Jamie so, when there's the sound of another car coming down the drive. I turn my head and frown.

Jamie grins at me. "Did you invite someone else?"

I shake my head. "No."

We turn and watch a sleek black car come around the bend. I narrow my eyes on the curved lines, the gleaming paint, the familiar design. That's a Bentley. A quarter-million-dollar car. Why is there a Bentley in Hollow Creek, at our house, and why do I know that Bentleys have glossy wood trim, butter-soft leather, a dashboard that spans like the wings of the logo across the interior and that driving one feels like steering a cloud? Was I once a car buff? I don't think I was.

I lift an eyebrow at Jamie as it pulls to a stop twenty feet away. The engine hums, a soft, expensive rumble that sounds loud and obtrusive amongst the country crickets and the background clucking of the chickens.

I tilt my head. Maybe they're here to see Jamie's work, maybe they saw her website and she'll have another sale. I smile down at her.

But instead of looking happy, her face has gone pale. She drops my hand and takes a step back.

I shake my head. "I'll go see what they want."

I walk across the gravel and dirt, a pleasant expression on my face. I'll help them out and then we'll get back to celebrating. Maybe tonight...maybe Jamie and I will finally—

The driver side door opens and a tall, brown-haired, firm-jawed, stern-looking man steps out. He's in a gray suit, a blue shirt, and a gray tie, and he looks as straight-faced and sardonic as ever. Of course he does.

I grin at him. "Hey Will. You here for the party?"

A black-haired woman with big soulful eyes steps out of the passenger door and gives me an impish grin.

"Oh. Hey Jessie. You came—"

I stop.

Stare at my brother.

My twin brother.

Everything is back. I remember everything. One moment the door in my memory was closed, and the next it swung wide open. It's all right there before me. I'm Gavin Williams. My brother is Will. I have a fiancée, okay, ex-fiancée. I travel the world, I like extreme sports, adrenaline, and I have a life, a history, a family.

My entire life spreads out before me and then beside it, jagged and out of place, is the last month. That's a life too. But it isn't mine. There isn't a single part of it that's mine.

When I stayed in the Arctic one winter, when the sun never rose, and the cold bit at your soul, there was a night that the wind howled and it sounded like a person weeping. It shook me, gave me chills to the bone. That is the exact feeling I have right now.

There's my life, and then there's this month, a piece that doesn't fit in the jigsaw puzzle of Gavin Williams, that isn't even part of the same set.

I turn and take in Jamie. Her face is pale, her eyes guilty. Oh, she knows. She knows what just happened. Any hope that this was all a mistake, that she isn't guilty as sin, well, it just disappeared.

I look back at my brother. "That's Will. That's Jessie," I turn to Jamie. "But who the hell are you?"

She looks like she's holding back tears. She quickly shakes her head back and forth. Then, there are tears at the corners of her eyes. They make me unreasonably angry. Why should she be crying? Why should she be sad?

Then I take a closer look. There's something familiar about her. Not from the month we spent together, but from before, when I was me.

She's a redhead in overalls, smelling like a chicken coop, dirt on her face, demanding I pay her what she's owed.

I stare at her in horror, take a step back.

"You're that woman."

Jamie steps toward me, her hand up, "Gavin—"

"Gavin? Really?"

"Let me explain."

I shake my head. "You're that woman with the wave sculpture. You hated me. You *hated* me."

I remember her now. She was...she was awful.

What is this?

Was this all revenge? Some sick joke? A way to pay me back for what she figured I'd done?

I feel a ripping, a tearing in my chest, and then I feel it, my heart, breaking, rending in half. I'm surprised, I'm stunned actually, that no one else seems to notice it happen.

Jamie wipes at her eyes and shakes her head. "I don't hate you. Please, let me explain. I didn't mean for it to go like this. I didn't plan to fall in love. I just…"

I take another step back. "Just what?"

"I just," she whispers, "wanted you to know what it felt like to have nothing."

To have nothing, and then have that taken away too, is what she doesn't say. But the meaning is there.

That's when I realize that Jamie was never the starlight, she was just another closed door. I never had her. I never had happiness. I never had kids. I never had a family. Just like when I was a kid, imagining my adventures in the woods while I was locked inside a dark closet, this wasn't real either.

I learned long ago, just because something feels real doesn't mean it is.

I look toward the kids.

By the guilty expression on Tanner and Elijah's faces, they knew too.

I never had kids. They were never mine.

I look at Grandma Allwright, at Diedre and Tom. They all knew.

Every single one of them knew.

Burning, flaming anger singes me, and I gladly grab onto it, because anger feels better than a breaking heart.

I turn back to my brother. He's giving Jamie his "I'm going to crush you in the boardroom and play with the entrails of your decimated business" scowl, and for once, I'm glad that smiling at people isn't his default.

I nod at him and a look passes between us. He doesn't know what has happened, but he knows I need him, and I need to get out of here fast.

"Let me just get my—"

I cut off. Get what? There isn't anything here that belongs to me.

"Never mind. Let's go."

I force myself not to look at the kids, not to look at Jamie, not to look at any of them.

None of it was real.

I yank open the backseat door, cold air conditioning and the smell of expensive leather rushes over me.

I hesitate, because dang it, there's a part of me that doesn't want to leave. It's yelling, "Wait, you can't leave your wife, you can't just walk out on your kids." But she isn't my wife. They aren't my kids.

I shake it off, shake them off, like smacking dust off a pair of dirty jeans.

The hell with them anyway. I'm Gavin Williams. I have houses around the world, private planes, exotic cars, I could buy this entire mountain in a second, but they had me pumping crap for a living, and sleeping with a mangy dog on a broken down couch. I'm sure...I'm certain they were all getting a good chuckle out of it.

Jamie, the boys, all of them really love to pay people back for their wrongs. That's all this was.

I duck my head to slide into the car when Shay throws herself against my legs and wraps her arms around me.

"You can't go." Her cheeks are bright red and her eyes are glassy.

I shake my head and try to force myself to remember that whatever I felt for her wasn't real. "Let go, Shay."

She grasps my legs harder. "No. You promised. You promised you wouldn't leave. I said some dads leave and you said you never would. You promised."

My eyes burn hot and I clench my jaw. "Shay, let go."

"No. I won't. You promised."

I can't look at Shay. A promise isn't a promise if you don't know who you are. Isn't that right? I finally look at Jamie, and I can't reconcile the woman I thought was my wife with the woman that made me the wave sculpture. I promised her I'd love her, that I'd never leave.

She bends down, crouches next to Shay and carefully pulls her arms from my legs.

"Come on, Shay. He has to go. You knew it wasn't forever, remember? You knew eventually he'd have to go."

Jamie's head tilts away from me, so I can't see her expression. Even so, she sounds wrecked. I harden myself against her.

Shay's hands slide from my legs. She buries her face into Jamie's shoulder. "But I made sure. I made him promise. I couldn't make Daddy promise, but I made him."

Jamie shakes her head, still not looking at me. "It doesn't work that way. I'm sorry. It's my fault."

She's right.

It is.

While Jamie pulls Shay into her arms, I climb into the car and shut the door. Will and Jessie climb in the front.

Will quirks an eyebrow at me and I shake my head. "I don't want to talk about it."

Jessie frowns, points at Jamie then at me, then back at Jamie.

"I'm not talking about it. Let's go. Get me off this godforsaken mountain."

Will shrugs. "If that's what you want."

He puts the car in reverse and backs out. That's when Tanner and Elijah realize that I'm really leaving. As Will pulls down the drive they sprint after me. For a moment, they're able to keep pace, and I think they're trying to stop me from leaving.

We had a lot to do. There's the camping trip. The contraptions we were going to build. The treehouse Elijah and I were going to make together. I was going to help Tanner study for his math test coming next week.

I don't look. I can't look.

Will keeps driving and eventually they can't keep up.

In the rearview mirror, I can see the boys falling back, Jamie standing in the drive, Shay in her arms, watching me go, then all of them disappear when we round the bend.

Somehow it feels like leaving them behind is the same as leaving myself behind.

"You alright?" Will frowns at me in the mirror.

I shake my head. "No."

And that, I think, is all there is to be said. I thought this was the happiest day of my life. In reality, it was the worst.

29

Jamie

THE CERULEAN GLASS SHARDS MAKE TINKLING, CHINKING sounds as I sweep them with a hand broom into the dustpan. My knees hurt from kneeling on the hard wood planks, but what does it matter? I want to get this glass cleaned up and the sooner it happens, the better.

After Gavin left, the party quickly turned to something more like a funeral potluck. It took all afternoon and most of the evening to convince Gran and Diedre that I was okay. Fine. Just dandy. Not hurting at all. That I'd expected it to happen.

Honestly, in the end I don't think either of them bought it, but there wasn't any point in them staying once I had to put the kids to bed. Seeing the look on the kids' faces nearly brought me to my knees.

"You're going to fix this, right, Mom? He'll be back, won't he?" Tanner asked.

I had to explain that sometimes when things broke, there wasn't any fixing.

"Like shattered glass?" Shay asked.

"Just like that," I'd said.

"Like when someone dies?" she asked.

"That's right," I'd said.

That was something they all understood. They stared at the ceiling for a long time before I turned out the lights, but when I did, Elijah said, *"I know you said it's not right to give just desserts, but I'm not sorry we did. If we hadn't, we never would've had him."*

Unfortunately, we never really had him anyway.

I kissed them all on their heads, tucked them in, and went to sleep in my lonely bed. When Scooter jumped up, I didn't push him off.

After the kids went to school, I decided even if I couldn't clean up the mess I'd made with Gavin, I could at least clean up the mess in his cabin. After all, I still had the door code, and my sculpture was still shattered on his floor.

His cabin is still as stupidly big and opulent as before. The tall, vaulted ceilings and the modern furniture make it cold and impersonal, and looking around, I don't think he actually liked this cabin. It's nothing like him. I can't picture him in a place like this. No, he'd want something cozier, with a quilt on a plush couch, a rug in front of the fireplace, toys on the floor, a project on the table, and cast iron pots in the kitchen.

Instead of lemon cleaner and varnish, it should smell like whatever's cooking at the moment, oatmeal or chicken or peach pie, and the windows should be open, with the sound of the wind through the trees, and the kids laughing in the yard.

I shake my head and scrape more glass shards into the dustpan. That's my vision of Gavin, that's not who he is. No. The real Gavin has a twin brother, which was a shock, who looks like he hasn't laughed a day in his life. He drives cars that cost more than I'll make in ten years working three jobs. He has expensive homes. And...beyond that, to be honest, I don't know anything about his life from before. I only know how he was with me. But that wasn't reality. He has a whole past to influence his likes and dislikes, and I don't know anything about it.

I dump another load of glass into my plastic bucket, the shards clinking against the edges.

Then, the electronic door lock on the front beeps. I look up, on my knees, the hand broom in my hand. Gavin steps inside and closes the door behind him with a sharp snick.

My heart stutters, I let go of the broom and it clatters against the floor.

He looks different.

He looks like the Gavin I first met. He's in expensive jeans, a cornflower blue sweater that molds to his chest and brings out the color of his eyes. He's clean shaven and his hair's been cut and is swept back from his forehead. When he sees me on the floor his lips twist wryly and he lifts an eyebrow.

I don't know what I expected, but I didn't expect him to look at me as if…well, as if we were strangers.

It feels as if a shard of glass is digging into my heart.

And I know, this is what I deserve. It's everything I deserve.

He looks me over, his eyebrow still lifted. I flush, my cheeks heating. I'm in an old pair of overalls, my hair is up in a frizzy ponytail, and I know, considering I didn't sleep last night, my eyes have deep purple bags under them.

I imagine he's wondering how it was that he ever thought he loved me.

"Just like our first time." His mouth lifts into a smile, but it doesn't reach his eyes.

I shake my head. "What?"

He gestures at me. "You on your knees, cleaning my cabin."

Oh. Ohhh. My fantasy. Our first time.

"Except, that never really happened, did it? Considering we never had sex."

A hot, reactive pulse hits me, when he says the word *sex*. Apparently, my body didn't get the memo that Gavin and I aren't together.

I push to my feet and wipe my hands on my overalls. All night, I thought about what I should've said, or what I could've said to convince Gavin to stay. I created a thousand different scenarios. I even replayed the day I told him the truth, but tried harder to convince him. But after all that night-time imagining, I can't make any of those should've saids or could've saids make it past my lips. Because now, with the real Gavin in front of me, I see what

I didn't in my mind. And that's the look on his face. The look that tells me that when Gavin remembers who he is, he also remembers that he'd never ever love anyone like me.

"I was just cleaning up, I can le—"

"Fine. Take your things and go."

His voice is hard and I flinch and turn my face away from his cold gaze, gathering the broom, dustpan, and bucket.

Then I stand and walk with my head down toward the front door, the glass clinking in the bucket. As I near him, I pause, then swallow down the hard beating in my heart.

"I just wanted to say one thing."

He frowns, staring hard at, I think, the freckles on my cheeks. "What?"

I grip the bucket handle in my hand, holding the cold metal for support.

"Thank you," I whisper.

He doesn't say anything, so I look up from the ground. His eyes are confused, he searches my features. "For what?"

I shake my head. For letting me love you, I want to say. But that's not quite right. For being an incredible person, but that's not quite right either. For loving the kids, for helping me chase my dream, for making me feel loved, for all that and more.

"Just...thank you." I give him a tight smile and move to walk around him, to the front door. The only darn door in this behemoth of a cabin.

As I walk past, Gavin reaches out and grabs my wrist. I

suck in a sharp breath. Him touching me, it still feels like sinking into a burning hot flame. My blood starts to sing and I sway toward him.

I lick my lips. My mouth is dry and hot. "What is it?"

He stares at my tongue tracing over my lips. "I wanted to see if I still felt it."

My stomach twists and I ask, "Do you?"

He looks at his hand cuffing my wrist, his calloused fingers rough on my skin. Instead of answering, he asks, "Why didn't you ever let me make love to you?"

I shake my head. "It wouldn't have been right. You didn't know. Plus, if...when you remembered, I didn't want you to hate me."

He gives a sardonic smile and lifts his eyebrows. "Maybe I would've hated you less."

"I don't think so." I look down at his hand on my arm. "You should let me go."

He makes an amused noise, like he's remembering the first time we were here, when I stomped on his foot for not letting me go.

I frown at him. "Why are you here?"

He should be back to wherever he came from, back with his brother, or his other family.

Gavin narrows his eyes. "I forgot my wallet and license on the kitchen counter. And as I'm sure you know, having identification can come in handy."

"Oh." Suddenly, I realize my subconscious was somehow hoping that he'd come back for us. For me.

He nods, like he heard my hope crashing and sort of liked the sound of it breaking.

"Jamie?"

"What?" My throat is raw and achy and I just want to get away so I can have a good, long cry, then wipe my eyes, put all this away, and then move on with my life.

"I don't like you very much."

"I know."

"I'm not going to forgive you."

"I figured you wouldn't."

His grip tightens on my wrist. "But I still want to strip you down, push you to the floor, and bury myself in you so deep that I forget everything except how you feel around me."

I suck in a sharp breath and quickly look into his eyes. They're bright blue, burning like hot glass, and he's watching me, like I'm the thing he wants most in the world. There's also a vulnerability there. I feel it in the tremble of his fingers on my wrist and the softness of his lower lip.

I realize he's offering me this.

He can't give us a future.

He won't give me forgiveness.

But he can give me this moment right now. The past and all its mistakes stretches in infinity behind us, and the future stretches just as long and just as lonely before us. But right here, right now, we can forget the past and not think of the future. We can have our first and only time.

I take his other hand and slowly set it over my beating heart.

Gavin lets out a relieved breath, and his hand curves over my breast. His lips rise into a smile, one that reminds me of how he looked yesterday morning, when he was making me my glass flower. His thumb grazes over my nipple and I let out a small whimper.

His eyes lock on mine and I couldn't look away even if the cabin were falling around us. "Is that a yes?"

I tilt my chin. "Yes."

He lets go of my wrist and immediately unhooks my overalls, letting them fall to my waist. Then he lifts my t-shirt and pulls it over my head and drops it to the floor. It lands next to me with a soft swish. He grazes his fingers over my breasts, his hands running over the fabric, pulling on my nipples. They bead, and ache, sending painful sparks down, down, down. I let out another moan, and he reaches behind and unclasps my bra, dragging the fabric over my skin and dropping it to the floor.

I reach up, almost hesitant, and run my hands over his abdomen, down the soft wool of his sweater. Through the fabric I can feel the tautness of his muscles, tense and straining. He makes an appreciative noise, so I continue to touch him everywhere I want. If this is the first and last time, I may as well touch him everywhere I dreamed.

I reach over his shoulders, drag my hands over his chest, feel his pounding heart. He bends down, the stubble on his jaw rubbing over my skin, and takes my nipple in his warm mouth. When he draws on it, I grip his shoulders and close my eyes. His teeth graze my sensitive skin and he drags his fingers along my breasts, over my ribs, down the slope of my waist.

I can't take it. I have to touch him. I tug at his sweater, make a sound of frustration, so he takes his lips from my breast and pulls his sweater over his head, then the t-shirt under it, until he stands before me, an expanse of maleness.

I reach out and greedily stroke him everywhere. He groans low in his throat, his eyes half-closed, as he watches me hungrily touch him. Then he takes my overalls and pushes them down my legs, cupping my behind, grasping my hips. I sway toward him and he grins at me.

I kick off my shoes and socks, let my overalls fall away. I slip out of my underwear and stand before him naked.

I think...I think he's as wrecked as I am.

He reaches out, puts his hand to my lips and runs his fingers over me. When he feels how wet I am, his pupils dilate and he breathes faster.

"Take them off," I say, tugging at his pants.

He shakes his head. "No. I've been dreaming about kissing you, and I'm going to do it."

Then he drops to his knees, takes my hips in a firm grip, and presses his mouth over me. To say that I was ready for what he does to me would be a lie. I could never be ready for how his hot mouth feels stroking me. I always wondered, and now I finally know what it feels like to be melted and reformed. I'm pliant, loose, completely at his mercy. He pulls on me, sucks, bites, forces me to stay in the heat of his mouth, while I grip his hair, his shoulders, while I call his name, and then as he's sucking on me, he takes two fingers and slips them inside, bending at the perfect angle, so that before I can prepare, before I can think, I'm made, I'm whole, and then suddenly, I'm shattered. I cry out, and he holds on to me, keeps me together, still pulling on me, to extend the feeling so that it feels like I'm coming forever.

My knees give out and he lays me gently to the cold, wood floor. I fall boneless beneath him, and he rises over me. His mouth is swollen and wet from sucking on me, his eyes are wild, and he's looking at me like he's never going to let me go.

I reach out and tug at the button on his jeans. His eyes go dark and I shove them down his thighs. He kicks them off. Gavin, apparently, goes commando. Because once his jeans are off, he springs free.

Looking at him, I realize that I didn't shatter, I only cooled, and just like glass, I just have to be heated again, molded anew.

I lean on my elbows and place a kiss on the tip of him, stroking my hand over him. He's so silken, so hard, so...everything.

He reaches for his wallet, pulls out a condom, and sheaths himself. Then I guide him down, and he settles over me, pushing me into the hard floor.

He positions himself at my entrance, staring down into my eyes, and I see that he wants to savor this moment, he doesn't ever want to forget it, and neither do I. Then he thrusts inside, and I'm catapulted up, I'm crying out, I'm spinning, I'm breaking again. It's as if I never came down. Gavin loses his restraint, and everything, everything that he's been holding in comes out, and he pushes in deep, harder and faster. Sweat runs down his back, over his brow, his muscles strain, and he pulls my hips around him and pistons harder, faster, he pushes in so deep that I can't think, I can't see, I can't anything, except feel.

"I love you. I love you." He's repeating it with each thrust.

I let out a sob and break apart, shatter around him.

He gives one final thrust and then I feel him pulsing, losing himself in me. He wraps his arms around me, kisses my neck, my temple, my lips, rocks slowly and gently in me now that he's spent and coming down from the wave. It's rolling to shore, but neither of us wants it to end, not yet.

I bury my face into his shoulder, breathing in his scent. It's different now, not the soap that he used back home, but an expensive cologne that smells like anise and autumn. I close my eyes tight and grip him as hard as I can, memorizing the feel of him inside me.

"I love you too," I whisper.

At that, he stills, then slowly he pulls away.

Looking up, I see it in his eyes, so before he can say anything, I gather all the shattered pieces of my heart, and say, "So this is goodbye?"

He looks down at his hands, then back to me. "It felt real, didn't it?"

I blink back the tears pressing at the back of my eyes. "It was real for me."

He nods, a small shake of his head. "I meant to ask, who is their real father?"

My throat is tight and painful. "My husband. Bobby."

Gavin looks at the wedding ring on my left hand. "What happened?"

"He died," I manage to push past numb lips.

Gavin nods and lays a comforting hand on my arm. That small gesture is almost too much. I close my eyes and concentrate on the feel of his warm hand.

"Good luck, Jamie. Tell the kids goodbye. I won't be coming back."

He stands, slips on his clothes, and I do the same, blindly reaching for my shirt and overalls.

As he moves toward the door, I realize that this is it, this is the last time I'll ever see him.

"Gavin, wait."

He pauses, then turns, his blue eyes searching.

"I'm sorry. I'm more sorry than you can know, but I'd do it all again, over and over, because if I hadn't I never would've known you. And even with all this regret, never knowing you is something I couldn't bear."

He doesn't answer, he merely turns and walks out the door. Leaving me to clean up the rest of the broken glass.

30

GAVIN

MY HEAD'S A MESS. DIVING IN BALI, SURFING IN SOUTH Africa, cliff diving in New Zealand, no matter where I go or how fast I run, I can't get away from the fact that I can't run away from myself. No matter which country I'm in, no matter what river I'm rafting or what plane I'm jumping from, I can't escape the fact that every time I close my eyes, the only place I want to be is with my family.

Which leads to swear words, jumping on another plane, and seeking another adrenaline rush, because *Jamie and the kids aren't my family.*

Somewhere between Jeju Island and flying to Patagonia, I realized that not even taking a rocket to the moon would get rid of the feeling that the only place I really wanted to run was back to an old A-frame on top of a remote mountain in West Virginia.

So twenty-two days into my self-propelled adrenaline-hunting frenzy around the world, I land back in New York, tired, jet-lagged, and determined to see the one person in the world who might be able to sort this whole mess out.

I hurry through the international terminal at JFK, dodging a family of five wearing fleece pajamas and lugging matching hot-pink suitcases. I tune out the constant stream of overhead announcements and the smell of garlic bagels, lukewarm pizza under warming lights, and coffee. I tune out the chaos of the terminal and the fact that I haven't slept in nineteen hours. I just need to make it to the exit, then to Romeo.

"Gavin?"

I brush past another group of travelers, talking so loudly their voices echo off the walls and the tile floors.

"Gavin? What are you doing here? I thought you never flew commercial."

I shake my head. Then turn when I realize that Lacey is here, in JFK, tugging on my sleeve, talking to me.

A man only slightly taller than Lacey, with glasses and curly hair, stands next to her, his arm around her waist. It takes me a minute to process everything. This is the first time I've seen Lacey since she gave me back her ring. She looks good. I'll amend that. She looks happy. Seeing her pink cheeks, the lightness of her expression, the way she smiles, I realize three things. One, I never made Lacey this happy, never made her glow like this. Two, I don't feel a trickle of want or love for her, I'm just pleased she's happy. Three, she and I were never meant to be.

The man sizes me up. It's apparent he knows exactly who I am. He doesn't need to worry, Lacey clearly is happier with him than she ever was with me. She lifts an eyebrow expectantly.

"I meant to call and apologize for how things ended. I felt guilty about the things I said, but your phone always went to voicemail, and then I reconnected with Abe at a conference and well..." She looks over at Abe and gives a goofy, love-sick smile, one she never, ever gave me, and then I see the engagement ring on her finger.

"Congratulations." I nod at the ring. "I'm happy for you."

Lacey's eyes light up. "Thank you. I hope we can stay friends."

Lacey might hope that, but by the look on Abe's face he clearly doesn't. I'm guessing he'd like me gone, the faster the better. I'm with him, I'm itching to get to Romeo.

"I'm surprised to see you here," Lacey says, looking around at the crowded, noisy terminal.

"I was in South Korea and had to get back, it was faster to fly through JFK than—"

"I see you haven't changed." Lacey gives me a wistful smile. "Always on to the next adventure. Always on the run." She lifts a shoulder in a small shrug. "Don't worry about it. I'm glad you're like that. When Abe and I have our kids, and then grandkids, I'm sure I'll be envious of you out there exploring the world on your own."

I nod, the roar of the people in the terminal echoing

around in my skull. It's a terrible picture, me at seventy, completely alone.

I'm not. I'm not meant to be alone. I'm not.

I lift my hand and give a stiff smile. "Congratulations, again. Nice meeting you, Abe. Bye, Lacey."

Lacey seems surprised I'm leaving, but Abe just lifts his hand in farewell. I hurry past, and as I go, I hear Abe, "He seemed nice enough. I thought he'd be arrogant, and—"

Whatever he says fades in the din of the terminal. And it doesn't matter. I'm hurrying through the hallways, making my way north.

"Twenty-two days? You lasted longer than I expected." Will smirks at me, and I try not to stare, because even though he's in a suit, looking stiff and supercilious, Jessie is currently perched on his lap, her arms wrapped around his shoulders. I'm pretty sure Jessie realizes how ridiculous it looks, her in a bright yellow polka-dot dress, Will in his stiff business attire, a smudge of her lipstick on his neck. She grins at me and winks.

I scoff and shake my head.

Apparently, I interrupted something when I busted into the old family house in good old Romeo, New York.

"I figured you'd take longer to come to your senses. You Williams boys are hard-headed." Jessie settles against Will's chest. He looks as if he's about to argue the point but then shrugs.

I sit on the edge of the settee in the formal living room.

This room always made me antsy. It's too stuffy, too fussy. What it needs is a broken-in couch and a table with a few nicks and...

Hell.

"I need to talk to that psychic. The one who predicted your match." I point between my brother and Jessie.

"Hmmm." Jessie's brow pinches and she considers me for a minute. "I'm pretty sure you don't."

I shake my head. "I'm pretty sure I do."

"Don't."

"Do."

Will scowls at me. "Gavin, listen to your future sister-in-law. If she says you don't. You don't."

Jessie flashes a smile at Will, and he smirks at her.

Jeez.

Is this what Jamie and I looked like when we were together?

I rub my chest at the thought.

"Will you tell me where she lives or not?"

"Not." Jessie shrugs. "And with that, I'm off. I have a computer class to teach." She presses a quick kiss to Will's mouth and hops off his lap. "Gavin. Listen to someone with recent experience. You don't need someone else to tell you what's in your heart. Okay?"

I nod and Jessie flounces out of the room, Will watching her every move until she's out of sight. Finally, with the click of the front door, he turns back to me, his eyes clearing.

"Where were we?"

I stifle a smile. I've never seen Will so happy. So settled. So himself. Not since before...before.

I lean forward, studying his face. "I've missed you."

Will cocks his head. "I'm here anytime you need—"

"That's not what I mean. I'm talking about before. When we were kids, when we did everything together and there wasn't anything that could separate us. It feels like you've come back. I missed you."

Will's expression shifts, emotions cross over his face, and then he nods. "I always thought you were the only one I never let be taken away. But I was wrong, wasn't I?"

I stand and nod toward the kitchen. "Come on, I'll make you lunch."

Will lifts his eyebrows. "Since when do you cook?"

CORNBREAD, NOT AS GOOD AS JAMIE'S. CHICKEN FRIED IN the pan, not as good as Grandma Allwright's. Iced tea, somehow not as sweet. But Will doesn't seem to mind. Over lunch, sitting at the kitchen table, I tell him what happened when I stopped coming to interrupt his tutors and break him free of his studies. I tell him about the dark closet, how I lied because I thought I was protecting him, how after a while the truth didn't seem to matter, how running became the only way I could live. How the both of us were trapped by what happened, and while Will had escaped the past, I never believed I had.

Will watches me solemnly while I retell the story of our childhood, reframing everything. His expression is as stoic as ever, but since he's my twin, and I can read his face as well as my own, I know that he's feeling everything again and he's hurting for the both of us.

"I'm sorry for not telling you when we were kids." My throat is so pained that not even iced tea can soothe it.

Will shakes his head. "No. Don't be. The thing about suffering. It always feels worse if you think you're going through it alone. But I promise, when you were there, I never felt alone. You've always been my best friend."

I scrape my chair back and stand. "Come on. Give me a hug."

Will scoffs. "I don't hug."

But I shake my head and motion my hand. "Come on."

When he does, he slaps my back, as stiff as ever, which makes me grin. "I don't know how Jessie puts up with you."

He shoves away and frowns at me.

I shrug. "Not that I can fault her."

Will takes the dishes and carries them to the sink, the smell of crisp chicken and the sweet scent of cornbread slathered with butter following him. He clatters them down on the counter and then turns, "Coffee?"

I shake my head. "No. Honestly, I just want to know where this psychic lives."

Will leans back against the counter, stretching out his legs. He looks so much like me, but so different. Our dad used to say that Will was the smart one, I was the dumb one, Will was the staid one, I was the fun one. That if he could combine us into one person, he'd have the perfect son.

Thinking about Elijah, Tanner, and Shay, I can't

imagine ever doing or saying the things that he did. Each of them is unique and perfect exactly as they are. Years ago, I'd wondered if my dad was right, if there was something missing in me. Now, having spent time as a dad, I know there wasn't any excuse for what he said or did. If my adult self could see me at age nine, I'd tell him, "You're a good kid, you're just as you're meant to be."

"I'm assuming you want to ask about the redheaded woman?" Will looks at me curiously.

"Jamie."

Will nods. "You never did tell me what happened. Why you didn't let us know where you were. Why we found you in clothes that looked like a ninety-year-old farmer wore them."

I snort and then cover it with a cough. Thinking back on that, I figure I was wearing Grandpa Allwright's clothing. He was pipe-smoker, and that smell clung to the clothes even after twenty washings.

"You were working on a lumberjack beard, and it looked like you had a wife, three kids, and a fat old dog. I imagine you didn't actually acquire a new life in a month. Right?"

I drag my hand over my clean-shaven jaw and let out a sigh. "It's complicated."

Will shrugs. "Uncomplicate it."

I take in a deep breath, my brain latching onto the cornbread smell, wishing the sparkling kitchen were a little more worn, a little more cozy, and say in one breath, "I hired Jamie to make Lacey a glass sculpture as an engagement gift, I didn't like it when she delivered, it shattered, I refused to pay her, then I fell off a cliff, hit my head, got amnesia, Jamie picked me up at the hospital, pretended I was her husband, and that the kids were mine, I fell in love, wanted to spend the rest of my life with her, make more babies etcetera, etcetera, then you showed up, I remembered, and voilà, here we are."

Will's brow furrows, and he lifts his finger, connecting imaginary points in the air, like he's trying to connect the dots. "Amnesia, wife, kids, lumberjack beard, fat old dog. Huh."

I cross my arms. "Will."

He nods. "Okay. Okay. I have one question."

I swallow painfully. "What?"

"How much money did you owe her?"

"Are you kidding me? I tell you I had amnesia and fell in love with a woman who lied through her teeth for a month straight and you ask about the money?"

He shrugs. "I am who I am."

I grin at him. "Yes you are." Then I admit, "Nine thousand."

He lets out a laugh. "She was having you work off the money?"

"By cleaning port-a-johns."

Will bends over at the waist, he's laughing so hard.

I glare at him. "It's not funny."

"It's sort of funny."

"It's not funny at all."

"It's kind of funny."

"Will, I fell in love with a lie. It's not funny."

Will wipes the humor from his face. "You're right.

Sorry." He claps his hand over my shoulder and squeezes. "She never tried to tell you? All of it was for revenge?"

My mind goes quiet, listening carefully for what that small, insistent voice inside me has been saying for weeks.

"She did tell me. I didn't believe her." Then I admit, "I didn't want to believe her. I liked being her husband. I loved her. I loved the kids."

Will studies my expression. "Love."

"What?"

"Love not loved."

I look down at the stone tile to hide the longing I know is evident in my expression. It's been twenty-two days, but I still wake up expecting to hear that darn rooster crowing before the sun is up, the kids scrambling down the ladder, Scooter snoring, and Jamie curling into my side. I shake my head. Speaking of that darn rooster, did they really name me after that jerk, one-eyed bird? I restrain a smile. Come to think of it, maybe Will's right, it is funny in a way.

Thinking back, when Jamie and I first met I practically told her she was an ignorant, banjo-fiddling, barefoot, chicken-rustling hillbilly. And then she made me exactly what I derided. She exaggerated her accent, I could always tell when she was putting it on. She doesn't even like bluegrass, that was all Grandma, and every time Jamie turned it on, there was a devious light in her eyes. The rotten eggs dumped on my head, the port-a-john job, sleeping with the dog, feeding the chickens, the clothes, all of it was to give me a taste of what I'd ridiculed. What I don't think they expected was that I'd love it, I'd love them. And what they didn't expect, I think, was to love me.

That's what that small voice deep down is telling me. They all love me. It didn't just feel real. It was real.

"Why are you here?" Will takes in the bags under my eyes, the tired lines of my face, the revelation coming over me.

I let out a huff of air. "I came to ask that psychic if Jamie's my soul mate. I figured I could forgive her if that were the case."

"You wouldn't otherwise?" His brow furrows, like this thought is foreign to him. I imagine it is. Will forgave our dad, but I don't think I'll be able to do that.

I don't answer, so Will says, "She lives at Water's Edge, her name's Erma Tanaka."

"Thank you."

A wave of relief washes over me. She'll tell me Jamie's my soul mate and then everything will have happened for a reason.

I love Jamie.

She loves me.

Erma will confirm everything.

"It doesn't work that way."

Erma Tanaka—"call me Miss Erma"—frowns at me while pouring a pot of tea in the recreation room of the retirement center. There's a rowdy game of bridge going on at the next table, and someone is baking chocolate chip cookies in the attached kitchen.

She's smaller than I thought she'd be for the amount of

weight she holds in this town. Miss Erma is even tinier than Grandma Allwright and probably just as old. Even so, she's sharp. She took my measure in a millisecond and I can tell she's not impressed.

I lean back in the squeaking metal folding chair, reminded of Ms. Crum and the unfortunate superglue incident.

"But you predicted Jessie and Will," I wave my hand around the rec room, "And from what I hear, hundreds of other couples."

Erma pushes the dainty cup of steaming black tea across the table. "Do you take milk?"

"Just sugar please."

She nods her approval and drops a heaping spoon into my cup.

"Thank you very much." Even though I'm impatient, and frustrated, I still have manners.

Miss Erma lifts her violet lined cup and draws in a breath of steam. "I love tea."

I nod and take a sip of the hot tea. It burns my tongue. I think about how it's almost, but not quite, as hot as the air coming off the furnace at Jamie's studio.

I set the cup down, and it rattles against the saucer. A cheer breaks out at the bridge table, and Miss Erma calls, "No cheating, Frank!"

An older man waves her off and Miss Erma's eyes twinkle. "He's a cheat," she whispers to me.

I shift in my chair and it squeaks again. "I'm sorry. I know you said you can't just tell me if Jamie's my soul mate, but can't you"—I wave my hands in the air—"look into the beyond or something?"

Miss Erma considers this, then nods. "Hold on. The tea leaves."

She peers down into her cup, concentrating deeply.

There are a few leaves floating in the bottom. I lean forward and look too. She must be reading the tea, I saw this in a movie once. You can tell the future by how the leaves fall to the bottom of the cup.

"What do you see?"

She frowns at me, the lines on her forehead wrinkling. "You won't believe this."

"What?" My chest tightens. What does she see?

"There are fannings, stems, and dust. I ordered Orange Pekoe, the finest grade. This is unacceptable. Who do they think they are, foisting subpar tea grades on consumers? Don't they think we'll notice? Well, I notice. I notice my tea. That's it. From now on, I'm only getting tea from Boden's." She crosses her arms over her chest and glares at the steaming golden tea in her cup.

I frown. "You weren't reading the leaves?"

"Reading the what?"

I'm an idiot. She has no clue what I'm talking about. "I'm sorry, I didn't mean to waste your time. I thought you could see soul mates if you met a person."

She purses her lips. "Do you know what I think?"

I shake my head.

She levels me with dark brown eyes. Ones that see too much. "I've been predicting soul mates for nearly eight decades. But what I see, or what I say, doesn't actually matter."

"It doesn't?"

"No." She reaches up and touches her heart. "This will tell you as well as I can. Ask yourself what it's saying."

I struggle to draw in a breath. "But what if I go back and realize I haven't forgiven her? That I can't?"

Miss Erma peers down at her tea leaves, her shoulders fall, and the shawl she's wearing suddenly seems like it isn't enough to keep out the chill of the room.

Finally she looks back up, a regretful look on her face. "Take it from someone who lost the only man I ever loved because of betrayal. Forgiveness isn't for the person who wronged you, forgiveness is for you. You'll never be free to love fully until you let the past go."

I search Miss Erma's face, taking in the meaning of what she's saying, the regret on her face, and the depth of sorrow. Then the group at the table next to us breaks into a loud cheer at the bridge game, and Miss Erma wipes the regret from her face. She smiles at me and claps her hands together once.

"Well, it was nice seeing you. Tell your brother hello. I hope everything works out."

I've been dismissed.

I shake her hand, tell her thank you, and leave her to join the game of bridge.

When I make it outside, the brisk air tugs at my coat, and a flock of Canada geese flies overhead in V-formation, heading south. Which is exactly what I'd like to be doing.

Forgiveness isn't for others, it's for yourself.

You can never love fully...

I have a few things to do.

Before I leave town, I stop by the bank and send an overnight check to Jamie for nine thousand dollars. The memo says, *paid in full.*

31

It wasn't so long ago that I claimed I'd take cold, hard cash over romance any day. Staring at the check for nine thousand dollars, signed Gavin Williams, I wish I could take that sentiment back. I'd take him over any amount of money, any day of the week.

I grip the wrinkled paper check and take in the words *paid in full.*

That's it then.

Nearly a month ago, when he said that he wouldn't be coming back, I believed him. But a part of me clung to the dream that he'd return. That he'd realized I may have started out with the intent to fool him, but along the way, it became real.

This check tells me he's not coming.

Ever.

As does the For Sale sign out in front of his cabin.

Pretty soon every trace of him will be wiped away. The kids are convinced he'll come back. Elijah and Tanner say he promised them a camping trip. Shay says he promised, period. I don't have the heart to tell them that just because someone promises something doesn't mean it'll come true.

I've stopped working on my glass sculpture. The hope in the floating spheres is a distant memory.

Gran slams a cast iron pot on the kitchen table. "Jamie Lynn!"

"What the heck was that for?" I shove the check in my pocket. I should cash it. That's what he'd want me to do. He'd want new clothes for the kids, little league, a new tent, new shoes, he'd want us to be happy. I'm sure of it. He just doesn't necessarily want to be here to see us happy.

"Enough is enough." Gran gives me a threatening frown. "Everything's catawampus and you're not doing anything about it."

The screen door clatters in the living room. "You tell her, Granny." Diedre walks into the kitchen, rubbing her hands together and blowing on them. "Dang. It's cold as Christmas out there."

Big Tom follows her in. I lift my eyebrows in surprise. I wasn't expecting anyone this afternoon. The kids are at school and I'm packaging up dozens of orders to mail out. In the past two weeks, I've had more than a hundred orders, my glass traveling to places all over the world. I never thought I'd be this successful, especially not this fast, but Diedre says she isn't surprised. Especially after she posed with my glass in a bunch of her photos.

It's funny, I've addressed packages to Hawaii, New York, Brazil, Australia, France, places all around the world. In the past my heart always yearned to leave this mountain and now even my glass is going. I wonder if in its travels, it'll ever pass Gavin.

I look at everyone gathered in my tiny, cluttered up kitchen. "Is this an intervention?"

Diedre nods. "'Course it is. We're tired of seeing you moping. It's time you went after him, right, Granny?"

The heat of the check burns in my pocket. "Sorry to state the obvious, but he doesn't want me."

Diedre glances at Big Tom, then at Gran, "Okay, now's the time you tell Jamie some old mountain saying that'll fix everything."

Big Tom nods in agreement.

Gran narrows her eyes. "When Bobby died—"

"Don't bring Bobby into this."

"When Bobby died," she says more firmly, "I let you mourn. I let you close yourself up into a tight ball and I didn't demand you open up. I lost your grandpa, I knew how it was. But I didn't expect you to stay closed up for six years. Nobody expected you to stay on this mountain, moldering away. Least of all Bobby."

"Gran." I shake my head.

"Don't you Gran me. That Billy..." She frowns at me. "That Gavin..."

I smile, because she used to call him Wilbur or Gilbert. I've never heard her actually use his real name.

She huffs. "That Gavin made you open up. I reckon that's scary. But Jamie Lynn, since when were you a coward?"

Gran levels a hard look at me and I think back over the last few years. Unfortunately, I see quite a few instances in which I've been a coward. Not selling my art. Not leaving Hollow Creek. Not letting in love after Bobby was gone. But in only a month, Gavin helped me shuck all those things. It's amazing how only a month can transform an entire life.

Diedre blows out a long breath, her bangs ruffle and she shakes her head. "If I ever had a man look at me the way Gavin looks at you, I'd marry him in a second."

The kitchen goes dead silent as Gran and I stare at Diedre, because...Tom.

In fact, he's looking at her that way right now. Diedre shakes her head, her hair falling over her shoulders, her tiny checkered dress barely covering her butt. "You have no idea. These online duds, they string me along, they just want to do the nasty, they don't care about who I am, or what I think, or that all I want is a little house, a backyard for a dog and some kids, and a man who will be there whenever I need a shoulder to lean on. And if I could ever find a man like that—"

"Diedre. Get in the truck. We're going to Charleston."

We all start when Big Tom says this.

Diedre puts her hands on her hips. "What the heck are you talking about? Why would I go to Charleston?"

Big Tom points at Diedre, then he points at himself,

and says in a gruff Scottish accent, "You. Me. We're going to the courthouse to get married."

A slow, sly smile spreads over Diedre's face and I get the distinct feeling that she's actually known all these years that Tom has loved her. "Are you saying you want to marry me?"

He smiles and shakes his head. "No, you daft woman. I'm saying I love you."

She grins. "About time. What took you so long?"

He narrows his eyes on her, steps forward, then picks her up and throws her over his shoulder. Diedre laughs then beats on his back. "Hey! Man oaf, put me down!"

He shakes his head. "No."

She cranes her neck, looks back at us and winks.

Tom carries her from the kitchen and the front door slams behind them.

Gran makes a noise of approval. "Now that's how a man does it."

I grin at her and shake my head. I'm happy for them, really happy.

"Now it's your turn." Gran gestures at the front door. "Pack up. Get the kids. Go after your husband."

I trace my hand along the edge of the cast iron pot. "Gran, we aren't actually married. Remember?"

She gives me a shocked look and plasters her hand to her head, looking frail and weak. "What? You aren't? Well I'll be! I plum forgot. Oh no, oh no, this old lady'll die of shock if you don't go out and fix this mess. You've been living in sin. You may have a child out of wedlock, oh dear—"

"Gran. Cut the bull."

She gives me a wicked smile. "Thought I'd try."

"Uh huh." I cross my arms over my chest and frown at her. "You'll never be able to play the frail old lady act on me. The day you get old is the day pigs fly."

She nods. "That's true. The only people that get old are the ones that are born old. Luckily, I was born young and I plan on staying that way my whole life."

I step forward quickly and wrap her in a hug. Her elbows poke me, and she smells like Grandpa's tobacco.

She hums and then says, "You've come to your senses?"

I step back and give her a firm nod. "Sure have."

I glance over at the windowsill above the kitchen sink. The glass flower Gavin made me shines in the spray of sunshine coming through the window. Gran was right. For years I've been closed up. It happened even before Bobby, although no one noticed but me. It happened when I lost my dad and then my mom and I just kept closing tighter and tighter. But since Gavin I'm as open as the flower he made me.

I can't go back to being closed up again. When you're shut down tight you can't get hurt, but you also can't get love.

It looks like I'm finally, finally going to leave this mountain.

32

Gavin

IT TAKES LONGER THAN I THOUGHT TO END ONE PHASE OF your life and start another. I put most of my foreign properties on the market. I won't be running so much anymore. I started negotiations with Will concerning what role I'll be taking in the family business. I have a new, burgeoning interest in establishing an endowment that supports young artists, inventors aka contraption makers, and sports lovers. Harder than any of that, I spoke with my dad and his new wife, and met my infant brother. As soon as I saw my dad, I knew Miss Erma was right. Hanging on to what he'd done had shaped my life and kept me from becoming who I was meant to be. Mainly, a man who wants a family, a wife, and a purpose.

I let all of it go. Everything that I thought was keeping me free was actually keeping me prisoner.

I pass the hand-painted Hollow Creek population two hundred and twelve sign and start smiling. It's hard not to. The sky's bright denim blue, the local radio DJ starts playing "Foggy Mountain Breakdown," which has to be a sign, and the smell of mossy wood, river stone and fresh air flies in the open window of my brand new SUV. I walked on the lot yesterday and bought it because it was big enough for a wife, three kids, a smelly dog, a brand new tent and five sleeping bags. Just in case, there's also room for a firecracker of a grandmother and a friend or two. It's the kind of car that someone would buy if they're planning on staying in one place, having a family, and a life. Which is why I got it.

I turn into the drive, the front of the SUV dips in the ruts and crunches over the gravel. The wind blows across my face and messes my hair, in the distance I can hear Scooter barking and Billy letting out a warning crow. To be honest, my heart's stamping, my chest is tight, and I'm more nervous than I've ever been in my life. Even breathing in the brisk fall air filled with the familiar pine tree smell can't keep my heart from banging around like rocks tumbling down a mountain.

When I pull around the bend, I lift my foot off the pedal, and let out a sharp, pained breath. I missed this place. The tall grass, the moss-covered A-frame, the chicken coop, the stone barn. Even more I missed the kids running and chasing each other in the grass, Scooter rolling in the mud, Jamie standing on the porch in her overalls, her red hair catching the sunlight, calling that it was time for supper. I think I expected everything to be exactly as I left it. That somehow when I pulled in I'd find the kids playing a game of baseball, Billy chasing Scooter, pecking at his legs, Jamie standing on the porch waiting for me.

Yeah.

That's not what's happening.

Not at all.

Instead, the kids are piled in the station wagon, Scooter with them. Gran's in the front passenger seat, shaking her finger at the kids, and Jamie...she's loading the final suitcase in the back. It's piled high. There are at least seven suitcases, two coolers, a few boxes. It looks like they're leaving for months, or for good.

Looking at the house, it's closed up, the shutters are drawn, the lights are off, and the chicken coop is empty. Which is shocking, because, did Jamie finally make good on her word and have Billy as chicken pot pie?

Are they leaving-leaving?

Jamie finally realizes that someone is here. She pulls her head from the back of the station wagon and raises her hand to her forehead squinting at the SUV.

It's been almost a month since I've seen her and looking at her flame red hair catching in the wind, the freckles on her cheeks, the way her lower lip curves into a questioning smile, the darn overalls she's wearing that I now know easily, too easily, come off, all of it punches me square in the chest.

I missed her so much.

How could I ever have thought that I wouldn't be able to forgive her? What's to forgive? She gave me a home, a family, and her heart. If I was given the opportunity to go back and change the past, I wouldn't change a thing.

I turn off the car and send up a prayer, *please, please, want me as much as I want you.*

When I step out of the car, I stop and smile at Jamie. Her eyes widen and her lip quivers as if she doesn't quite believe what she's seeing.

Then Tanner flings open the backseat door and sprints toward me. Elijah is right behind him and Shay's running as fast as she can.

And it's that scene again, the one from the hospital parking lot. The kids are running toward me, shouting how much they missed me, throwing themselves into my arms. This time though, the difference is my arms are wide open, and I catch them, hold them to me, and say, "I missed you too. I missed you."

I drop to my knees and pull them all in, gathering the three of them in my arms. Scooter joins the fray, barking and running in circles around us.

My eyes are blurry when I look up and see Jamie standing next to us. Her hands are on her hips and although she's trying to school her expression, I can see the joy in her eyes. That gives me enough hope to stand and hold out my hand.

"What're you doing here?" she asks, eying my extended fingers.

The kids look up at me, waiting to hear my answer.

"I heard fall is the best time to go camping and since I promised a trip—"

"I knew it!" Tanner jumps up and down.

Elijah tackles him and they start to wrestle, tumbling through the grass like two jubilant puppies let free. I shake my head and Shay tugs on my hand, the one I was holding out for Jamie.

"What is it?" I ask, leaning down.

"Are you staying now?"

I smile at Shay and then look at Jamie, taking in the tears at the corner of her eyes. "That depends."

"On what?" Shay frowns.

I look into Jamie's eyes. "On whether you'll have me."

For the longest few seconds of my life Jamie stares into my eyes, measuring me, weighing what I'm saying.

"'Course I do." Shay tugs on my hand again.

I smile at her. "Thank you."

"You're welcome." And with that, Shay nods and then runs after her brothers, circling them and joining in the tumbling.

There's a beat of silence and then I say, "Were you going somewhere?"

At the same time, Jamie says, "Why did you really come back?"

She shakes her head and flushes. Grandma Allwright slams the front door of the station wagon. This time though, instead of spitting on the ground, she takes one look at me and says, "About time you came to your senses." Then she waves her hand and starts down the driveway. "I'm going home. I've got zucchini to pick."

Jamie watches her grandma leave with a stunned expression.

"I think she likes me." I smile at Jamie, showing her that dimple she likes so much.

She nods. "I think so too."

"Do you?"

"Do I what?"

"Like me."

She shakes her head. "Not so much."

I feel like I've just been tackled and the breath has left me.

Jamie takes my hand. "I don't like you. Like doesn't even begin to describe what I feel about you. That's like describing a sunrise that takes your breath away as pretty. How could pretty describe everything you feel?"

"It couldn't." I reach out and tuck a strand of hair behind her ear; my body rejoices at finally touching her again.

"So no, I don't like you. I...do you remember when you asked whether I'd ever left this mountain."

I wince. "I'm sorry."

"No, it's okay. I haven't." She nods her head. "I was just about to leave for the first time, to come find you. Not because I like you, but because I love you."

I feel winded, like I just ran up the mountain to reach her. I thread my fingers through hers and never want to let go.

"I'd really like to kiss you." I stare at the lips that have haunted my dreams since the day I met her. "But first..." I take a step back, letting go of her hand, and then, "Hello.

My name's Gavin Williams'. I think you're the most beautiful woman I've ever seen and I've never felt this way about anyone. I want to marry you. I want more kids with you. I want to give you everything you've ever dreamed of. When I'm with you, I feel like there's nowhere else I'd rather be." I smile and hold out my hand. "It's nice to meet you."

Jamie bites her bottom lip and then takes my hand. "Hello. I'm Jamie Sutton. I have three kids, a horde of chickens—"

"You didn't eat them?" I interrupt.

She laughs. "Diedre's watching them."

"Good." That darn rooster grew on me.

Jamie smiles and then squeezes my hand. "I have a dog. A feisty Gran. And the first time I saw you I fell right into love."

"And then I spoke."

"Quit interrupting. And then you spoke." She winks. "But then, I knew you were the reason I felt alive again. You were the reason I dreamed. I want to marry you. I want to spend the next seventy years in your arms, because there's nowhere else I'd rather be."

My chest expands and I tug Jamie into my arms, tipping her chin up. "I'm going to kiss you now."

Her lips soften and her lavender blue eyes warm. "I wouldn't expect anything else. But Gavin?"

I brush my mouth across hers. "Yes?"

"What are we doing after we go camping?"

I nibble at her lip and span my hands around her waist, breathing in the orange blossom scent of her.

"We're getting married, you're becoming a world-famous glass artist, and we're having a baby."

She smiles against my mouth. "In that order?"

I laugh. "The last two are interchangeable."

"You can kiss me now." She wraps me in a hug.

And then I kiss her and kiss her. The kids run by, laughing and shouting, Scooter chases them, and the door that was closed in my heart opens wide and lets all the light in.

From now on, I know it's going to be a good life.

THE END

GET A BONUS EPILOGUE

Want more Jamie and Gavin? Get an exclusive bonus epilogue for newsletter subscribers only.

When you join the Sarah Ready Newsletter you get access to sneak peaks, insider updates, exclusive bonus scenes and more.

Join Today!

www.sarahready.com/newsletter

ABOUT THE AUTHOR

Author Sarah Ready writes contemporary romance and romantic comedy. Her books have been described as "euphoric", "heartwarming" and "laugh out loud". Her debut novel *The Fall in Love Checklist* was hailed as "the unicorn read of 2020".

Sarah writes stand-alone romcoms and romcoms in the Soulmates in Romeo series, all of which can be found at her website: www.sarahready.com.

Stay up to date, get exclusive epilogues and bonus content. Join Sarah's newsletter at www.sarahready.com/newsletter.

ALSO BY SARAH READY

Stand Alone Romances:

The Fall in Love Checklist

Hero Ever After

Josh and Gemma Make a Baby

Once Upon an Island

Soul Mates in Romeo Romance Series:

Chasing Romeo

Love Not at First Sight

Romance by the Book

Love, Artifacts, and You

Married by Sunday

My Better Life

Stand Alone Novella:

Love Letters

Find these books and more by Sarah Ready at:

www.sarahready.com/romance-books

Sign up to receive bonus content, exclusive epilogues and more
at: www.sarahready.com/newsletter